"Worie Dressar isn't your typical heroine—she's tough, she's opinionated, and she's loud. But at her core she wants to love and be loved—just like the rest of us. Cindy's special talent is in telling about life the way it is—hard parts and all—while preserving the beauty and wonder of love shining through even the darkest night. As my grandmother would say, 'Worie's full of beans!' That grit and gumption let her pass through the fire not only to overcome her own pain but to bring joy and life to those around her."

Sarah Loudin Thomas, Christy Award–nominated author of
Miracle in a Dry Season

"Seldom does a story move me to tears and encourage me to examine my life. A powerful story. Highly recommended."

DiAnn Mills, author of *Fatal Strike*, www.diannmills.com

"In Cindy Sproles's newest novel, *What Momma Left Behind*, we embrace one unique family from the very first heart-wrenching scene to the surprising and satisfying epilogue. This story is both gritty and grace-filled. The adventure includes amazing lessons in forgiveness, integrity, restoration, calling, faith stories, and Christ's mandate to care for 'the least of these.' As with all my favorite Sproles novels, the descriptions and humanity of the characters came alive and left me wanting the rest of the story."

Lucinda Seacrest McDowell, author of *Soul Strong*
and *Life-Giving Choices*

"Cindy Sproles has a way of placing readers inside the Blue Ridge Mountains. Her ability to transport readers into her Appalachian adventures is nothing short of genius. Leaving us hanging on every word, Cindy writes with feeling and incredible historical knowledge. This book is a must-read!"

LaTan Murphy, writer, speaker, decorator, and lover of people
and strong coffee; author of *Courageous Women*
of the Bible; latanmurphy.com

WHAT MOMMA LEFT BEHIND

CINDY K. SPROLES

Revell

a division of Baker Publishing Group
Grand Rapids, Michigan

Published by Revell
a division of Baker Publishing Group
PO Box 6287, Grand Rapids, MI 49516-6287
www.revellbooks.com

Printed in the United States of America

Library of Congress Cataloging-in-Publication Data
Names: Sproles, Cindy, author.
Title: What momma left behind / Cindy K. Sproles.
Description: Grand Rapids, Michigan : Revell, a division of Baker Publishing Group, [2020]
Identifiers: LCCN 2019036337 | ISBN 9780800737047 (paperback)
Subjects: LCSH: Appalachian Mountains—Rural conditions—19th Century—Fiction. | GSAFD: Historical fiction.
Classification: LCC PS3619.P775 W47 2020 | DDC 813/.6—dc23
LC record available at https://lccn.loc.gov/2019036337

ISBN 978-0-8007-3871-6 (casebound)

Scripture quotations are from the King James Version of the Bible.

Published in association with the Hartline Literary Agency, LLC.

20 21 22 23 24 25 26   7 6 5 4 3 2 1

Dedicated to my mother,

Velma Frady

Mom mothered more children who didn't belong
to her than any other woman I know.

She took them in her arms and loved each one exactly the
same. I am grateful to have a mother who, with Christlike
faith and wisdom, loves and cares for so many.

And to my niece and her husband,

Erin and *Devin Thomas*,

who willingly listened, prayed, and trusted until God laid
a special little girl in their arms. We witnessed a miracle.

Historical Note

Though the isolated life in the Appalachian Mountains was hard, for many years it protected the people from many of the illnesses that ran rampant in other places. Rivers and streams were clean and clear, the air fresh, and illness at a minimum. During the 1800s, as the industrial age entered, isolation became the enemy. As railroads and coal mining made their way into the remote areas of the Appalachian Mountains, woodlands were cut, streams were polluted, and the air grew dark from black smoke. The purity and protection of isolation turned deadly. Typhoid fever, dysentery, tuberculosis, and influenza spread through the valleys and hollows, taking lives by the hundreds.

With no records kept until the mid-1900s, there is no way to estimate how many lives were lost to these diseases. Given that, we draw our history from the stories given to us by our grandparents and great-grandparents. We know influenza ran wild and spread quickly. With few doctors, isolation, and the lack of trust in modern medicine, the mountain people seemed doomed.

According to local historians, influenza spread through the Smoky Mountains and across Cumberland Gap, killing more adults than children, with the only reason being that adults had more interaction with one another than the children. This, of course, is only speculation since records were scarce. However, the theory makes sense.

This story is loosely based around two diseases that plagued the mountain people—typhoid and influenza, both referred to as the fever. Devastating and deadly, they changed life in the mountains forever.

But Jesus said, Suffer little children,
and forbid them not, to come unto me:
for of such is the kingdom of heaven.

Matthew 19:14

CHAPTER
ONE

1877 — Sourwood Mountain, Tennessee

"They was nothin I could do for her. Her eyes was fixed on the sky and she never moved again. Despite me shakin her, she was gone."

Ely slipped his worn hat from his head and pressed it hard against his chest. "Miss Worie, thangs is what they is. Ain't nothin you coulda done."

The spring breeze whipped my hair around my face, brushin the clay trail of tears from my cheek.

Just the day before Momma was hangin clothes on the line and singin. She didn't seem to have a care in the world. Today she was dead. This didn't make a bit of sense. "Like you said, Ely, it is what it is." I swallowed hard, tryin to be strong.

Ely shoved a flat rock into the soft clay. "This'll mark her till we can make her a cross like your daddy's."

"I never knew what a chore it was to bury a person." I dropped to my knees and gingerly swept the clots of dirt to one side, smoothin the mound that covered Momma. I wasn't sure if I was to be angry or hurt. Either way, my heart was achin.

Ely grunted. "Uh-huh. 'Tis a chore. But you was smart to drop that quilt over her. Kept the buzzards away whilst we dug that hole." He placed his hat back in its spot, pushin his dark, tight curls from beneath.

I stared at Ely, his skin blacker than the rock coal Daddy would bring home from time to time. He was a good friend. Stood by Momma and Daddy through thick and thin.

The sun peeked through the newly formed leaves of the old oak tree, castin a shine on ever one of those curls that boasted around Ely's ears. "You're startin to look a little shabby there, Ely." I smacked at a curl.

He busted into a guffaw that shook ever bone in his body. "You always make a man laugh, Miss Worie. Even now, in the shadow of your own troubles."

"Lordy, lordy. Like you said, it is what it is. Ain't my fault. Leastways I hope not. But I don't understand, Ely. I did everthing Momma ever told me. Never give her no reason to pull such a stunt. I thought my bein good would make up for the boys."

"You stop right there, girl. Ever man makes his own choices. Calvin chose his swindlin and connivin. Justice made his bed with a bottle of hooch. Them ain't your doins. And I feel right sure Miss Louise was proud of you. Ain't many young girls would choose stayin home to help their momma over bein a wife and mother."

I laid across the mound of dirt and commenced to sob. Long, hard wails. Ely stood solid by me, bendin down ever once in a while to pat my shoulder.

It wasn't long before the buzzards went to squallin overhead. "Get way!" I hollered. "Go on. Can't you see we buried Momma?"

Ely took my arm and lifted me to my feet. "She's safe. We buried her deep and covered her with stones and more dirt on top of that. Ain't nothin can get to her." He tugged me toward the house.

"But I've seen them beasts peck at the ground until they dig up what's buried. Buzzards don't care what the meal is, just so it's fresh."

"Like I done said, she's safe. She'll sleep unbothered."

I clapped my hands together and knocked the red clay loose.

"You need to get yourself cleaned up." Ely yanked a dress off the clothesline as we passed. "You stoke that fire in the fireplace and hang the pot. I'll pump some fresh water for you to boil, then I'll send Bess along after a while to bring you some supper."

My legs grew weaker with ever step to the house till my ankles finally twisted and I sat on the ground with a thud. They was no quiet in my stomach either. My gut twisted and churned until I couldn't hold it no more. Ely held my head while I vomited.

"Miss Worie, you been through a lot today. Help me get you inside, now. Come on. Let's go. Get your feet under you. Come on." He slipped his arms under mine and lifted.

I tried to stand but I couldn't. Ely hung the clean dress over his shoulder, then scooped me in his arms and carried me. He turned his head to one side, tryin to get a good breath. They wasn't nothin to say. I knew I smelled like sweat and blood. And I knew the only reason them buzzards was circlin Momma's grave was because they caught the vile scent from my clothes.

Ely stood me by the screen door. His face said everthing his mouth wouldn't. Like what happened here to rip the screen outta the door frame, but in his kindness, he didn't ask. He pulled open the broken screen door and pushed his shoulder against the heavy inside wooden door. It sounded like a wildcat screamin as it swung open on its rope hinges.

"I'm gonna set you in this here chair while I stoke the fire. You ain't in no shape to mess with a fire."

"The pot is already filled. Momma was ready for me to wash clothes."

Ely nodded and headed into the back room. I heard him movin and stackin wood in the fireplace, then they was the puff of the billows. The smell of hot embers filled the house as the fire caught and went to burnin.

Ely laid the dress he'd yanked from the line on the table, then he squatted at my side. "Miss Worie, I'm goin on home. Get yourself cleaned up. You reek of blood. Your purty skin is tainted red." He brushed my hair from my eyes, then kissed me on the head. "Me and Bess will be back later on. You hear me?"

I heard him, but words wouldn't work their way out.

"Worie. You hear?"

I nearly jumped outta my skin. "Yeah, I hear." The words quivered as they come out. He squeezed my shoulder and left.

It didn't seem real. None of it. Worse, it made no sense. I'd gived up everthing—a husband and a new life—to stay and help Momma. She couldn't count on the boys after Daddy died. Half the time Justice was laid out drunk, and Calvin spent his time bein what he called a slick businessman. Daddy called him a liar and swindler. Momma, she called him lost. I couldn't bear her tendin the farm alone. With Daddy dead, it was just me and her.

I ain't sure when I laid down on Momma's bed, but I did. I suppose it was somewhere betwixt exhaustion and agony. I dozed a spell. When I woke up, nothin had changed other than the wet blood all over me had dried. The hope that this was a horrid dream vanished and reality set in hard.

I scrounged up one of my own skirts and an old shirt of Daddy's, then headed to the creek. Despite Ely's best intentions, Momma was smaller than me and her dress wouldn't cover one of my legs. She was a small woman. Tiny in height compared to most folks, but despite her size, she could move mountains when she was riled.

A while back Momma had the boys dam up the creek so we had a clear pool of water. It would fill to the brim of the stacked rocks and spill over. The water Ely set to warmin over the fire woulda been nice, but dried blood washes better in cold water. My clothes was stuck to me, and when I went to pull them off it was like I was tearin ever bit of the hide off my legs. I stepped into the icy waters of Tender's Creek and my skin went numb. It was just one more callus, cause my heart had numbed earlier in the day. Slipping under the water, I opened my eyes to see the streaks of sun and deep blue sky through the clear glassy ceilin.

It would be easy to just take in a breath of cold water, close my eyes, and never see the light of day again. Was it that easy for Momma? What was she thinkin? How could she pull the trigger?

My lungs went to burnin, longin for the spring air, and despite my thoughts to breathe in the creek, I found I didn't have the courage. My head popped above the water and I took in a gulp of mountain air. I wasn't good enough for Momma to make her want to live, and I was too much of a coward to take my own life. "What use am I?"

I scrubbed the blood from my face and arms. My teeth went to chatterin like a squirrel gripin at its mate. Easin out of the pond, I pulled Daddy's shirt over my head, then slipped on my skirt. My skin now harbored a grayish blue. I run my fingers through my wet, curled strands of hair, then quickly braided them. The damp from the braid soaked the back of my shirt.

How does a person do such a thing? How do they get in such a dark hole that they can't see the light of day, the sun bouncing off the summit, or even hear the soft song of the mockinbird? How can they possibly want to let go of the tender smell of honeysuckle or not want to savor its sweet nectar?

Ely's words echoed in my head. *"This here ain't your fault."* And he was right. If I was one thing, I was strong. Momma raised me to be just that. She always said, "Take a day to mourn your lot, then shovel it over your shoulder and move ahead."

I'd missed my chance to be a wife and a mother so I could help her. That was water under the bridge, as Momma would say. But I was no quitter. Never had been. At seventeen, I'd manage just fine.

The longer I pondered the choice of givin up so much, the madder it made me. Momma was always a givin woman. She always took others over herself, until today. Today she turned selfish and greedy. Today she took ever dream I ever had. All my hope. All my desire. And she bled it out on the ground with one pull of the trigger.

I wiped the tears from my eyes, straightened my shoulders, and walked to Momma's grave. In one swift motion, I drew back my foot and kicked the stone Ely had stood at the head of her grave. It toppled over. As I walked away, I spit.

TWO

The sun peered over Taylor's Point, turnin the sky an eerie orange. Signs of a storm brewin. I held my hand in front of me and twisted it from side to side. The orange of the sky reflected onto my skin, turnin it a brassy color. When the wind kicked up, they was no question what was comin. Rain. I took in a deep breath and the scent of a storm wafted through my senses. It would behoove me to carry some extra wood in the house and fill the wood box.

I looked over my shoulder at Momma's grave and dreaded a hard rain washin the red clay mound level. "Well, bull." I kicked at a rock. "Reckon I better shore up that mound."

Next to the barn sat Daddy's wheelbarrow. It wasn't nothin fancy. Just a wood wheel and an open-ended box with handles. Harder than kraut to push, but I wheeled it away from the barn and went to pickin up hand-sized rocks to lay around the edges of Momma's grave. Even though Ely made sure Momma was covered, I didn't have a desire to shovel washed-away dirt over her again. I picked up the rocks and dropped them with a thud into the wheelbarrow, back and forth, workin my way to Momma's restin spot. With each rock I pulled from the dirt, I dug my toes into the ground to help put some push behind the worthless wheelbarrow. It took me a spell, but I got them rocks wheeled next to Momma.

"I ain't rightly sure why I'm botherin to shore up your restin spot. Why should I?" Every rock I laid around Momma's grave landed hard on the ground. "Don't do me no good to talk to a dead woman, but I can throw these rocks at you." Two more hit the dirt hard, and I shoved them tight against the others. "This oughta keep your dirt in place until it settles. Pile it high now and in a few days it's gonna sink." Once I got them rocks seated I stepped back. The stone I'd kicked the day before lay tilted on its side. "I reckon I oughta fix that too."

As I bent to straighten the heavy stone, tears dripped from my nose. Wasn't somethin I expected. I was tryin my best to be miffed at Momma, but the truth is, I couldn't be mad. I loved her too much.

I tugged at the stone until it stood upright, took one last looksee to be sure Momma was safe in her spot, then turned and grabbed the wheelbarrow. Two steps later, I stopped.

"Momma. I love you. And I hope when the gates of heaven opened, Daddy was standin there waitin. So, I'm obliged that you'll understand if I move on now. After all, it was you that taught me to buck up and shovel my feelins over my shoulder."

I made my way to the barn and rested the wheelbarrow back in its spot. The barn door was gapped open, so I shoved it to the inside. Sally, Daddy's old workhorse, shook her head and lumbered through, nudging me as she walked past.

"I reckon you're hungry, ain't you? I plumb forgot to let you out with all the goins on." Sally nuzzled me with all the forgiveness the pastor talked about on Sundays, then she made her way out to pasture. She didn't need no coaxin, and with the barn door open she knew the way. Silly horse could care less if it was rainin either.

I scooped several ears of corn from the wooden bin into a

bucket and followed her to the field. "Here you go, girl." The horse snorted and latched her teeth onto one cob.

A rumble rolled over the mountain behind the house, and the sky that direction turned a misty gray. Rain was comin for sure, and I needed to do one thing before it hit.

"Life ain't easy in these mountains," Momma would say. "When the messes happen, you swallow the ache and do what has to be done."

I was swallowin a heap too. Hurt, anger, pain. It was like takin a bite of dry biscuit and tryin to choke it down. The bread splinters and the pieces get just damp enough with spit to stick like molasses to your throat.

I went back to the house and went to eatin that dry biscuit.

There are times when we do things without thinkin, and when I'd stretched out on Momma's bed, soaked to the hilt in her blood—well, that was one of them things. My clothes was wet plumb to the skin from holdin her . . . and that odor. Blood-soaked stench covered her bed and filled the house. First things first. Get this rancid-smellin mattress out. I wrestled the heavy mattress on its end and pulled.

"What in tarnation are you doin?" a voice boomed through the tiny cabin.

I nearly come outta my skin.

Calvin kicked a stool out of his way. "I said, what are you doin?"

Sweat beaded across my brow as I fought the large straw-filled mattress from the back room and into the kitchen. I swiped my arm across my forehead. "What's it look like I'm doin?" Calvin was always good at figurin things, but right this minute he was provin hisself wrong. "And you can just turn your rear around and get out of my house."

"Your house?" He took me by the arm and yanked. The bloody mattress slipped flat onto the slatted poplar floor. "Who died and made you the queen?"

"Momma died. Or did you even know that, Calvin? Momma died."

For a moment he stood quiet. His head hung whilst he took in the news. "She was half crazy anyhow. Ain't no surprise."

I eyed him. His answer didn't offer me no shock. It was common for idiot things to drop outta his mouth. I pondered my next words. They needed to be just right. Strong enough to let him know I meant business. Steady enough to show him no fear. Any signs of fear on this day and he'd just as likely kill me as look at me.

"I reckon since I buried her without your help, that makes me the one to say what's what."

A snide smile tipped the edges of his mouth. "Ain't you the cocky one?"

"No, they ain't no cocky to it. Neither of you boys was around to help bury Momma. I had to get Ely Merrell to help me dig a proper hole. Took the better part of the day to do it." I took a step and planted my feet solid. "Now get out!" My heart raced. Despite my attempt to hide my fear, I could feel my knees knockin.

Calvin slung threats for years, but they was nothin but hot air. From the time we was youngins, he had no trouble lyin or makin nasty threats to scare a body into doin what he wanted. He was best at pitchin fits and flappin his jaws. Stompin and ravin, slingin his head from side to side if he didn't get his way. Them actions by theirself was enough to scare a body into givin in. But not today. I was in no mood to give.

Calvin snagged the stool he'd kicked with his foot and pulled it over. He planted hisself firm on the wooden seat. "Like I said. What in tarnation are you doin?" He had no intention of movin.

We stared eye to eye for a short time before I finally broke the silence. "Well, Calvin, if you really must know, this here is the mattress I got blood on. I was tryin to save Momma. The odor makes me want to vomit, so I got plans to light a fire to the thing." I stepped on the mattress and pointed to the tainted material covered with dried blood. "And this here is about ever ounce of blood that spurted out of Momma. Do you see it, Calvin? Do you? You happy now? That what you wanted to know? Cause the truth is, you boys is the reason Momma is dead." My own anger boiled like a pan of water over the fire.

"My, my. Ain't you growed a smart mouth. And I did no sucha thing. I wasn't the one who pulled the trigger and took her life."

It took a second before his words hit me. How did he know Momma shot herself? I didn't tell him. Questions commenced to rise in my mind. Today was not the day to make this fight. I didn't have the strength.

"My mouth ain't smart. It spits out truth. No thanks to y'all, our momma is dead." I squatted and grabbed the edge of the heavy mattress. "I'll thank you to get out of my way so I can get this stench outta the cabin."

I heaved the straw bedding past him and out the door. Calvin picked at his teeth with a twig and watched.

"Of course you won't help, you lazy, good-for-nothing . . ." The mattress landed hard on the ground a few feet from the cabin. Taking the flint from my apron, I clicked it together until the corner of the tickin caught fire. A black smoke took to twistin and twirlin before I could lean down to blow up a good-sized flame.

"I come home to get Momma's Mason jar," Calvin said. "I need it."

I stopped dead but never uttered a word. I thought that was Momma's secret. A memory come to me.

"Come on, Worie, I got something special to show you," Momma had said. "It's just for you, so don't you dare tell a soul." Momma led me into the back room by the fireplace. She smiled and pulled my hand over the stones. "Count four from the left. One, two, three, four." She slid my fingers across the rough rocks. "Then four up. One, two, three, four." Momma went to giggling. "This has been here all along, and even after twenty-eight years your daddy never once knew about it. Now push." She pressed my hand beneath hers, and the rock, loose in its stack, slid to the right just enough to leave an open hole. She reached back into the hole and pulled out a jar. "Here it is." Momma unscrewed the lid and dug at some folded papers crumpled inside. She fished the contents out onto the hearth, then quickly scooped them up and placed them back in the jar.

Three nickels. It wasn't much at all, but on the mountain, them nickels would buy flour and grain. That was it. The jar was Momma's secret. It never amounted much to me, but to Momma it was the world, so I kept her secret. I promised her I'd never let a soul know about it.

"When I'm dead and gone, that jar is yours. One day you'll see why it's so precious." Momma gently pushed the jar back into its home and moved the heavy stone into place. "Remember, four and four."

Things with Calvin got to seemin a bit queer, and that made me determined to not breathe a word about the jar. I'd play as dumb as Calvin thought I was.

"Ha!" I slapped my knees and laughed. "What jar?"

The flames eat at the straw mattress like a dog after its last meal. They stretched high into the sky.

"You can't even come here and say you're sorry Momma is gone." I pushed my finger in his face. "Ain't you the least bit sad? Just a little?"

Calvin pushed his hand into his trouser pocket and pulled out a dollar bill.

"Where'd you get that?" I snatched the bill from his hand, dodging his attempts to take it back.

"Give it here." He chased my hands, tryin to nab the bill. "I got ways of gettin money ever once in a while."

I broke out laughin. "I might only be seventeen, but I ain't stupid. You're like a mountain lion lookin for the weak prey. Lyin all the time. Stealin. I'm right sure you'd not know the truth if it bit you." I slammed the bill hard against his chest and shoved. "Now take your bill and get from here."

"Where's it at?" Calvin snapped. He took me by the arm and wheeled me around.

"Where's what at?" I knew he meant Momma's jar, but I had no intentions of makin his takin it easy.

"Stupid girl!" he shouted. "I asked you where Momma's cannin money was. I want to know and I want to know now."

"You really think if Momma had money she'd keep us poor as dirt? I ain't the stupid one here."

Calvin's eyes showed me he was desperate. I ain't sure why or what he'd got hisself into, but he shoved me against the house and pressed his forearm against my throat. Between the smoke from the straw mattress and Calvin pressin my neck, cutting my air by half, I began to choke. You coulda slid a piece of paper between my toes and the ground. Calvin had to be bad off to even start to carry out a threat.

"Where's the jar?"

"Want in one hand and spit in the other. See which one gets full fastest." I squeezed the words through the choke, then gagged and coughed.

Calvin shoved me to the ground. "Smart mouth. I know she told you where she kept it. You was her favorite."

Anger crawled from my gut. "Calvin Dressar, Momma never had no favorites. If she did, she'd never have killed herself. She'd have never let me find her dead. That ain't showin favorites." I slapped my hand against my chest. "They ain't no money, you idiot." I rubbed the pain from my neck. "All I got is this house. Now crawl back into the hole you came from. You ain't welcome here."

Calvin stomped through the cabin, yankin open pantry doors and lookin under beds like we had some sort of mansion. "Where's the jar?"

"We just got two rooms, Calvin. And since you done tore through them both, it ain't right hard to see they ain't no jar. And bein them mattresses is just lifted off the ground by some blocks of wood, ain't gonna be nothing slipped under them. What more do you want?"

Despite his rantin, my mind wandered back to a time when our family wasn't so splintered. In the far corner of the back room two mattresses rested on small wood blocks. Long, thin slats laid across them held the down-filled tickin inches from the floor. It wasn't fancy, but it kept Momma and Daddy off the cold floor in the winter. The boys took the other mattress, and I slept on a pallet next to the fireplace. Momma's rocker butted against a small window by the fireplace, and a quilt she'd sewed hung over the arm. Her Bible rested in the seat.

The fireplace opened into the cookin room, and if you bent down far enough, you could see clean through the cabin. Daddy was right smart to open it on both sides. One fire served to heat and cook.

Evenins after we'd eat around the small table Daddy'd made, I'd wash the dishes whilst everone else gathered around the fireplace. Momma made no bones about it. We'd all hear the Word from the good book come hell or high water. The cookin room held a wood bin and a pantry, and in that pantry Momma kept jars of canned beans and spinach. A screen door stood in front of a heavy wood door. I won't never forget how it warmed Momma's heart to have that screen door.

"I done ask you thrice. Where is the jar?" Calvin tossed Momma's quilt onto the floor, then stormed to the pantry, nearly tippin the rocker over. It was hard to keep my eyes from scannin across the room to Momma's secret place. I was just thankful Calvin didn't think to take Daddy's shotgun.

I eased inside, sleeked around the broken screen where the shotgun hung, and lifted it off its hook. Calvin stepped behind me. I rested the gun against my shoulder real quick like and pulled back the hammers. "Get out, Calvin. Now!"

He lifted his hands. I aimed the gun just to the right of his head and pulled the first trigger. It fired, blowin a hole the size of your fist in the wall behind him. The color drained from Calvin's face. He bore a resemblance to that raccoon Daddy had snagged after a week of it stealin our corn. The look in his eyes was nothin short of disbelief.

"I said, get out. I was clear and I meant it. I got one more shot. And remember, Daddy taught me to shoot, so do you wanna chance me missin?"

He eyeballed me for a minute, then stormed outta the house. "Watch your back, Worie. Watch your back!"

THREE

"Idiot," I said. Calvin's threats never held no water. He was, after all, a liar. When he lied his eyes flitted. With all that flappin, he could have took flight just now. And that kinda scared me. It was a different way about him . . . a desperation.

Sadness took hold of my heart. Momma loved us. She loved Calvin despite his meanness. She loved Justice through his drinkin, and they was no question she loved me for givin up all I did to stay with her and help.

I miss you, Momma. I surely don't understand why you felt the need to drain the life from your body. "Didn't I do things right?" I felt my mood darken. *I don't understand. I don't know if I can ever forgive you.* "Ever!"

Fear took hold. I was the one thing that scared the socks off me . . . an orphan. Just like all them other youngins—like them eleven Olsen children. No momma. No daddy.

I remembered when George and Martha Olsen died. He got sick first, and when the fever finally snuffed out his light, they was so poor that Martha quit eatin in order to have enough food to feed her children. Momma'd carry food down to Martha, but it was hard for her to feed Martha's eleven and her own brood. When

Ellie Olsen come knockin on our door to tell us that her mother was real sick, Momma said she knew Martha's time was counted.

"It's the fever, Miss Louise!" Ellie wrapped her arms around Momma's waist and buried her head into her stomach. "That fever is like ants. It swarms everwhere." Her shoulders shook as she cried.

There was always a pot of soup simmerin over the fire, so Momma pulled a bowl off the shelf and poured Ellie some. "Here, child. Eat you something. You're gonna need to be strong for your brothers and sisters."

Whilst Ellie slurped on that soup, Momma went to roundin up canned goods to take to the Olsens.

"Ellie, you hurry up and finish that soup. We need to get back to your momma."

"Yes, Miss Louise." She turned the bowl up and gulped down the warm liquid.

I won't never forget the look on Momma's face when we saw Miss Martha's eyes was sunk deep into her head and her lips favored blueberries. And her skin was a pasty gray.

"Lord have mercy, Martha, they ain't enough meat on your bones for a buzzard to pick." Momma lifted Martha's head and dribbled warm broth into her mouth.

"Had to d-do wh-what I h-had to d-do to be s-sure my k-kids was f-fed."

Martha did what any momma would do to care for her children. She sacrificed so they could live. If it meant more work, she'd work. If it meant not eatin, then she'd miss a meal so them youngins could eat. They was lots of times Miss Martha did without so her youngins could have what was necessary. This time, betwixt the fever and starvation, her life was snuffed out.

We didn't have a lot, but Momma always made sure we had what we needed. If we was lackin, she'd commence to can anything she could to sell.

I wondered if they was a reason Momma might have done the same. Did she do without so us youngins had what we needed? What did we lack that was so important Momma felt like she needed to take her life? What?

"Have mercy!" Momma had gently dabbed a drip of soup from Martha's chin. "They was only one person to make this kind of sacrifice. All you had to do was ask for help. You ain't the good Lord." She wheeled around to me. "Worie, this fever is runnin wild on the mountain. People is dyin left and right. You best be prayin that the good Lord will have mercy cause it seems the devil hisself is wreakin havoc, takin the parents of the weak and knowin that without care them little ones will die too." Momma swiped her forehead with her sleeve. "Get me a bucket of cold water so I can cool Martha down."

Martha was no different. She was another soul captured, and her children would be orphans. I felt sorry for them little ones. What would they do without their momma and daddy?

"Martha, we need to break this fever so you can get on to carin for your family." Momma rubbed a cold rag over Martha's face, but her life was all give out. She sucked in a long breath and it hissed outta her lungs. Death carried her away.

"Martha!" Momma shouted. "Martha, what about these youngins?" But she was gone.

The memory burned hard in my mind. Layin on that slat floor, still damp from scrubbin up blood, I choked back the sobs. Here I am now—an orphan myself. My worst fear had come to pass.

I reckon I laid there a good part of the afternoon. Smoke from the burned mattress seeped through the door. Horrible thoughts scrambled through my head. I remembered how them Olsen children was left in the cold to fend for theirselves. I was afraid. Afraid of bein alone. Not afraid of bein by myself, but of bein alone—

with nobody that cared. My brothers sure as whiz didn't care. They was too busy makin out for theirselves.

I loved my brothers despite their stupidity, but in the same breath, I hated how they treated Momma. I hated how they left her alone to fend, expectin her to give, give, give and never get nothin in return. Not even love. She did the best she could to care for us, and them Olsen children, and the others. All the others . . . I remembered all the families Momma tried to help where there was no help to be had.

"Bring me them jars from the root cellar so I can start cannin these half runners," Momma'd say. "Get them brothers of yours to stoke up the fire. I need it hot to preserve them beans."

That was when Momma started to can. We didn't have much in the pantry when Martha Olsen died, but Momma took what we had.

"This is the last time I'll be caught with my drawers down. I'll have more food canned. They'll be something—some sort of food to feed all these hungry children when they come knockin."

And Momma did. After Martha died, she commenced cannin all she could from June until October, and when winter come, she could at least try to feed the little ones who lost their parents.

I crawled to my feet and shoved open the door. The ashes of the burned mattress simmered. What would I do? How would I manage?

In a fit, I went to kickin and stompin them ashes, bellerin like a sick goat. Anger crawled up from the deepest part of me, hurt seeped outta my heart, and fear eat at me like a hungry buzzard. Momma had left me in more ways than one. She'd left me with two brothers that wasn't worth their weight. And then there was the secret of that blessed old jar. I knew Calvin would be back after Momma's cannin jar, and I had no intentions of bringin it out of its hidin spot to see what was in it. It'd stay in its hole. After all I'd been through the last two days, I wasn't sure I wanted anything Momma had to give.

"How could you, Momma? How could you?"

FOUR

I sat on the porch step, watching the sky go from blue to yellow. A hawk circled overhead, and with each pass he made, it was like he was draggin new colors into the clouds. I watched as they melted into gray. The sun slowly slipped behind the mountain, takin what light was left to the evening away. Crickets rubbed their legs together, makin the song that danced on the night breeze.

Alone. They was no singin from the kitchen. No one to set me at the table and continue to teach me words and letters. Nothin. I could read some, but I needed to know more. My dream to be a teacher was gone. Faded with the end of daylight.

I didn't need no lantern to make my way to the smokehouse. I'd done it so many times I knew ever rock and hole in the path. The plank door creaked on its rope hinges when I pushed it open. To the right hung a fresh side of smoked venison. Justice and me had tagged a small deer days ago before he got to drinkin. A knife, snug in its sheaf, hung on the wall. My fingers crawled up the wall and wrapped around the handle, slippin it free from the leather case. Bracing one hand against the meat, I sawed through the toughened carcass, still warm as it smoked. Just enough for supper and a tad for breakfast.

"Thank you, good Father, for the blessin of this provision. I'm much obliged." I swiped the knife clean on the tail of my skirt and placed it back in its holder. *Though I ain't rightly sure how thankful I am for this mess I'm in.*

I didn't feel right close to the Almighty right now. My anger was as much at Him as it was Momma. But Momma always prayed over the food. I reckon I orta. I dipped the meat in the bucket of water that sat by the door, then shook it dry.

"You hear that, Lord? I ain't real fond of You right now. How's a person supposed to trust a body who lets this kind of mess happen?"

Momma'd read from her Bible and tell us about the amazin sacrifice the good Lord made on our behalf. I never rightly grasped why He saw a need to die. And right about now, I wondered what that "big sacrifice" Momma talked about had to do with this ordeal.

I slipped the meat in my pocket, then reached over to one side and grabbed two chunks of applewood, tossing them in the smoker hole filled with embers. It only took seconds for the wood to catch, and a new sweet-smellin smoke went to fillin the room. "That oughta last through the night."

Takin hold of the knotted rope handle, I slammed the door closed behind me. Ever step I took landed hard against the ground, and for a little bit I'd have sworn I was digging holes with my heels.

They was so many feelins rushin through me, I couldn't catch a good breath. "Can't You see what You've done to me?" I shook my hand toward the stars. "If they is a good Lord, You sure can't prove it by me!" My chest felt like it would rip open and spill my heart out on the ground.

In the midst of my own pain, I heard a whimper.

"Hooch, that you, boy?" I clicked my lips together for the old hound to come. "Hooch! Come on!"

The whimper grew louder.

I ain't one to get spooked easy, but seein as I found my momma dead, then buried her, I was a little skittish.

"Calvin? That you?" I inched toward a stand of grass just off the path. "I ain't scared of you. Come on out and stop playin games."

The weeds rustled and I rubbed my eyes. I couldn't believe what I was seein. A child—a girl—crawled from the weeds.

I squinted hard to see. "Who are you?"

"Doanie. Doanie Whitefield."

"What?" I couldn't be sure I heard her right. "Get outta them weeds and let me see you." She stepped closer and I took her by the arm. "Let's go to the house. I can't make heads or tails of who you are." I wrapped my hand around her arm and my fingers kissed. "Lawsy, girl. You ain't got a bit of meat on your bones."

We stepped onto the porch, and I grabbed the lantern off the hook and held it close to her. The child's cheeks was caved in, her eyes sunk into her head, and her frame frail. "Lord have mercy," I whispered. "This here is what I'm talkin about, Lord. Why would You let this happen? This here is a little one."

"I come lookin for Miss Louise. She's been bringin us beans and such. Can you get Miss Louise?"

I stood starin at the girl. She had no idea Momma was gone. It was hard to speak the words that needed to be said, but I mustered up the courage. Pushin her hair behind her ear, I leaned next to her and whispered, "Doanie, Miss Louise is gone."

"Reckon when will she be back?"

I swallowed hard, then took in a deep breath. "No, you don't understand. Miss Louise passed."

The girl lifted her head toward the sky and bellowed like a hurt animal. She yanked her arm from me and shouted, "What am I supposed to do now? They's three of us at home. Farrell is five, T. J. is just three. What will I do?" Her legs buckled and she grabbed at me to steady herself. "I got no way to feed 'em. They'll die. I'll die."

I knew Momma was keepin up the Olsen youngins, but I had

no idea she was feedin the Whitefield children. This didn't seem real. Now this one child stood toe to toe with me. She laid her face in her palms and cried.

How many children was Momma feeding?

It was hard to know what to do. I was still harborin my own grief. It had only been three days. Now here I was, about to do something I never imagined I'd do. I always dreamed of makin my way to Knoxville to learn to be a teacher. To learn good enough to be able to come back to the mountain and teach the wee ones. Momma told me about some fancy folks who lived there. They might take me in and help me get the extra schoolin. Now that Momma took her own soul . . . my working hard at my chores, huntin when the boys was nowhere to be found, doin what Momma told me, seemed all wasted.

I'd never get to learn better. Momma's teachin at night was a start, but it wasn't enough. Now it'd never be no more.

Words seeped outta my mouth like molasses drippin from a jar—slow and thick. I tried to convince myself this was a mistake, but it was like the good Lord stuck His hand down my mouth and pulled them words right out. They was no doubt I'd regret it. Anytime words come thick and slow, it was a mistake.

"Where's your brother and sister?"

"I left them down the path."

"Lord have mercy. Go get them."

Doanie stood workin out a good excuse why they was down the path.

"Go get 'em! Now."

The girl took off down the path like a flash of lightnin.

"Lawsy, lawsy. Where will I put them?" I slapped my arms against my sides. *Answer me, Momma! Where am I gonna put these youngins? Where?*

A cool breeze brushed past me, and when I looked up I could have swore I was starin at Momma. *"It's warm out, they could bed down in the hayloft.*" I covered my ears. Momma was dead, and the dead don't talk. My mind was messin with me.

I dug my knuckles into my eyes and rubbed. When I took down my hands I saw what I thought was Momma—the outline of a bent-over tender cedar.

They wasn't no desire in my heart to take care of these . . . these . . . The word stuck in my craw. "These orphans."

I felt my legs commence to shake. Orphan. I'd done become what I feared most of bein. My heart went to racin and I bent down, snagged a rock, and threw it as hard as I could at that cedar tree. "Liar! You wasn't Momma!"

The shadows of the night can twist a body's sight and make us see what we want to see, not what is really there. I reckon what I wanted was to see Momma. Seein as that wouldn't happen, I needed to move past my grief and on to what would be the reality of my life.

I was an orphan who had to pick up the work of her momma, whether she wanted it or not. And that made me mad.

Doanie made her way back up the path, brother and sister in tow. I eyed them for a minute, then let them sticky words slide out. "Don't you worry none. This here can be your home."

This here can be your home. It was like I'd stepped on the mountaintop and shouted them words down into the valley. They bounced off every rock and crevice on the ridge and come back on me. Back at me like a lie.

Doanie reached down and scooped up little T. J. His pants hung heavy with manure. Farrell, the middle child, wrapped her arm around her sister.

I knelt and reached out my hand. "You Farrell?" Her eyes dug into me like a cat clawin to get away. "How old might you be? Six? Seven?"

She burrowed tighter against her sister.

"Oh, I see, the cat's got your tongue. Well, seein as the cat has your tongue, I reckon I can snitch your nose." I gently took hold of her nose and tugged, sliding my thumb between my first two fingers. "There! See! I took your nose."

The child swatted at my hand. "Ain't no sucha thang. You can't steal my nose."

"Why, I reckon I did. Right here. See?" I showed her the end of my thumb barely poking through my fingers.

Her eyes widened. "Give it back!"

"You answer my question and I'll see if I can hook it back to your face. How old are you?"

Farrell stared hard at me, then steppin behind Doanie, she answered, "I might be five."

I thought I'd lose my stomach. This wee one was five. Doanie was ten. T. J. three. These was just babies. Babies without a momma or a daddy . . . without a home. And Momma had been feedin them. How'd she keep this such a secret? Like it was no ordeal?

"Hey! You promised to give me my nose back."

"Well, let's get somethin straight right now. I made no promise. I said if you answered my question I'd see if I could hook it back." I rubbed my hand against my skirt and then blew on my thumb so she'd think I was cleanin off her nose, then I gingerly twisted it against her face. "Stand back, let me look." I took her cheek and turned it from side to side, eyein her nose. "A body has to be sure we got it on straight. Don't want you walkin around the mountain with a crooked nose."

Doanie smiled. Silent like, she nodded. I felt a rush of tears fill my eyes, so I coughed and spit to try to fight them back. I pulled the slice of meat from my pocket and held it up. "Supper needs to be cooked. Let's go." I pointed to the tore-up screen door. "It might be broke, but you still open it to walk in."

Farrell pulled open the rickety door frame and stepped inside. Doanie followed.

I grabbed her shirttail. "Hold up there, girl. That boy reeks.

You wait here and let me find some cheesecloth. I'll clean him up before you take him in."

She smiled again. "He is ripe, ain't he?"

"Ripe ain't the word." I glanced into the darkness. The moon give off a haze that shadowed everthing. And there she was again. Momma. Standing at the edge of the woods.

It was like the wind carried her voice. *"You're doin right."*

I blinked and squinted. "Doanie," I said. "Remind me to cut that cedar down tomorrow."

FIVE

It took a while for the stew to make. Longer than Farrell could hold her eyes open. I didn't have the heart to put them little ones in the barn, so I made my way into Momma's room and looked over the wooden slats to be sure they was no blood left on the floor. I took some quilts out of the cupboard, made a pallet, and carried Farrell into Momma's room and laid her flat. She balled the corner of the quilt in her hand and rammed it into her mouth. I reckon suckin on a blanket was the step after suckin on your thumb.

"Good Lord. What have I done?" I kept askin myself that question. Takin in these youngins was more than I could manage. How can one orphan take care of three more? My knees went to wobbling and my hands shook. I knew the ways of housekeeping. Momma taught me to cook, can, sew. But motherin wasn't somethin I had planned on. It wasn't somethin that could be taught. I guess it just had to be experienced. What I wanted was to teach. That had gone by the wayside.

I spied Momma's Bible on the small table in the corner. Its edges wore, pages the color of the fadin sun. And writin. Momma always wrote smart words in her Bible. I bent open the book and the pages fanned past me like a peacock spreadin its tail. When the pages stopped I pulled the book close to my eyes and commenced to sound out the words.

"'Suffer little children, and forbid them not, to come unto me . . .'" I struggled to sound out the words, but as I thought on them, my anger toward Momma kindled. It burned sucha fire in my heart that it singed my soul. She took her life, and when she did, mine went with it.

I slammed the book closed and tossed it back in its place. "Stupid book." I never imagined this thought would cross my mind, cause I loved my Momma. But right now, right at this minute in my grief, I hated her. Despite its words, I didn't want no youngins brought to me.

Doanie rocked T. J. in the old pine rocker Pawpaw built. I wasn't sure what creaked more, the rungs on the rocker or the floor. Before I knew it, Doanie had the youngin sound asleep.

"Lay him by your sister, then come get you a bite of stew."

Her cheeks was stained with trails of dirt left from her tears. She snuffed and whimpered as she passed by me.

"It'll be fine, Doanie. We'll go to your cabin tomorrow and bring up what belongins you and the others need. We'll make do."

She sniffed again. "Yes ma'am."

I nearly fell outta my chair. I was seventeen, and though I'd courted Trigger Townsend once, we never married. I was still nowhere near old enough to be called ma'am. That made me even madder. I realized I lost more than my momma, more than my dream for schoolin, but I lost my childhood too.

The embers in the fireplace glowed a faint yellow. And when I leaned down to stir them, ever breath I took in and blew out fed them. It was like they was as hungry as Doanie and hers. I dropped on a log, then took the bellows from the nail and probed the embers. One pump, two. A twist of smoke twirled from the log. Damp wood makes smoke, and since we'd had rain the day before, we was bound to have a house full of it.

I raised the window just a bit and fanned the smoke toward freedom. My eyes burned as the white fog worked its way out of the house.

Thoughts of Doanie's plea bored deep in my mind. *"What am I to do? They'll starve. I'll starve."* Them words eat at me hard. I loosened the smooth stick that held my hair in place, and it fell in strands around my shoulders. My fingers rubbed through the lengths of hair, twistin and turnin it. "What will I do? Me?"

Ely Merrell told me a body needs to mourn the dead for seven days. "Give a body time to take in the loss and feel the hurt." But from what I could see, they wasn't no time for mournin. I was gonna have to figure a way to take care of these youngins. A way to rid myself of Calvin. A way to help Justice. A way for an orphan. The words dug deep. I was beginnin to see the burden Momma carried. Ain't no wonder she snuffed out her life.

I remember Daddy getting on Calvin when he lied. "All a lie does is breed another until a body is so full of untruth they can't see light. The truth will set you free, boy. Set you free."

Momma and Daddy read from the good book ever night. But me, I wasn't so sure about all that malarkey. So far all I'd seen was hardship. I'd come to figure, the truth might set you free . . . but not before it rips a body apart.

Doanie never made her way back to the kitchen for supper. When I called for her, she didn't make nary a sound. Scared the dickens outta me.

"Doanie, honey. Where are you?" I crept through the house and peered into the back room. There she was, layin on her back holdin one child in one arm and the other in another. I pulled a second quilt over them and tucked it. They was tired. Worry does that to a soul. Reckon I oughta know. Momma musta known I'd be a worrier and that's why she named me the same.

For an instant, I gazed over them three babies and my heart opened up. Compassion seeped from ever crevice of my body. I knew they was no way I'd let them little ones starve. What kind of person would turn their back on these youngins?

There was only two split logs left by the fireplace, so I took the hook and shoved around the embers, then seated them two logs tight. The wood caught fast, and before you could say apple butter them flames popped and crackled, licking at that wood like a thirsty dog lappin water. The room warmed. I dusted my hands and made my way through the broke door to get an armload of wood.

Lightning lit the sky, showin the outline of the ridge above the house. In the far distance, I could hear a soft rumble. Best take in two armloads. If the rain made it over the mountain it would soak the wood. I propped open the door and stacked a waist-high rack of wood. "That oughta do."

A breeze whipped up, carryin the scent of rain. It give me precious memories. Daddy loved to sit in the rocker on the porch during a spring rain. "Ain't nothing sweeter than the smell of rain. It washes the soul," he'd say. "Go ahead. Lift your nose in the air like a hound and sniff. Take in a big ole breath." He'd stick his nose straight up and snort real loud, then cough. Momma patted him on the arm and laughed while me and the boys did just what Daddy told us.

My heart ached for my folks and my brothers. There was a time we was a real family. Daddy, Momma, Calvin, Justice, and me. Seems we was happy until Daddy died. That's when Calvin took a hankerin for money and Justice took to drinkin. Momma did her best to protect me from the death on the mountain. She kept me home, teachin me to read and write, and when she did mention the sickness on the mountain, it was to the point. "The fever is runnin wild. Keep everthing clean. You hear me? Boil the water. Wash the dishes and clothes in hot water." It was like she knew somethin nobody else knew.

The wind brushed my hair around my face, and I took in a gulp and filled my lungs with air favorin honeysuckle and lavender. The fragrance made me hunger for a taste of both. I closed my eyes and pictured them times on the porch with Momma and Daddy. Despite the memories, one thing was for sure. They really wasn't a sweeter smell than a spring rain.

Turning to go inside, I stopped short. A crack of wood. Then another. I reached inside the door and grabbed the shotgun. "Who's there? Now ain't the time to be hush-hush lest you want a backside full of buckshot. That you, Calvin? Done told you to find you someplace else to light. You ain't here half the time anyhow." I pulled the gun to my shoulder and pulled back the hammers. "Calvin, come on out. Show yourself."

"Put that thing down." Ely stepped to the porch, totin a child by the wrist.

"Ely?" I rested the gun against the house. "Whatta you out wanderin around this late for?" Taking the oil lamp from the hanger, I held it up. A warm yellow glow lit the porch.

"Well, set me a trap to snag that ole coon that's been raidin my henhouse. Come to find out, it wasn't no coon. It was this here youngin." He lifted her arm above her head. She twisted to free herself.

"That ain't tellin me why you're here."

Ely stepped onto the porch. The wrist he held belonged to a young girl. Her face was dirty. Stringy locks of long dark curls wrapped around her shoulders.

"I took the wife over the mountain this mornin to visit her sister. Didn't think it would look right for me to take this girl in . . . me bein a man and all. Especially with the wife not around."

I knew what he was achin to say, and after all he'd done for me, I'd not be able to tell him no.

"I's wonderin if you could keep her here tonight. I'll take her home tomorrow."

I took in a deep breath and blew it out. "Just like you to be a gentleman. Refusin to keep a young girl in your house without your wife bein home. Momma always said things like that showed a man had integrity."

He smiled.

I bent over the edge of the porch to get a better look at the girl. "You got a name?"

"Abeleen. Abeleen Wallen."

Wallen. That name rung a bell. "You John Wallen's girl?"

She nodded.

"Your daddy forges. That's right. He forges. I got two knives he made for huntin. Why you stealin' Ely's chickens? Your daddy's a good provider."

Her eyes begin to water. "Daddy died. Been gone close to a month now. He got the fever. Momma went last year."

Ely sat down on the porch and pulled the girl close. "Youngin, why didn't you just tell me John died?"

This was the hardship on the mountain. Folks was spread so far apart, unless they met up when the pastor come over, you didn't always get news. Unless it was gossip, and that seemed to travel on the wind.

"I was sceered and hungry. Miss Louise's been droppin me dumplins by. She's good like that. Then all of a sudden they wasn't no more dumplins. I thought I made her mad."

I stepped off the porch and took the girl by the shoulders, twistin her toward me. "Abeleen, Momma died three days ago. When was the last time she brought you dumplins?"

"A few days ago." The girl stared at the ground. "Miss Louise is de-aa-ddd?" She went to sobbin.

Momma's mood had changed about that time. But why wouldn't she tell me about these youngins? Here stood another one she'd been takin care of for a month.

42

I pressed my face into my hands. "Lawsy mercy me."

"Miss Worie, can you manage a youngin for the night? I can pick her up and take her to the pastor in town tomorrow. Youngin don't need to be alone."

That just run all over me. What did he think I was? Burnt bread? I was a girl alone. What made me any different than this youngin? Jealousy took hold of my heart, squeezing like a snake with a mouse. For a minute, my own selfishness of being without Momma come out.

"Miss Worie, I realize you's by yourself too. But the way I see it, you're a young woman. This here is a child."

I took Abeleen by the shoulders again. "How old are you?"

Her eyes called out to my heart. "I . . . I'm eleven."

Eleven. She was a youngin. I pushed hard to shove back the tears and get my wits about me. Words wouldn't come out, so I cleared my throat. I was ashamed and my face growed warm. How could I be so selfish?

"You'll have to share the floor. I got three more youngins inside."

Ely come to his feet. "Three more. Who?"

"The Whitefield children. Doanie, Farrell, and T. J. Now, John Wallen's child. Next thing I know, them Olsen youngins will be here."

"Lordy, lordy. This mountain is ravaged by the fever. People is droppin like flies." Ely brushed the girl's hair behind her ear.

"I'll take her tonight, then you best get your wife. It's gonna take all three of us to figure out what to do. Go on now. Go home. Then get back here tomorrow."

Ely tipped his hat and headed into the darkness.

"And bring me a couple of them chickens for stew when you come."

The thunder cracked. This time loud and close. Abeleen jumped like a scared squirrel. "It's fine, honey. Just a storm brewin. You're safe here." I give her a little hug. "Let's feed you and go dig you up a blanket." I nudged her through the door. Lightnin hit, this time lightin up a tree at the edge of the woods.

I'd heard folks talk about lightnin striking twice in one place. I reckon it had done struck me twice and then some.

CHAPTER
SIX

The sun crept through the shutters, warming my cheeks, bringin me out of my sleep. I pushed back in the rocker and stretched. It seemed ever bone in my spine cracked. Sleepin in a rocker ain't easy on the bones, despite my youth. Resting my hands on the arms of the chair, I lifted myself up. "Oh, Lordy mercy." I was stiff as a board.

I coulda slept in my bed, but I feared one of them youngins would raise up in the night and lose their bearins. They looked a mess layin there. Their bodies twisted and contorted over one another. I rubbed my eyes and smiled. I had no intentions of gettin attached to this bunch of youngins, but I had to admit, they was sweet piled up like a litter of pups huggin their momma's teats.

The fire still harbored a small flame, so I stoked it tight and pulled the hook close to hang the coffeepot. I grabbed my knife and headed to the smokehouse to shave off some bacon.

The rain through the night left the path muddy. My shoes sunk into the thick mire and popped with each step. I knew pullin that smokehouse door open would be a test with deep mud. It scraped the dirt as it was. Mud would just dam it up, so I shoved the knife into my boot. Takin the rope handle, I wrapped it tight around my wrist and planted one foot on the side of the building.

"Uhhhhh!" I grunted and heaved. The door drug hard over the mud, and when I stepped inside my heart hit rock bottom.

"You had me blocked outta the house."

I stepped back against the door. "Calvin, what in the name of all that is good are you doin here? I done told you to stay away. Go sleep where you spend the most of your time. Which, by the way, ain't here!"

"I could stay down at the boardin house."

"If that's where you been stayin anyway. Now, get out." I put my finger in his chest. "I mean it."

Calvin busted out laughin. "Ain't you tough?" He shoved my shoulder and bounced me against the side of bacon hangin from a hook. I slid to the dirt floor. A ham hock swung overhead, smackin me in the face.

"I'll thank you to keep your hands to yourself." I slipped my hand to my boot and fingered the knife. They was no reason to think Calvin would really hurt me. Outside of some bully-pushin, he never offered to do me any real harm. Leastways, not till Momma died. The things in that jar of Momma's had his hackles up. Nowadays, I couldn't be sure what Calvin would do. He'd gone from all hot air to varmint. Greed does dire things to a person.

"Whatta you want, Calvin? I ain't got nothing."

"I done told you I'd be back to get Momma's jar. Ain't nothing gonna stop me."

"Your head is harder than a wood block. I told you they ain't no jar." I grabbed his shirt as he started out the door. "Where you goin?"

"Now that you got the door unbarred . . . to the house."

Fear shot through me like a bullet. Them youngins was in the house. I couldn't let him in. He'd scare the devil outta them.

46

"Let go!" He wrapped his hand around my wrist and twisted it behind my back. My arm stung like I'd stuck it in a hive of bees.

"They ain't no jar, Calvin. Take the side of pork from the smokehouse, take Daddy's tools—I don't care. But they ain't no jar."

Calvin stomped through the mud to the house. No amount of me tuggin or yankin stopped him, so I made my way around him and planted myself in front of the door.

He roared laughin. "You protectin a busted screen door?" Calvin took my arm and slung me away. He took hold of the screen door frame and jerked it off, sending it sailin into the mud by the porch.

"Look what you done! Calvin, why don't you just go? Momma is gone. It's just me. They ain't nothin here for you."

"They's a jar here, and I don't plan on leavin till I turn it up. Even if that means rippin ever door, shelf, or cabinet outta this house."

Calvin turned to kick open the plank door where the screen once stood. Just then, the door come open and there stood little T. J.

Calvin's eyes darted down to the child standing in the door. He squatted to look the boy eye to eye. Fear crawled up my back like a stinger bug. I knew Calvin. Knew what he was thinkin.

"Don't you touch that child." I pushed past him, knocking him to his rear and scoopin T. J. into my arms.

Calvin climbed to his feet. "Where'd this wee one come from? You been holdin out on your family, Worie? Hidin a youngin? When'd you become a momma?" The words slid out of his mouth like melted butter.

I hoisted T. J. onto my hip. He laid his head against my neck. A yawn stretched across his lips. "This ain't my youngin, you smart mouth."

"Looks pretty incriminatin to me. You standin there with a

youngin on your hip and all. Where's the daddy? Maybe I need to seek him out and make a righteous man outta him."

I rolled my eyes. "Smart skipped you, didn't it, Calvin? Ain't a lick of sense in your body." T. J. was small but solid. I boosted him up higher on my hip. "Let's get you inside, little one." I leaned against the wooden door, shoved it open, and slipped inside. Try as I might to shut the door fast, Calvin managed a foot inside.

I squelched raisin my voice. "Get out." The words squeaked through gritted teeth. I set T. J. down and patted his rear, sending him into another room.

"Who's the daddy?" Calvin snapped.

"You idiot. I told you, he ain't my youngin. His momma and daddy is Rennie and Elbert Whitefield."

"So, why you got him?"

"I got him because him and his two sisters was starvin. Elbert and Rennie died from the fever. Them youngsters come here lookin for Momma."

"Our momma?" You could see curiosity wrote on his face.

"Yeah, our momma. Seems she'd been carryin food down to these youngins after their momma and daddy died. Momma was a good woman. Kind. Somethin you don't know nothing about."

Calvin went to prowlin through the cupboard, slingin plates and bowls everwhere.

"Stop it, Calvin. Just stop it. I done told you—"

"Miss Worie, is somethin wrong?" Doanie stood swipin the sleep from her eyes.

I run to give her a hug. "Mornin, sweetie. Things is fine. Why don't you take your brother and sister out to the outhouse. A night's sleep is a long time to hold your water." I pulled some cheesecloth from the shelf and handed it to her. "They's a bucket of water by the outhouse. Wash up before you come back. Clean up that boy. He's soakin wet." I smiled, tryin to hide my frustration.

Doanie picked up T. J. and took Farrell by the hand. "Yes

ma'am." The child was obedient. Her folks had taught her well, and it drew tears to my eyes to think she was takin on raisin her siblins when she was just a youngin herself.

"Set that boy on the hole. It's time he starts learnin to do his business in the outhouse instead of in his drawers."

A grin tipped the edges of Doanie's lips. "Yes ma'am."

I knew once them little ones was out of the house, Calvin would start in on me. And he did.

"Three! Lands a Goshen! Is they anything else I need to know?" Calvin squawked.

I walked into the back room and nudged Abeleen. "Abeleen, honey. Get up. Go on out to the outhouse. Doanie's out there with the others."

The girl stretched and stood.

"Four! There's four youngins."

"Good to know you can count, Calvin. Now get out. Trust me, if they was any money in this house, don't you think I'd be usin it right now to do something with them children?"

Calvin drew back and spit on the floor. I thought my stomach would turn. "What do you plan on doin with these youngins?"

I dropped a rag over the wad of spit and dried it. "I don't know, Calvin. But I do know I got no plans of letting them starve." I couldn't believe what I heard myself sayin. The words just fell outta my mouth before I could stop 'em. "I reckon I'll bed them down in the barn and give them a place to stay."

Calvin went to laughin. "You! You're gonna take to raisin somebody else's youngins?"

I could feel my anger risin. It wasn't enough Calvin was selfish and sneaky, but he still seemed to have no sadness for the loss of Momma or what she'd been doin on the mountain. That was hard to take in. A woman who give all she had to raise him, make him a home. Love him despite his meanness—and he didn't have an ounce of sadness. Just greed.

"Yep, Calvin. There is four youngins. They got no folks. Neither do I. I reckon all us orphans might as well put our heads together and make a way to survive. Now, unless you got plans of plowin up the field this mornin . . ." I picked up Daddy's gun and once again pulled back the hammers. "I suppose you might orta find you someplace else to go." My heart raced. I knew Calvin could yank that gun from me at any second.

"Stand your ground." That's what Momma used to tell me when Calvin picked at me. "Stand your ground." A skunk don't have to spray his stench. He just has to raise his tail and folks take heed. I dug my heels in and pulled the gun to my eye.

"Now might be a good time to make yourself a decision, Calvin." My insides quivered.

He stared hard at me, then stomped outta the house. I could feel the sweat beadin on my brow. Calvin was gone for now. But he'd be back. He was always like a cat—findin his prey and then playin with it before he bit down on its neck. For now, he was gone.

Abeleen headed outside with the other children, and I watched as she walked, twistin her hair into a bun behind her head. There was a twinge of determination in how she walked that moved me.

Here was this child. All alone. Still carryin herself with determination. Right that second, I learned a lesson from a youngin—one that would change my life forever. I'd be like Abeleen. Determined to make a way for me. Determined to make a way for these youngins. Determined to keep that blessed jar hid away.

SEVEN

I took T. J. from Doanie's arms and rested him on my hip. "There's a wagon at the side of the barn. Either of you two ever hitched a horse?" I pointed at the girls.

"I have." Abeleen raised her hand. "Daddy showed me how."

"Good, take Doanie and show her. She needs to know how. Hitch up ole Sally. Bring the wagon around."

"Yes ma'am."

The hair on the back of my neck raised ever time that child called me ma'am, but I couldn't rightly fuss about manners.

"We'll load up and head to your cabin, Doanie. Get what you need. Bring it back here."

"But what about Momma?"

"You don't worry yourself about that. Mr. Ely and me will give her a proper burial. You focus on helpin take care of your brother and sister." I tinkered with her braid. "Now, go on. Get Sally."

Doanie stood, mouth gapin. "Miss Worie, does that mean we're gonna stay with you?"

I rested my hands on my hips. "Well, unless you think you can manage on your own."

"We're grateful. All of us." Water filled her eyes. "They's something you need to know."

"What could that be?" I asked. "They surely ain't no more surprises, are they?"

"Momma is still in her bed. I didn't have no way of buryin her."

I felt my stomach turn. How could my momma have been takin food to these youngins and not know Mrs. Whitefield was dead in her bed?

Since she brought up the subject, I commenced to feel out what we was in for once we got to the Whitefield cabin. "How long has your momma been passed?" It was an answer I dreaded to hear. I was sure the house reeked of rotten flesh.

Doanie dropped her chin to her chest. "About two weeks."

It took me a minute to gather my thoughts before I spoke. There was nothin I wanted to say to make this child feel like her momma's dyin was her fault. I knew the sting of that guilt, and I wasn't about to lay that burden on Doanie. All I wanted was to get Ely and maybe the sheriff and see how to manage buryin the child's momma.

I pulled her close. "Go help Abeleen hitch up Sal."

I loaded the youngins into the wagon. Sal was all hitched up and we headed out. A half mile down the bumpy road Ely met up with us.

"Where you off to? I told you I'd be up to take Abeleen down to the pastor. He's in town."

I pulled Sally to a halt and lifted my face toward the morning sun. The early sun always felt cleansin. Like it could take hold of what was in a body's soul, be it sickness or sadness, and suck it out. I felt them same words I told Calvin seep to the surface again. I was gonna say it again. I was gonna push the words out for Ely to hear.

"Ain't no need to take her to town. She can stay with me. I got these Whitefield youngins. What's one more?" I shrugged.

"You're gonna need help. Want me to tag along?"

"Much obliged. I ain't ashamed to take your help. Besides, they ain't stayin for free. They have to help with chores." I raised my voice and turned to the children. "That clear? Everbody has to help with chores in exchange for a bed and food."

They nodded.

"We ain't gonna be called a bunch of misfits. We're gonna do what we have to do. Ain't we?"

"Miss Worie, I gots to say, this is mighty big of you," Ely said.

I snapped the reins against Sal's rear. "You think this is big. Just wait till we get to the Whitefields."

They wasn't nobody more taken back than me when I pushed open the Whitefields' cabin door. Flies buzzed in the cabin, and there was still the stench of death. Ely went to openin the windows. There was no need to guess what shape Mrs. Whitefield was in. Leastways, not with all them flies. Where they was flies, they was maggots. The thought made me gag.

"Lord have mercy." Ely pushed his nose into the bend of his arm, then held up the other hand. "Make them youngins stay in the wagon."

My eyes burned from the smell as I turned toward the children still in the wagon. "Stay there till I call you."

Doanie promptly set down. T. J. went to cryin for his momma, and Farrell buried her face in Doanie's lap.

"It's gonna be fine. You'll see. Just sit still." I pulled my shirt around my nose and followed Ely through the cabin. Sure enough, there laid Mrs. Whitefield, one arm across her eyes and the other across her stomach. Maggots crawled all over her, and it was all I could do to not vomit.

"What do you need outta here?" Ely covered Mrs. Whitefield with a quilt, partly to cover the sight, partly to cover the smell.

"Uh . . . what beddin and clothes these youngins have. Extra plates and cups." I scanned the small cabin. Pickins was slim. A rocker by the fireplace, a small table in the corner. Blankets in the cupboard. We didn't have much at our cabin, but lookin around this house, I could see Momma had left me plenty.

Ely helped me load a hay-stuffed mattress in the wagon, and I gathered what few things the children had. As I started out the door, my eye caught a rag toy layin in a basket by the fireplace, made from scraps of old clothes with button eyes. I could see Mrs. Whitefield had intended it for T. J. I set in the rocker and drew my fingers over the tattered toy. The needle still hung from the button eye. I pushed it through the cloth, tied a knot in the thread, and bit it off with my teeth. T. J. would want this sweet gift. It wasn't nothing fancy, but a body could see the love in each stitch. Every one exactly the same size. Carefully darned together. Kissed with tender lips.

I could see there was more to motherin than birthin and feedin. There was tendin to, carin for . . . lovin. There was things I'd took for granted with my own momma. And I wondered for a minute if I could come close to bein what was needed for these little ones.

The words from Momma's Bible come back to me. *Then were there brought unto him little children, that he should put his hands on them, and pray . . .*

Brought to Him. Brought to me. My heart ached. The sting of death was still fresh in my own heart. Could I manage this?

Ely tapped my shoulder, and I jumped like I was jabbed with a prod. "Miss Worie, Pastor Jess just rode up. He was passin by, so I hollered at him."

"Oh. Alright. Don't reckon I've ever met the pastor."

"Good man. He is for sure. He can tell us what to do with Mrs. Whitefield."

I walked onto the porch, clutchin that rag toy tight. The pastor slid off his saddle and walked toward me. He stopped at the wagon and hugged the children, pullin T. J. outta his sister's arms and tossin him into the air. It was the first time I'd heard the boy giggle.

"They ain't nothin sweeter than a child's laughter. No wonder the good Lord wanted them brought to Him." The pastor set T. J. back in the wagon.

Brought to Him? They was brought to me. Leavin little children without folks didn't sound like a person who wanted them brought to him. It was strange the pastor spoke the same Scripture that was on my mind.

"Ely." He tipped his hat.

"Pastor Jess. Good to see you. You're just in time."

The pastor stuck out his hand. "And who's this here lovely lady?" He cupped my hand between both of his, his touch gentle, his smile kindly.

"Worie. Worie Dressar." I eyed his hand, then gently pulled mine away.

"Dressar. Dressar. Any kin to Justice?"

I felt the color leave my face. "Yes sir. He's my brother."

The pastor cocked his head, his eyes readin me like a book. "Justice is a good man. He's just burdened. Visited him at the jail yesterday. He's about dried out."

I wasn't sure what to say. He was right. Justice was never a bad child. But when Daddy died, he went to drinkin and that become his lover. Daddy's passin was hard on Momma and me, but Justice suffered. Momma tried over and over to veer Justice away from the hooch, but it had its grip tight on him.

Justice looked like Daddy. Tall, rusty-colored hair. Eyes as green as the summer fields. When he was dry, he was a hard worker. Kept the farm up. Watched over me and Momma. But when he give in to the hooch, it'd take him away for days. Leave him in a hard place.

"What am I in time for?" Even with a puzzled look the pastor was handsome. He was younger than I expected. To hear Momma talk about him, he was older than her, but he wasn't much over me. A squared chin lined with a short, well-kept beard sprinkled with white. His hair was cut neat around his ears and neck. His shoulders were broad and his hands large and strong. I wondered if he was anything like he seemed. I could tell he worked at more than preachin the good book.

It took me a minute, but I managed to muster the words. "Mrs. Whitefield is dead. Died from the fever."

Pastor Jess wheeled around and looked at the children. "Oh no. When?"

"Ain't sure, but these youngins come to me yesterday huntin for food. When we come here to see what could be done, we found her dead in the bed. From the looks of her, she's been gone a spell."

The pastor bowed his head. His lips commenced to mouth a silent prayer. "These children are . . ."

"Orphans." I finished his sentence. Nobody knew what that meant better than me.

The preacher pushed his hair back and reset his hat. His fingers scratched at the hair on his chin. "It might take me a bit to find a place for them to stay."

"No need, Pastor. My own momma died a few days back. It's just me now. I'll tend to them."

He took my hand again. "I'm so sorry for your loss, Miss Worie. Are you sure you wanna take on youngins? You're mighty young yourself."

"My age ain't got nothin to do with the needs. But what we want here is knowin what to do with Mrs. Whitefield. We can't just leave her to be eat by the varmints."

The pastor walked into the house, and I could hear his voice. "Oh Lord, I pray for this woman and her soul. She was a good woman. Special in every way. Take her soul into Your arms and give her peace."

After a bit, he come from inside. "The house reeks. I don't reckon it can be lived in now. We sure can't pick up the body without it fallin apart. So you got all you need for them youngins from inside?"

I nodded.

"Then you take them children and head home. Ely, can you stay with me?"

"Indeed, Preacher."

"Go on now. Take them children home. I'll be along later. Help you settle them in."

I climbed into the wagon and nudged Sal to move. Just as we made the bend at the top of the summit, I caught a whiff of fire. When I turned to look behind me, I could see flames risin above the treetops. I reckon they did the only thing they really could. Set the house ablaze. That would be the best way to do away with Mrs. Whitefield.

That sweet smell of rain was took real quick by the scent risin from the Whitefields. Just one more ugly memory. Burnin wasn't somethin folks did unless the ground was so froze they couldn't dig or they was some bad sickness. I hated for them youngins to see such a thing, but it was the right thing to do. The whole mountain would know soon.

We set there for a spell, watchin the smoke curl into the sky. Them youngins had a minute to take in that they didn't have a home no more.

The mornin passed quickly. I pulled the wagon to the edge of the summit and climbed down from the seat. Walking to the edge of the rocky path, I took in a deep breath. The clouds looked like tufts of white snow floatin across the miles of mountains. In the distance, I could see the remains of the storm from the night before, makin its way over the ridges. A bird soared on the breeze above, dippin and divin, and his call echoed over the pass.

T. J. lifted his finger and pointed. "Bird."

"That's right, baby. Bird. Beautiful bird."

T. J. raised his arms for me to pick him up. I brushed his hair from his eyes and gently kissed his forehead. "Look, honey. Look what Miss Worie found." I pulled the toy from my dress pocket. "Your momma made you a rag toy."

He snugged the toy under his arm and poked his fingers into his mouth.

I set the boy on his sister's lap and crawled back into the wagon. "Hup, Sally. Hup." Sal leaned into the yoke and groaned. "Good girl. Hup."

We turned the bend, and I had a strange feelin in my gut. Like I was bein watched. I turned real quick to look over my shoulder, wonderin if my mind was playin havoc with me again. Maybe I'd see my dead momma. I shook the thought from my head. A rustle in the bushes give me a jolt. I thought for a second I'd got a glimpse of someone followin us.

EIGHT

How much more could I take?

"Carry the boy in and put him on that pallet." I pushed Doanie's hair behind her ear. "It's been a long day for him."

Doanie hoisted the child, limp as a wet rag, and hung his head over her shoulder. She snugged him onto her hip and climbed from the wagon. Farrell followed. She stopped and eyed me.

"What's on your mind?" I asked.

Farrell stared, never utterin a word, then trailed behind her sister. There wasn't much reason to ask what she had on her mind. It didn't take a real smart person to know. She could only watch the smoke from her home, along with her life, whirl into the sky. Her momma and daddy gone. Maybe she was angry. Maybe afraid. But broken for sure.

I could only hope she didn't blame me for her momma dyin. It didn't take much to know that grief could skew the truth. Farrell might not see me as the woman who was willin to take her in. She might only twist the flames of her home and her momma's dyin to me. Even when I had nothing to do with either.

Still, her silence spoke louder than a scream. And to me, that wasn't anything good. Pent-up pain was never good.

"Miss Worie, she'll be fine." Abeleen squeezed my shoulder, wakin me from my thinkin. I nodded and patted her hand.

This youngin was wise beyond her years. Momma used to tell me there was some folks who were helpless on the outside but fearless on the inside. All it took was a push to set the inside part free. Once it come out, they were strong. Real strong. Abeleen looked to be one of them people. She'd lost her folks, learned to fend on her own to survive. Even at eleven, she'd figured how to make do.

"Abeleen?" I asked. "How did Miss Louise know to bring you dumplins?"

The girl hung her head, her fingers drawin circles on the wagon bench. She pondered for a while before she finally spoke. "She was carryin corn from town, saw me haulin rock."

"Rock?"

Abeleen wrapped her arms around herself. Her voice quivered. "I was buryin Daddy. He was so sick. He died on the porch tryin to call to me. They was blood comin from his mouth. All I knew to do was tie a rope around him and let the mule pull him into the woods."

"They ain't no need to say no more," I said. "You're a brave child."

"Miss Louise helped me finish stackin rocks over Daddy, then next thing I knowed she was bringin me dumplins 'bout once a week. Sometimes I'd see her, other times she just left them on the porch."

I pulled her close to me and squeezed. "Poor child."

She pulled away. "I ain't poor. Ain't nothing poor about me. My daddy always told me we was rich with the love of the good Lord and that was all we needed."

I wasn't about to argue with her even though I couldn't say I agreed. I was still strugglin to understand how allowin a good woman to take her life was love. Still, the thought pacified Abeleen, and I figured I might as well start choosin my battles now. This wasn't one to take on.

"Well, don't you worry none. You'll stay here. We'll manage this brokenness together." I pulled her braids behind her head. "And I don't mean no disrespect, but you need a good scrubbin. So help me put this wagon in the barn and then make your way down to the creek, wash that hair, and clean your skin."

We unhitched Sally and set her loose in the pasture, then put away the wagon. When we was done, I pulled Daddy's overalls off a nail in the barn and tossed them to her. "Go on now. Get washed up. Scrub them clothes too." Abeleen's mouth hung open like it was some big surprise I'd told her to bathe. "Go on now. I know your daddy would never let you go nasty." I pointed toward the creek. "And shut that mouth lest you catch a few flies."

She hesitated but made her way to the creek.

I set on the milkin stool and buried my face in my palms. Sobs welled up from the deepest part of me. The pictures in my head was about more than I could manage. Momma killin herself, fightin with Calvin, findin these youngins. Mrs. Whitefield. What more could happen?

Though my heart ached, it only fueled my determination. This mess won't get the best of me. "It won't." I wiped my face with the tail of my skirt and come to my feet. Takin a deep breath, I pulled my shoulders back and straightened up.

Momma had managed to fill the corn bin. She'd helped Justice slaughter a hog and a deer—the meat hung in the smokehouse. There was hens that laid. Flour in a sack. That made for enough food to last a couple of months. Spring was fresh. There was plenty of time to get a garden in the ground.

"I can do this." And I could. Momma taught me all I needed to know to make do. All but doin it without her. "I miss you, Momma. And I still don't understand how you could do this to me." I lifted my fist into the air.

"That sounded like a battle cry."

I yanked my hand to my side and wheeled around. My heart dropped into my gut. "Pastor Jess. You scared the tarnation outta me."

He stepped into the barn and pulled his hat from his head. "Wasn't my intention . . . to scare you, I mean." He stuck out his hand. "Friends?"

I tried to find words. "Friends, I reckon."

He motioned to the bale of hay. "Can I sit?"

"Sure. That's about the best seat I can offer you."

"I suppose it'll do. We need to talk about these youngins."

This pastor was comin across a little pushy. It wasn't clear to me just what he was getting at. Maybe it was his tone. I ain't sure. He wasn't hateful, but it riled me that after his howdy ma'am, the next words outta his mouth was talkin about the children. We was managin just fine. The man seemed kind enough and Ely trusted him, but I guess I wasn't to that place yet. Nice as Pastor Jess seemed, he hadn't earned my trust.

"What's to talk about? There's four youngins. They're welcome here. We'll fare just fine." I crossed my arms to show him I meant business.

"You ain't prepared to take on little ones. You're a child yourself."

That was all it took to raise the hair on the back of my neck. I stepped closer, my finger straightened to a point. "I ain't sure who you think you are, Pastor. But I'm seventeen. I ain't no child. I'm a grown woman with plenty of know-how. Just cause I chose not to marry don't mean I'm not prepared. So whoever give you permission to judge me, just take their words and—"

"Hold up there. Just wait a minute. Don't get your hackles up. I ain't here to judge you. I'm here to help."

"Your idea of help is tellin me I can't manage these children?" I could feel my temper crawlin from the depths.

"All I'm sayin is you just lost your own momma. It might be too much for you to take on four children who has lost theirs."

"Ever think it might make us more alike, Pastor? I might just understand the pain them little ones feel. I might just understand the anger, the hurt, the frustration of becomin an . . . orphan." I huffed. "I might just be more prepared than you think."

"Let's start this conversation over." Pastor Jess stood and pressed his hands deep into his pockets. His head twisted from side to side. "Can we try this again? I done messed up."

I walked to the barn door. "We sure can, Pastor. You can take the mess you made and scoot right on outta my barn. Get on your horse and leave."

The pastor dug the toe of his boot into the soft dirt of the barn floor. He drawed a line and stepped back. "I reckon I crossed over the line. Can you forgive me?"

I was breathin like I'd run a race. It was all I could do to be stern but nice. What I wanted was to backhand him. Pastor or not. I took in a deep breath and swallowed. The pastor never looked up. It was like watchin a whipped dog cower. He never opened his mouth, and the silence was killin me.

"Aw, alright. We can start again. But you don't make no more assumptions. You hear me?"

He smiled. "How can I help you settle these children in?"

I squinted. Then a thought come to me. "You can help me build some beds. You any good at building?"

"Might be."

Daddy's hammer hung on the barn wall by the claw. I took it down and tossed it at the pastor's feet. "Take off that fancy coat and get to work. I need four for the back room in the barn. That would just about do it."

CHAPTER
NINE

After the children was bedded down, I filled the coffeepot with water and hung it over the fire. We didn't have much, but Momma bartered her canned foods for coffee down in Wears Cove. I pulled the can from the cupboard and popped the lid open. The scent of a woody grind filled the room. One thing she taught me was how to make a good strong brew. "It ain't good coffee unless it makes the hair on your arms stand straight," she'd say.

Between the katydids and the frogs, the noise comin through the windows was enough to wake the dead. Despite the confusion of chirps and trills, these critters still managed to somehow come together in perfect harmony. I closed my eyes and listened as the song made the mountains come alive, then stepped outside and gazed toward the heavens. The sky filled with stars blinked in rhythm. It was like the night sky had a heartbeat. I smiled, thinkin of them times Daddy talked about the heart of the mountains. "The good Lord give these hills life. From the stars to the clouds to the breeze and the sun. If you lay your head on the ground and be right still, you can feel it beat—the soul that lives here. Ain't nothin like it, Worie. Nothin."

That was the sweet thing about Daddy. He had a hardy love for the world around him. To him, every inch of the mountain lived. "We owe ever stitch of this beauty to the good Lord."

I never really understood how Daddy could give such attention to somebody he couldn't see. But him and Momma both give a lot of credit to the good Lord. Me . . . what I did believe went to the wayside when the good Lord let an angel shoot herself.

The lid on the coffeepot commenced to jiggle so I headed inside, but not until I kissed my fingers and blew it toward the heavens. "That's for you, Momma. Daddy." A body could only hope they caught the kiss on the breeze.

I strained the dark liquid into a cup and made my way to the rocker, snugglin in. Steam twirled in soft designs as it rose off the cup. I leaned back in the rocker and sipped. My eyes scanned the room to the stone that kept Momma's secret. Momma sure didn't hoard money. It was hard enough to come by. What she got, she used to buy necessities.

My knees bent and the rocker swayed forward. I sipped again. What if I pulled that stone outta the hearth? Reckon what I'd find? It had to be something special for Calvin to be so fired up.

My fingers gently rubbed the tin cup. "Hummm. Wonder if . . ."

There is somethin to the sayin "curiosity killed the cat," but even that warning didn't stop me from wonderin. I set the cup down and walked to Momma's secret spot. She had her way of countin them stones and openin up that hole. A body had to press on just the right spot to get that stone to slide. She was good at hiding things . . . them youngins she was feedin, the jar. Her secret was more than the jar. It was in what it meant.

My fingers climbed the stones. One, two, three, four up. One, two, three, four over. I pushed the stone and slid it out. There in the hole laid a blue Mason jar.

I slid my fingers around the jar and twisted it around. Slips of paper spun inside. A small cloth bag no bigger around than a watch flopped in the bottom. Three nickels. Certainly not the treasure Calvin thought. What was so important about this stupid jar?

I could have just pulled the jar out, and the next time Calvin come around threatenin me, just give it to him. Wouldn't he be surprised? It ain't always about who wins the prize, sometimes it's all about principle. And though I ain't right proud of it, I was stubborn.

Calvin always had a gift of twistin the truth, lyin, swindlin folks to get what he wanted. Didn't matter how many times Daddy would blister his rear as a youngin, Calvin just took the punishment and then went right back to the same ole thing. What burns my britches is how he found out about this jar. What could he have possibly seen that made him want a jar full of notes? Three nickels might buy two bags of flour. It sure as whiz wasn't no treasure.

"One of these days I'm gonna be rich. Ain't nothing gonna keep me tied to this place," Calvin would say after he had a tannin. He'd stomp off and look for a new way to get what he wanted.

I turned the lid and the metal scraped the glass jar, sendin chills up my arms. Reachin the tips of my fingers inside, I grabbed the roll of paper scraps and pulled it out. Gingerly I unrolled the papers. Notes. That's all they was. Notes wrote in a neat hand.

Trust in the Lord *with all thine heart; and lean not unto thine own understanding. From the good book's Proverbs, chapter three. Verse five.*

My heart is broken. I buried Evan today. I gave up everything to be with him. What do I do but trust, even when I haven't got the understanding? But how is it, when a person gives up all they have, does things only get worse? Folks are dying everwhere.

Good Father, help me understand.

It took me a spell to read the note. They ain't been a schoolteacher in the gap for several years, so most of what I learned,

Momma taught me betwixt her cannin and gardenin. It was enough to make me hungry to learn more.

Each note listed words from the good book, then Momma's trouble. I suppose of the few I read, I was taken back by her pleas, her prayers. They was somethin about threadin them letters together like threadin a needle that made me want to stitch together more and more sentences.

Momma was right about one thing. Folks was dyin all over the mountain. It was like the fever was pickin and choosin who it wanted to snuff out, and it looked to be the adults. I glanced through the door at the youngins on the floor. They didn't get the fever, but it didn't stop them from bein victims.

I glanced again at the papers. *I gave up everthing.* What did Momma give up? Why?

More questions. More things I didn't understand. *Lean not unto thine own understanding.* My head felt like it was gonna split open like a dry log.

I rolled the papers and tied a piece of twine around them, then slid them back into the jar. It was like that jar got hot in my hands. So hot I couldn't hold it. I twisted the lid, stuck the jar back in the hole, and covered it with the stone. I looked at my hands. They was just regular. The burnin was in my mind, just like seein Momma was.

I reckon worry and grief does queer things to a body. But here I found myself hung between being a child and being a woman. Part of that was Momma's fault—keepin me home instead of sending me on my own after I said no to marryin Trigger. It tore me between wanting to stay a youngin and becoming a woman. It was time to be a woman. I had these youngins now. I needed to be grown. Mountain women shovel their feelins over the shoulder and go on. It's what they do. It was what I would do. I kept tellin myself this just so it would sink in.

I picked up my coffee and sat back in the rocker, my toes pushin the chair enough to make it sway. My mind started to rest when a gasp raised from my chest. "Pastor Jess!" I'd left him in the barn workin.

Grabbin up a quilt and tossin it over my shoulders, I lit the extra lamp and headed to the barn.

"Pastor, I done got so busy with them youngins, I plumb forgot you."

The pastor was nowhere to be found. His horse stood, head in the food trough, still saddled. I walked the inside of the barn, holdin the lamp over darkened crevices to see where he mighta ended up.

"Hard to sleep with a lamp burnin."

I nearly jumped outta my skin. "Where you hidin?"

Strands of hay fell from the loft, and when I looked up a set of feet hung from the loft floor.

"You ain't even unsaddled your horse."

The feet disappeared and footsteps clomped down the loft ladder. "Yep, that'd be right. I'm guessin he's as tired as me."

"Why didn't you come up to the house?" I asked.

The pastor wiped his face on his sleeve. "I wasn't invited, for one. And I was busy building beds." He pointed to the far side of the barn. "Four beds. I set them together by twos. Saw something like this in Knoxville one time. Stacked beds wasn't your idea, but I thought it right clever."

And it was right clever. Pastor Jess managed to build a bed for each child, and he'd even added some sides to T. J.'s so he didn't fall out.

"I gotta say, Pastor. You're right handy. These is real nice." I walked around the wooden beds, eyein the handiwork. "Real nice. I ain't never seen anything better." A smile come across my lips. "I suppose a thank-you is in order."

He moseyed next to me and crossed his arms, admirin his work. "They are real nice, ain't they?"

I rolled my eyes. "I done said they was. Don't you believe me, or are you just fishin for kind words?"

Pastor Jess went to laughin. "I was lookin for both, but seems I ain't gettin that. So can I at least get a bowl of that vegetable soup I smelled earlier?"

My face grew hot. "Uh, Pastor, I'm sorry. Wasn't my intention to forget you. Of course you can have some soup. Unsaddle that poor horse and draw him a bucket of water to wash that hay down. I'll go heat you a bowl."

"I'd be much obliged." He went to unsaddling his horse.

I run to the house and pulled the pot of soup closer to the fire, then ladled a bowl out. They was no excuse for me forgettin the pastor. He was a little pushy, but all in all he seemed kind. I never put much stock in a pastor, but that didn't mean they couldn't be kind folks.

They was no real reason for him to offer his help, still he did. Took it upon hisself to help Ely decide what to do with Mrs. Whitefield. And he didn't have to stay and build beds. But he did. I reckon that made him worth his salt.

I pushed open the barn door. "Pastor, here's your supper. I brought—" I stopped mid-sentence. There he laid in the hay on the floor, sleepin like a bear in winter.

I cocked my head. He was a handsome sort and, I suppose, a bit more than just kind. I set the bowl of soup on Daddy's work-bench, then took the quilt from around my shoulders and gently laid it over him. Pickin up the lamp, I snuck outta the barn and closed the door.

The lamp was dyin down, just like the embers in the fireplace. My coffee had done cooled down. The same way my heart felt—a little cold. I'd lost my family, and without askin I found this passel of youngins.

A song come to mind. *Was lost but now am found.*

TEN

I hadn't done much but cook and tend youngins for the past few weeks. Ely and Bess helped get the children put into doin chores, and betwixt us all, we got the garden in the ground.

The sun fought to find its way through the gray noon clouds. Spring rains come and go with the breeze, and today the water hung heavy in the sky.

Them youngins was doin their chores. Abeleen and Farrell fed the chickens, and little T. J. handed clothespins to Doanie so she could hang his washed pants. I put my two little fingers under my tongue and let a whistle whoop out. "Come on. Hurry for the barn before the rains hit." There wasn't a long breath between my whistle and holler before the rain come, the wind blowin it in long sheets across the field.

Squeals and giggles rung through the barn as them youngins darted in, shakin like wet dogs to get the water off. It was somethin to see a little laughter fill them wee ones' hearts.

T. J. flopped onto the barn floor and went to rollin in the hay. His drawers hung to his knees.

"Oh, for Pete's sake, T. J." I lifted him gently by the hands. "Look at your pants. You already filled them."

His smile drooped.

"I ain't mad at you." I squatted in front of him, takin him by the shoulders. "But you're a little man, and little men quit messin in their pants when they hit your age. Think you can work on askin for help to the outhouse *before* you turn rank?" I touched his nose with my finger. "You think you can do that?"

He stuck his finger in his mouth and nodded.

"Good. Now go tell Doanie you need your drawers changed."

I smiled as he lumbered across the barn to Doanie. It was becomin more apparent every hour that passed how much work it was gonna take to manage these little ones.

Abeleen took to pushin the huge barn door shut against the rush of the wind and rain. Just as she got the door nearly closed, a shout rang out.

"Worie, I told you I'd be back!" Calvin pressed his shoulder against the barn door and shoved, knocking Abeleen to the floor.

I rushed to her, liftin her to her feet. "Calvin, what is wrong with you? You nearly busted her head open." I dusted the hay from her clothes. Anger bubbled in my stomach . . . anger and fear. There was somethin different about Calvin this time.

He shook the rain off of his hat and pushed the barn door on open. Two more horses walked inside. I recognized the sheriff but drew a blank on the other man.

"What are you doin? Who is these men?"

"I been down in Hartsboro doin some business."

I busted out laughin. "You got business? What *business* brings you here? I done told you to find someplace else to live."

Calvin come right to my face. His breath smelled like a mixture of bad meat and liquor.

I winced. "Get outta my face." I put my palm against his chest and shoved.

He took my wrist and turned me toward the men. "I know you know the sheriff. But this here is Jordan Sikes. Mr. Sikes here runs the bank in Hartsboro. And this here . . ." Calvin pulled a folded paper from his pocket. "This is official and legal papers that says this place belongs to me."

I took a step backward, not sure whether to laugh or cry. Calvin was known for his swindlin and lyin, but I never thought he'd do somethin so mean. I whipped the paper from his hand and unfolded it.

This document certifies, that the land be left to the family.

I couldn't read no further. My stomach turned as I looked toward them youngins. There was no words that could say what was on my mind.

"You ain't serious? You can't take this place away from me."

"Yep. I can and I did." Calvin leaned against my head and whispered, "I told you I'd get Momma's jar."

I yanked away from him and turned to the sheriff. "You can't let him take my house away from me. What about these youngins?"

The sheriff looked past me. "I'm sorry, Miss Worie, this is all legal."

"Since when did 'all legal' matter on the mountain?" The sheriff stared at his feet. "Yeah, that's what I thought. You can't look me in the eye. What's this snake holdin over you, Sheriff?"

I could see shame all over his face. He didn't want to boot me off the land, but somethin or somebody was forcin his hand.

"This is on you, Sheriff Starnes. The lives of these little ones is on you." I swung around to Calvin, balled my fingers into a fist, and popped him in the jaw. "You can't do this to me." I couldn't imagine what would happen to me or these youngins. "I told you they wasn't no jar. I told you to take what you wanted from the house. Do you think if they was any money anywhere, I'd be livin in such dire straits?"

Calvin wiped a drop of blood from his lip. The sheriff grabbed my raised hand. "Now, now. They ain't no need for hittin."

I twisted to free my wrist from his grip.

"You're right, Calvin, she's got fire in her."

"I'll make you think fire." I yanked my arm hard, breakin the sheriff's hold. "Calvin, why are you doin this?"

"I did take what I wanted. The whole place. Now, me and the sheriff are here to make sure you make your way out."

"You can't do this!" I shouted. "Momma and Daddy are buried here. You can't do this." My voice quivered as I fought back the tears.

Sheriff Starnes put his hand on my shoulder. "Miss Worie, I'm afraid Calvin is right. I got papers that won't allow me to do otherwise. You got a day to pack up and leave."

"A day! That's it? A day!" I scanned the barn to the new beds the pastor had built, then I looked at them youngins lined up in a row. It felt like my chest would crack open. My legs weakened and I dropped to my knees. "What about these youngins?"

"Oh, ain't no need to worry about that. I done took care of that too." Calvin squatted in front of me. "Mr. Sikes here will take the two least ones and find them homes. The two older girls can stay with you for now."

"What?" I come to my feet and rushed in front of the children. "You ain't takin a one of these children. You hear me?"

Doanie swung T. J. on her hip and pushed Farrell behind her. "You ain't touchin my family!" she screamed.

Calvin reached for Farrell and I run at him, hittin him in the gut.

Sheriff Starnes took me by the arms. "Don't make this no harder. Let Mr. Sikes take the two."

I went to screamin as loud as I could, fightin to free myself. Doanie was hollerin and both the little ones were screamin bloody murder. Abeleen went to kickin at the sheriff to turn me loose, but all my fightin and screamin didn't help one iota. Mr. Sikes scooped

Farrell up under his arm and climbed on his horse, the child hollerin until she vomited down the side of the horse. Calvin tore T. J. loose from Doanie, leavin her on the floor sobbin.

Once the sheriff let me go, him and Sikes turned them horses and trotted outta the barn, both of the youngins bellerin and squallin.

"You got a day to get out. Understand me? A day." Calvin mounted his horse and left. I could hear his nasty laugh echo off the mountain.

There I was on my hands and knees, my heart torn outta my chest, and when I looked at them two girls bleedin tears, my grief turned to anger. I crawled to my feet, the rain gushin through the barn door in sheets. "Get up, girls," I snapped. "Come on. Get up. We can't get Farrell and T. J. back layin here on the floor squallin." I took Abeleen by the hand and helped her stand. I couldn't begin to feel how Doanie felt. Losin her momma and daddy, seein her house burned to the ground, and now havin her brother and sister took from her.

"Come on, Doanie." Abeleen pulled at her. "We're sisters now. Get up. We gotta help Miss Worie get them little ones back."

Doanie could hardly stand. Her eyes was sunk in her head, partly from her hardships, but mostly from havin her heart ripped out.

"Doanie," I said, "we're gonna fix this. It's gonna take some figurin, but we'll fix it. But right now we have to shovel the pain over our shoulders and get on with business. You understand?"

Her head wobbled like an apple teetering on a split rail. When she got her feet under her I saw somethin I never thought I'd ever see. That girl's face changed. It went from hurt to anger. Her eyes turned from a soft brown to black, and I could see the fire in her.

"Abeleen, take Sally and go down to Ely's. Tell him what happened and get him up here to help us pack up. A house is just a place to stay, it ain't our life."

She bridled the horse, then climbed up. "I'll be back, Miss Worie.

I promise." She leaned down from the horse and rubbed the tears from my face with her thumb.

"I know you will. Now go on. Get Ely." She pulled Sally around and bolted out of the barn into the driving rain.

I took Doanie by the hand and headed to the house. "We need to load up what we need to cook with. Start carryin things out to the wagon. Hurry."

Ever step she took, she stomped. Mud splashed up her legs and all over her skirt. But the child made haste.

I walked straight to Momma's secret place, lifted my fist, and slammed my hand against the loose stone. It popped free. I put her jar in my apron pocket and took an empty jar from Momma's shelf, jammin it into the hole. Then I replaced the stone and straightened it perfect.

"There you go, Calvin. I hope you find it." I had no intentions of makin his search easy, and all I really wanted was to see the disappointment on his face when he finally found the hole. That is, if he was smart enough to find it.

Doanie and me stuffed all we could into the wagon. When we left, I aimed to take all I could just to spite Calvin.

"Ho there." Ely's voice lifted above the roar of the rain. "Miss Worie!" He climbed from his wagon and run hard to the house. "Abeleen come to the house. Is you alright?"

"I'm fine, but we . . . we . . ."

"We have to leave. Them men took my brother and sister." Doanie stepped in front of me.

Ely pulled her close and hugged her. "Don't you worry none. We's gonna figure this out. Right now we need to load them beds the pastor built."

One more time I realized I'd forgot the pastor. "Where is Pastor Jess?"

"He's down at the cabin helpin Bess. Come down right early this mornin, huntin for Bess's biscuits and gravy."

The rain went from a hard wash to a soft sprinkle, but it didn't help the mud that was made. We traipsed out to the wagon. Lord bless her heart, Abeleen had done hitched Sally up. Ely wrapped his arm around Doanie and picked her up. Her head seated against his neck.

I walked into the house and looked around. I realized what I'd told Doanie was truer than I knew. A house is just a place, it ain't a life. We'd make a way. My mind was made up. I took the quilt Momma made and wrapped her Bible in it, then without a second thought, I kicked open the door. Lightnin cracked over the back mountain, and thunder echoed through the gap. One, two, three, four . . . and another rumble of thunder. Four miles till the rain made its way here again.

I lifted the covered Bible to the sky. "Momma prayed all the time. I reckon it can't hurt to try."

Ely winked. "I always believed the good Lord was faithful."

"Well, that's good to know, Ely."

Shakin the Bible at the sky full of black clouds, I shouted, "Seein as You are the good Lord, I just ask one thing. Strike this house with lightnin and burn it to the ground."

Thunder shook the ground and a bolt of lightnin hit that blessed ole cedar tree.

ELEVEN

The rain finally quit. All that water that fell over two days left the mountain lookin like it was weepin. Streams poured down the side of the mountain like tears. Put me in the mind of Doanie. The child cried ever time a body looked at her. I could understand. She'd lost her family. Then so had I.

They wasn't no comparin losses. Not one soul had ailed any greater than the next. We'd both lost people we loved. Whether you was a youngin or somebody like me, a loss was a loss.

But poor Doanie . . . that little girl was sufferin. She was sufferin because of greed and selfishness. My anger begin to boil. There was nothing I could do. I ain't sure what made me maddest. The fact that Calvin did this to spite me or that I was the cause of her hurt. I shoulda seen something like this comin. Calvin is good at what he does.

The sun was dippin toward the mountain. Underneath the rain clouds a gentle breeze eased over the pass, givin the hawks what they needed to soar from peak to peak without flappin their wings. For a minute, I was lost in the haven of the Smoky Mountains.

"I hate we couldn't get them beds the pastor made before the trail washed out." Ely leaned against an elm tree close to the edge of the mountain. "Them mountains is beautiful, ain't they?"

I crossed my arms and stretched my head upward. "They are somethin. And Ely, it ain't your fault. The trail will dry in a day or so and we can dig the wagon loose. Besides, dusk is settin in. We did the best we could despite Calvin and the storm."

"Yes'm, we did." Ely nodded. "We got you and the girls. You's safe."

I smiled and slipped my arm through Ely's. Him and Bess was good to Momma and Daddy. They was the kinda people who loved folks despite theirself. When Daddy passed, Ely helped Justice bury him. Then Momma. I remember when Bess give birth to them twins. They was born lifeless. Momma tried to rub life back in them, but them little ones wasn't meant to live. I won't never forget the wails Bess let out. They was never able to bring no other babies into the world, so Miss Bess always loved extra on me.

By the time me and Ely hauled what we could to his barn, night had closed in. We'd made countless trips on foot to the wagons mired down in the thick red mud of the mountain. We was tired. Worn clean down, but Ely helped me do what needed to be done.

Bess rocked Doanie most of the night by the fire. She understood the loss and made no attempt to put Doanie to bed. Instead, she untied the child's braids and kept running her fingers through her hair. Ever now and again, I'd see her rub her knuckle softly over Doanie's cheek.

Ely followed me onto the porch. "Bess said the child never stopped cryin. She's brokenhearted." He wrapped his hands around mine and squeezed. "We'll figure somethin out."

"I know. Her spirit is broke. I'm much obliged for y'all puttin us up whilst I figure things out." I leaned against the porch rail and took in a long breath. Tears hung in my eyes, but I wasn't about to let them fall.

"Worie, I've knowed you since you was little. And I knowed your momma and daddy. They was good people. And cause I knowed them like I did, I feel like I can speak to what they'd say." He pulled his arm away and buried his hands in his pockets.

I blinked back the tears. "Say your peace, Ely. Just spit it out."

Ely looked out over the ridge, ponderin his next words, then he spoke. "This ain't your fault, but it is the hand you's been gived. Good Lord tells us He won't never let us be tempted more than we can bear without givin us a way out."

My stare told Ely I wasn't sure what he meant.

"I can tell you is tempted with vengeance in your heart. It ain't hard to see them wheels turnin in your head. You's thinkin of a way to get even. And as much as you wanna do that, take my word on it. Nothin good comes from vengeance."

My anger was at a slow burn, just waitin for fuel to be shoveled on. "And what's that supposed to mean? You think I'm gonna do somethin foolish?"

"Don't get your drawers crumpled. All I's sayin is you's been through a lot. It's what people do when they's been run through the mill. Vengeance is what naturally works its way outta us. I can see what's normal workin its way up on you."

"Ain't you the wise one?" I snapped.

"Now that you mention it, I *is* the wise one here. I's the one who made my way from the Georgia plantations to the mountains, first a slave and now free. I know what pain does to a body. And I know what runs through your head." He took the cup I was holding and pointed over the ridge. "Them mountains, they's like the hills and valleys in our souls. We can't have one without the other, but we can figure the best way to climb."

How could I fix this? What could I do? My mind went to turnin. I could only see one way and I couldn't do it with youngins in tow. "Ely, can them girls stay here? I can't mind them now. I need to figure what to do."

He stuffed a chaw of tobacco in his lip, chewed a bit, then spit. I could tell he was thinkin.

"I don't think Abeleen will steal your chickens anymore if that's what you're thinkin on."

Ely spit again. "Ah, once I knew what was wrong, I forgived her. Can't blame a child for tryin to survive."

"Will you and Bess watch over them? At least for a while." I felt the pain of hurt well up in me. "I got no home no more, Ely. I got no place to go."

Ely bumped against my shoulder. "Sounds like what the good Lord's Son suffered. No place to lay His head, but He come round to do some mighty powerful things. I'm guessin you'll do some powerful things too."

I wasn't sure why Ely felt such a need to keep pressin his wisdom on the good Lord at me, but it was growin irritatin. Right now, I couldn't see no good in a God that allowed these children to suffer—or me, for that fact.

"You know you can stay here. Me and Bess, we's find a way to make room."

I slipped my arm through his again and rested my head on his shoulder. "You done so much already. It was more than any man should have to do, helpin me bury Momma. And then the way we found Mrs. Whitefield. I ain't sure I'll ever let that thought loose."

"Times is hard. But they's one thing for sure. Most folks are good people. Reckon the lot of them take to their knees and pray. Good Lord made us to take care of each other."

"Makes a body wonder what happened to Calvin," I said.

Ely shook his head. "The Lord knows about them few bad apples. He's give us all free will to make our choices. Calvin's made his choices."

"Ahh, law. I can't see no light yet."

"Miss Worie, a person's gotta trust. Yes'm. The good Lord knows and He works in His own time. Your job is to trust."

I couldn't stop the words before they spit out. "If He knows so much, why didn't He see this mess acomin and fix it? If He knew them youngins was gonna end up on my doorstep, why, Ely . . . why would the good Lord let them suffer again?" The words from Momma's Bible come to me. "What about them words in the good book that Momma had dog-eared? 'Suffer little children.' Seems the good Lord wants the children to pay a price."

Ely scraped his lip with his finger and flipped what little tobacco was left to the ground. "I ain't no preacher and I sure as whiz ain't gonna waste my time arguing with you about the Almighty. But I can tell you this, Worie Dressar, them children comin to your doorstep wasn't by chance. You can believe what you want, but I can done see there is a purpose for you."

I'd got Ely's hackles up, and it wasn't hard to see his frustration with me. A man never empties his lip before he's done with a chew unless he's riled. Ely's faith was more than I could or wanted to live up to.

"I got one more thing to say to you, Miss Worie, and I want you to take it to heart. The good book tells us the Lord knew you before you was put in your momma's belly. He knowed the color of your eyes and"—he lifted his hand and rubbed my cheek—"the tint of *your* skin. Good Lord don't turn His back on His children. No sirree."

I stood silent. Ely's words dug deep into my craw. There wasn't no reason why I felt so ill toward the good Lord, other than seein my momma die. I wanted to smart off to Him, but I kept my thoughts to myself. After all, I couldn't even count losin my cabin, havin a rotten brother, bein an orphan. No, they wasn't no real reason for me to carry a grudge against the good Lord. Nothin at all.

"What about them girls? I don't believe Doanie will give you no trouble. And Abeleen is strong-minded—determined."

Ely took my arm. "Look in there. Just look." He snapped me toward the window. There was Bess, Doanie on her lap, wrapped in a quilt. Bess rockin her and hummin. Abeleen laid on a quilt at her feet. "My guess is, you's gonna have a hard time pryin them children away from Bess."

I looked Ely in the eye. "And Abeleen? She might need a firm hand."

"I can manage her."

"The youngin is bitter. Angry. Bound and determined."

Ely pulled me close. His fingers tightened around my arm. "Sounds like the same girl what come got me to help her bury her momma."

Better words couldn't have been spoke. Abeleen was a lot like me. That might be why we got along from the start. She was determined to survive. I was too. But now I had to find my way, and I couldn't do it with them girls in tow.

"I reckon you know what I need to do," I said.

"Yes'm. I just pray you use good sense."

I left early that morning while the water still trickled down the mountain after the rain. Sally sloshed through the puddles of muddy water on the trail to the back side of the mountain. Her hooves sucked in and out of the mush, putting me in the mind of milkin a cow—ever pull on an udder, splattin milk in the pail. I wasn't sure where I'd go or what I needed to do to get where I needed to be, but I figured the best place to start was with Justice.

The pastor said Justice was about dried out, so I reckon he oughta be about ready to get back to livin his life. I couldn't be sure he knew Momma was dead . . . or that Calvin had run me off. Knowin Calvin and his selfishness, he could have done blindsided Justice.

"Ho there, Sal." I pulled the reins. Leaning down from the saddle, I wrapped my arms around her neck. "Walkin in this mess is tirin. You need a rest."

She slung her head from side to side.

"I reckon that was a yes." I eased from the saddle and stretched to get my footing on a rock stickin out of the mud.

"Real toad choker yesterday." A voice come from a dark part of the trail.

"Who's there?" My heart skipped. I stepped behind Sally and run my hand down her side, feelin for Daddy's shotgun.

"After all that work, you don't know who I am?" Pastor Jess let out a big guffaw. "I was just headin up to your place."

I slipped my foot in the stirrup and pulled myself up in the saddle. "Ain't no need to bother, Pastor."

"I'm guessin they's a reason. You don't hit me as one who would let a body off from doin their work."

"Ain't no need for your help now. My brother Calvin went and got papers to take the homestead from me." I turned away.

"What?" The pastor got right testy. "Don't turn away from me." He nudged his horse to one side and stepped toward me.

"I don't reckon I stuttered. Calvin give me a day to get out."

"What about the children?"

"What about 'em? Ain't nothing I can do."

The pastor's voice grew stern. "Worie, I ain't funnin. Where's them youngins?"

I rested my hands on the saddle horn. "I figured you for smarter, Pastor. They ain't nothing we can do for them. Calvin brought some fancy man from the bank down in Hartsboro, and he took Farrell and T. J."

"He can't do that. What about the others?"

"I left them with Ely and Bess. It was best. I ain't got a spot to lay my head, much less put up youngins." I dug my heel into Sally's side. "Hup there, girl."

She snorted, flipped her ears, and stepped off. It was clear Pastor Jess was in the dark.

"You was eatin with Miss Bess. How could you not know all this?"

"I left and headed down the path to visit the Thomases before I come back to you. Reckon I missed all the excitement."

I believe he had a good heart, and it seemed he was rightfully upset. After all, he did work buildin them beds.

"Pastor, you seem like a right nice fella. Take leave. Go preach or whatever the—"

"Hey. Hold it just a cotton-pickin minute. You ain't able to handle this mess alone. Now, like it or not, I'm trailin along with you. We're gonna find out where them youngins are, and we're gonna get your cabin back."

"I'd thank you to know I am able. Darned able. I buried my own momma. I'm able." I huffed.

The pastor stared, never speakin a word. His eyes spoke for him. It took him a minute, but he finally spoke up. "Looka here, Worie, I don't feel sorry for you and I know you can figure things out. All I'm sayin is you don't have to. You don't have to do this alone. What's happened is a terrible thing. Terrible for you and for them youngins. They ain't no need to suffer."

And there it was again. *Suffer*. But for how long?

"Town's that way. Path is muddy," I said.

"I can see that." The pastor pressed his hat tight against his head.

"You still wanna go?" I nudged Sally and she commenced to lumber, her feet poppin in the mud.

The pastor nodded and followed.

As we rounded the summit, I pulled Sally to a halt. The gap laid ahead. There, like a piece of raw meat temptin a hungry dog, in the crevice of the mountain, was home.

CHAPTER
TWELVE

It took the better part of the day to make our way to Hartsboro. I could count the times I'd been there on one hand. There was some pretty fancy folks in the Cove, especially since the railroad come through these parts.

I slipped off Sally and tied her reins to a rail. I never remembered this town bein busy, but somehow it had growed. I could see where Calvin found that fancy-pants banker.

"Pastor, where's the jail? I need to find Justice."

The pastor scrubbed his hand along his trousers, dustin off little splashes of mud. He pointed his finger in my face. "Worie, you can start by callin me by the name my momma give me. I'm right proud of it. And it fits me better than Pastor."

"I ain't sure it's right for me to call you by your given name. You're older than me. Momma always told me to be respectful."

The pastor went to laughin. "Lawsy mercy, sakes alive. I've heard it all. You're seventeen and you're callin me older. I ain't much past twenty. So it ain't like I got a lifetime on you."

Despite what he said, it didn't feel right callin him by his given name. Leastways he didn't call me a child this time.

"Alright, Pastor, you want me to call you Pastor Jess?"

He tightened the slide on his necktie and straightened his shoulders. A body would have thought his name was some big secret. "Pastor Jess is fine."

I felt a giggle inch up. It wouldn't be right to laugh. I could hear Momma's voice in my head. *"If you ain't got nothing nice to say, don't say nothing at all."* A half cough, half laugh shot out of my mouth.

"What? What's funny?"

"I'm guessin 'Pastor Jess' ain't nothin special."

The pastor stood starin me down. He went to drawin lines with the toe of his boot.

"You always dig your foot into the mud?" I asked.

"I reckon they ain't a whole lot more I can say or do that you won't rip apart and throw on the ground." His lip pooched like T. J.'s did right before he let out a sob.

I busted out laughin. "You gonna pout over me teasin you about your name?"

A grin stretched across his face. "There, now that's what I wanted to see. A smile. Laughter. If you're gonna visit Justice, he'll need you to look strong."

I shook my head. This pastor was a smart one. He could see my frets, and he was right kind about letting me know I needed a new attitude.

"I know. You're right." I stared at the muddy ground. "I don't know if Justice even knows Momma is dead."

"All the more reason to let him see you are fine despite this mess. You understand? Justice is a good man, but he's mighty weak. When a body's soul gets weak, they have a hard time takin in rough news."

I was quiet for a spell before I spoke. "I knew what it was that made the change in Justice. Him and Daddy went huntin one day, and the next week Daddy was dead. It shook Justice to the bone." It was hard to think on the past.

I was tired . . . and muddy. A body can't ride a horse through the kinda mud after a gully washer without gettin filthy. I looked around for a small stand of grass to wipe my boots.

"You wanna clean up before you see Justice?"

I wondered how Pastor Jess could read my mind, but then my tryin to clean my boots off mighta been a good hint. "Cleanin up would be nice, but I ain't got no money for room at the boardin house, so I reckon Justice will have to take me as I am."

"The church is just down the road. There's a water pump." He pointed ahead.

"That'd be right nice, Mr. Pastor Jess." I hiked my skirt up to my knees and tiptoed through the mud to the wooden walk.

The pastor went to laughin.

"What are you findin so funny?"

"I guess that you'd tiptoe through the mud when you done got it all over your shoes."

"Oh shaw! I reckon I was tryin to be somewhat ladylike." I reached out and gently punched the pastor's arm.

We walked to the end of the boarded walkway and stepped into a grassy patch that wound around toward the church. They wasn't many folks out and about. I guess the heavy rain kept them inside. The sheriff's office was across the muddy road, along with the general store. A fancy-dressed man stepped outta the store and sucked on his pipe. The sweet smoke twirled on the breeze, catchin my nose. He stared me up one side and down the other till I felt like his eyes was burning holes in me.

Pastor Jess raised his hand and waved, and the man nodded.

"Good thing you waved at him. I was ready to tell him when he got his eyes full, open his mouth."

"Mercy, no. Don't be sayin smart remarks like that. You never know who you'd be smackin with an insult."

I pulled the heel of my boot across the grass, scrapin loose a chunk of mud. "He was starin a hole right through my soul," I snapped.

"Worie, that's the mayor. We might need his help to find them children. You need to find a way to keep your snide remarks quiet."

"Well, I . . . uh . . ." I stopped in my tracks. There in front of me was the forge. John Wallen's forge. Abeleen's daddy's forge. I lost my words for a minute. The strength that girl held inside her was put there by the man that run that forge. John Wallen did good.

Momma always said guilt was a rotten bedfeller. She was right. Them two little children was ripped outta their sister's arms because of me. Abeleen was tore away from the beginnins of a home, again. It was my fault, and they seemed to be nothin I could do to fix this mess.

I stared at the forge whilst tears filled my eyes, then I could have swore I heard Momma's voice. *Shovel them feelins over your shoulder. Buck up. It's the mountain way of doin things.*

"That's John Wallen's forge. Abeleen's daddy." I pointed toward the barn. "You know, the child buried him a stone at a time." My heart hurt for her. Still, Momma was right. Buck up! I pulled my shoulders back and dug my heels in. "I'm gonna figure this out, Pastor. I will."

Pastor Jess reset his hat. "I know." He took hold of my shoulder and squeezed. "I know you will."

"John died from the fever. Beats me why Abeleen didn't get sick," I said.

"The fever don't seem to care who it does or don't take. Poor child. She's lucky to be with you."

I couldn't imagine how Abeleen was lucky to be with me. Seemed like my luck had done washed out. "I ain't got her, Pastor. Remember, I got no home. These girls are with Ely and Bess."

The pastor did his best to comfort me. He took my hand in his and gently squeezed. "Them children will be back with you soon, and you'll have your homestead back."

"I hope so. But right now it ain't lookin so good." I hadn't much more than got the words outta my mouth when the barn door on the forge opened. A puff of smoke bellowed out. The awfulest coughin rang from inside.

"What in heaven's name?" The pastor headed across the road to the forge. It was only minutes till he come from inside the barn with a tall, lanky man coughin up his guts.

I waved the smoke away to see who Pastor Jess had pulled from the forge. I squinted hard. "Well, slap my knee. Trigger? Trigger Townsend?" My heart sunk. He hadn't changed a bit since I'd turned him down two years before.

He rubbed his eyes, trying to clear the fog. I wanted to rush across the road and wrap my arms around him. But I couldn't. Momma had needed me back then. She couldn't manage the homeplace alone, and it wasn't fair to ask Trigger to give up his life to work our farm, not with Calvin and Justice. So, the day he asked me to marry him, my heart broke. I was torn between bein his wife and helpin Momma.

I watched as Pastor Jess patted Trigger's back, tryin to get him to suck in some good air, and when he stood, I saw them long strands of hair that hid his eyes. A smile come to me as I remembered walkin the river with him. I could still feel the tenderness of his touch.

Trigger and the pastor made their way across the road. The look on the pastor's face was like a fat possum scarfin down the last bit of corn in the bin.

"Worie Dressar, I'd like you to meet—"

"Trigger," I whispered.

"Worie?" Trigger slapped his leg. "I'll be. Talk about a surprise."

I'd be lyin if I said it was nothing short of awkward, so I did what I was good at. I got snide. "What on earth are you doin in John Wallen's forge?"

Trigger straightened his shoulders and snapped back, "Not that it's any of your business, but I been learnin smithin. John ain't been around for the better part of a month. Somebody had to step up and shoe the horses."

"You idiot. Did you never think to check on John if he ain't been around?"

Trigger wrung his hands. "Well . . . I . . ."

"That figures. So, you don't know. John Wallen is dead."

"Dead!"

"Yes, dead. And if you'd even used your head, you'd have checked on him. His little girl buried him by herself."

Trigger stuttered around, trippin over his tongue before he got out the words. "I'm sorry to hear that. What about the forge?"

I felt my hackles lift. John was dead. His girl was an orphan, and all the words Trigger could spit out was, "What about the forge?"

I drew back my foot and let it fly, catchin him in the shin. "What about his child?"

THIRTEEN

Momma used to say what Trigger missed in brain, he made up for with good intentions. Trigger was kind, gentle. A hard worker. Lookin at him brought back a flood of memories. Some good. Some bad. But they was memories I didn't have time for.

"Worie, what in tarnation are you doin here?" Trigger asked. He took me by the shoulders and pulled me into a hug.

I wiggled free. Despite a sweet memory of Trigger's arms around me, now wasn't the time. "Let go." I pushed him away. A body could have blowed him over with a feather. I reckon he thought we'd just pick up where we left off when I told him I wouldn't marry him.

Pastor Jess stepped between us. His arm stretched in front of me like a fence rail. "Whoa there, friend. Let's leave the little lady to herself."

Trigger cocked his head. You could see what smarts he had, workin to figure the pastor's protection. He pulled his hat from his head and nodded. I admit, I wondered myself. I never ask the pastor for protection.

"I never meant nothing. Me and Worie go back a ways."

Pastor Jess dropped his arm but kept his stance hard in front of me. I pressed against him, shoving him to one side. "It's fine, Pastor. Trigger is a . . ." I stuttered, unsure what to call him. Ely's words come back to me. *Honesty is always the best row to hoe.* So honesty it was. "Pastor Jess, I reckon I owe you a proper introduction. This here is Trigger Townsend. We was set to get hitched when we run upon a disagreement."

"Disagreement?" Trigger slung his head like a horse fightin a bit. "You couldn't let go of your momma. No matter what she said."

I felt my nose flare. "They *was* a reason, Trigger."

"Reason? Twernt no real reason other than you was scared. Daddy called you cold."

"Well, ain't that just nice? I wasn't scared."

"You was."

I balled my fist and punched Trigger in the arm.

"Hey, hold up here." Pastor Jess took hold of my wrist. "There's obviously some bad blood here, and mudslingin, hittin, and name-callin don't settle nothin. We're all grown-ups here and this ain't grown-up behavior."

I hated to admit it, but the preacher was right. I was actin like a child. I snorted and dug my toe into the grassy patch.

"Let's start this conversation over." The pastor set his hand out to Trigger. "Pastor Jess Martin. I'm the pastor on this side of the mountain."

Trigger stared at the pastor's hand, then took hold. "Pleased to make your acquaintance."

Pastor Jess took a solid hold on Trigger's hand and shook. "So you're tryin to fire up John's forge?"

"Yes sir. People need shoes for their horses. Knives. That sort of thing. And John was teachin me when he just quit comin into town."

"Like I said," I snapped, "it never entered that thick skull of yours to check in on the man. Especially with so many folks bein sick on the mountain."

Pastor Jess's hand raised in front of me to shush me. "Worie, this ain't getting us nowhere." His hand dropped to his side. "How long have you been workin with John?"

Trigger scratched his chin. "I reckon a couple of months. I met him for the first time when Daddy sent me to Hartsboro. I didn't get to this side of the mountain often till then."

"I reckon this is startin to take some shape, now ain't it, Worie?" Pastor Jess patted my arm. "I'm guessin you ain't known John long enough to know his homestead."

"No sir. He was lettin me stay in the back room of the barn here as long as I'd get the fire stoked and hot before he got here to start work. If that was all it took for him to let me stay, to teach me his trade, then I'd stoke or build a fire anywhere he wanted me to."

Pastor Jess turned to me and smiled. "There, Miss Worie. The man didn't know where John lived." He looked right proud that he'd killed my suspicions of Trigger.

It didn't help the uneasiness of seein Trigger again. It made me madder than a wet hornet to think he might just be right. I hadn't wanted to leave Momma. It wasn't that I was hooked at her hip, but truth was . . . it was fear for Momma. Once Daddy was dead, Momma couldn't count on the boys to step up. Calvin's only goal in life was to get what he wanted, when he wanted it. Poor old Justice was a hard worker when he was sober. Course, *when* he'd be sober wasn't nothin a body could count on. Momma needed help. Daddy wasn't a rich man, but he did have the land. Acres of it. Somebody had to tend it. Somebody had to lay the garden and set the tobacco. Momma couldn't do it by herself, and her being the kind of woman she was—lovin my daddy like she did—things would have to be done just the way Daddy did it. Momma needed me, and Trigger didn't take light to it.

I watched as the pastor conversed with Trigger. It was like the two was best friends for havin just met. It sorta riled me. And ever time I went to step up and speak, Pastor Jess would step in front of me. I finally quit tryin to edge a word in and hushed.

"Miss Worie here wants to clean up before she goes about her business in town. I was gonna show her to the pump by the church."

Trigger stuttered around and finally spit out a few words that made some sense. "I got a back room in the barn. There's always hot water by the forge. Worie, you are more than welcome to partake of it."

It was awkward, but I could see Trigger's heart was in the right place. "Alright. I'm obliged."

He motioned then pointed toward the barn. "This way."

I smiled, and it only took a minute for Trigger's cheeks to turn the color of cherries. That sweetness was what drew me to him. I watched as he took the lead, dodging the puddles of muddy water like a child at play.

He stopped and stuck out his hand. "Let me help you over these here puddles."

The pastor took hold of my elbow to guide me. "Much obliged, but I think we can make it fine."

Trigger stood there starin like a deer caught at the crack of dawn. "Alright." He took a couple more steps and pushed open the barn door.

The smell of heat come at me like a fox after a squirrel. Daddy used to talk about heat and fire bein livin things. "Depends on the fire and its purpose," he'd say. "A fire meant to keep a body warm smells like applewood or hickory. One meant to destroy carries the odor of fir or pine."

The forge fire smelled like pine, hotter than blue blazes. Hot enough to melt iron. A barrel filled with water sat close to the firebox. Swirls of oil formed rainbow-colored streaks in ever-changin patterns on the surface of the liquid.

Trigger snatched a rag off the anvil and gently dropped its edge into the water, pulling it over the slick film. "This here will get the oil from the iron off the water." He grinned right proud, like a child who'd just learned a new trick. "Pastor, if you can pass me that ladle hangin on that nail." Trigger swiped his hands on the wet rag, then rung it out on the floor. "Worie, would you kindly reach me that bucket?"

I handed him a bucket that rested upside down on a bench. Trigger ladled some of the warm water into the bucket, then carried it to the back room. "This way," he said. "You can wash up in my room." He slid open a rickety door and motioned me in. "Ain't much, but it's all a body needs. A place to lay his head." Trigger pointed to a beautiful glass bowl perched on a stand. A mirror raised high above the bowl.

My eyes scanned the piece. Painted flowers circled the top of the white glass, with green vines dripping down the sides. And them same vines lined the edge of the mirror, reflecting their own images.

"Trigger, this is beautiful. A little out of place in this barn, but mighty pretty."

One side of his lip raised, and his eyes brightened. The dimple on that cheek deepened. "Thank ye much. It was Momma's, and her momma's, and her momma's. All I got left of her after she died from the fever. When John said I could come to work here, I brung it with me." He took in a breath and blowed dust from the mirror.

Odd as it was, I begun to see Trigger in a new light. Though it befuddled me why the fever was takin so many folks and causin their little ones to be left behind, I could see that it was takin its toll on folks just like me and Trigger. We was grown, but we was left without a momma and daddy too. Orphans—the both of us. I reckon we still had things in common.

He run his finger along the edge of the wooden stand. "You know Daddy died last fall, not long after . . ."

I knowed what he was gonna say, so I shushed him before he could go any further. "I know how you feel. Momma died a few weeks back."

Pastor Jess leaned against the door. "It's the circle of life. For ever life that leaves the world a new one comes in. All this reminiscin is nice, but Worie, you got business here in town. Best get to washin up." He nudged me away from the door and waved Trigger out, slidin the heavy door closed. "You just holler when you're ready and we'll be waitin." He tapped the door with his hand. I could hear the two of them conversin as they walked away.

A yellow glow from a low-lit lantern broke up the darkness, and the smell of oil filled the room. I'd never seen anything as beautiful as the wash bowl and mirror. It seemed a shame to pour water in it and chance messin up the tiny blue and yellow flowers, so I doused the rag in the bucket and wrung it dry. They was no need to dirty such a pretty bowl with muddy water. I could tell it was precious to Trigger.

I stripped off my muddy skirt and rinsed the clay from the tail, then hung it on a nail to dry. My bag was small, but I had stuffed a clean change of clothes and what little money I had inside. I dipped the rag in the bucket of warm water again and twisted it damp dry. What little warmth was still in the rag felt wonderful against my face. It took me a spell to scrape the mud off my boots, but once I got the thick paste loose I was able to clean them too.

I unfolded the clean skirt and pulled it over my hips, tying a small rope around my waist to keep it snug. I folded a small handkerchief and snugged it in my pocket. I guess, like Trigger and his flowery bowl and mirror, this was all I had left of Momma. This and that blessed old Mason jar.

A small window, cracked open in the corner of the room, let in a sweet, fresh rainy smell. I raised it a little further and dumped the dirty water and clots of mud from my boots out. I took hold of the door to slide it open when I caught sight of a reflection in that mirror. It took me back for a minute.

"Momma?"

Silence. The hairs on my arms stood straight as I took in a gulp of air. Mirrors was rare on the mountain. Momma had a little one that fit in her palm, and when Calvin took it and sold it for a few nickels, she was both hurt and mad.

I walked to the mirror and touched my fingers to the cheek reflectin back at me. It wasn't Momma. I never knew she left me such a gift. Brows that framed deep-set dark eyes, a heart-shaped face. Long, silky strands of chestnut hair that fell over the shoulders and onto the arms like a shawl. I looked like Momma.

I felt the water gather in the corners of my eyes, and I remembered Momma sayin her Scriptures when Calvin would lash out at her and make her cry. "'My tears have been my meat day and night, while they continually say unto me, Where is thy God?'" She'd swallow back her tears and say, "That's what it says in the Psalms, and the Psalms is hope."

Calvin would mock her. "I thought the good book was supposed to give a body hope. That just sounds plumb, downright hopeless."

I pressed my hand against the mirror, prayin for one last time to touch Momma's face. A tear spilled from my eye. "Momma, I miss you. Why did you have to go and do such a horrible thing?"

I took my hand from the mirror and placed it on my neck. My fingers tightened and the air snuffed out of my lungs. I winced. With each thump of my heart, I could feel my blood shoot through my veins. I wondered what it took for Momma to pull that trigger.

"Worie, you 'bout ready? I saw the sheriff go into his office."

Pastor Jess's voice brought me back. I coughed, then gagged. Was this how Momma felt as her lifeblood drained? Did she feel it gushin from her chest . . . count the beats as her heart run down and stopped? I gagged again and let loose of my neck.

"Uh . . . yeah. I'm comin." I pushed open the door and stepped toward the pastor.

"There she is." He eyed me for a minute, cockin his head to one side. He lifted his forefinger and pointed. "Why's your neck so red?"

CHAPTER
FOURTEEN

"What business you got here in town?" Trigger shoved open the barn door, and we stepped through and onto the plank walkway. He pressed his hand against my back.

Feelins stirred in me and I leaned into him. I didn't answer.

"I've missed you, Worie."

Pastor Jess slipped his hand around my elbow and gently guided me away from Trigger. "We ain't got much time, Worie. The sheriff don't hold up long in his office."

"Sheriff? What's wrong?" Trigger nudged me back to his side.

"It's been a long few weeks. With Momma dyin and all, Calvin put me out."

"What? Put you out? You mean, took you outta the cabin?"

I nodded.

"You ain't pullin my rope?" Trigger took my hand, and his grip tightened. I could feel his eyes starin into my soul.

"Ain't right sure Worie's need to see the sheriff is any of your beeswax." Pastor Jess reached his arm around me.

"Alright!" I snapped. "Enough is enough. I ain't a cheap ewe meant to be tugged from field to field." I pushed away from both men. "Both of you! Let me alone. Hear me? I got business to tend."

I straightened my skirt and pulled my shoulders back. Takin in a deep breath, I remembered what Momma would say. "Suck in some air, count to ten, then walk away."

She was right too, though I might need to count to more than ten.

It befuddled me why the pastor had got so protective over me, and it bothered me even more that Trigger still stirred my heart. I had work to do. I had them youngins and a fight to finish with Calvin.

I wheeled around and started toward the sheriff's office. "I ain't got time to bicker with you two. Justice needs me. Them children need me. And Calvin's gonna wish he hadn't ruffled the feathers on this hen."

"No need to get snippy, Miss Worie. I'm just tryin . . ." The pastor stumbled over his words. "I mean, I . . ."

"Don't matter the why, Pastor. I ain't a wishbone that needs to be split." I stomped toward the sheriff's office. "Let's hope Justice is sober." I left both men standin with their mouths hung open. My heels clicked against the wooden walk as I made my way to the sheriff's office. My shoulder pressed against the heavy door. "Well, you comin?" I shouted.

Pastor Jess snapped to his senses, and him and Trigger both hightailed it to the sheriff's.

"Let me get that door." Trigger reached behind me and shoved it open.

A lanky, bearded man sat leaned on two legs of his chair, his feet propped by the heels on the desk. His hat covered his eyes and his arms were crossed.

I shoved his dirty boots off the desk, startlin him awake. The sheriff's hat flew to the floor and he come to his feet.

"So, this is what the sheriff does? Rears back and sleeps when bad men are stealin the home right from under their families. Is that your job? Maybe your job is puttin a poor drunk that ain't hurtin a soul in jail." I knew my bad side wasn't polite. It rarely made its way to the surface, but I was fed up. There was Momma dyin, Calvin stealin my home, Justice drunk, them children, seein Trigger, the pastor bein so protective . . . and that blamed old jar that had took on the shape of a ghost haunting me. Something had to come out.

The sheriff scooped his hat from the floor. "Ain't you something?" he said. "Bein judge and jury and all." He extended his hand. "Sheriff Bud Starnes. What *can* I do for you?"

"It ain't what *can* you do for me. It's what you've already done."

He cocked his head and leaned across the desk. "Do I know you?" He squinted, tryin to place me.

"Let me think on that, Sheriff. Does runnin a girl and a handful of children off their property mean something? Does rippin two of them little ones away from the only family they have stick in your craw?"

Sheriff Starnes walked to the front of his desk and parked his rear on the top. "I might remember something about that."

The anger boiled in me like Trigger's fire in the forge. "Reckon you might remember them screaming children cryin after their sister?"

"Now listen, missy, a man has to do the job he's been assigned. It ain't always pleasant."

"I guess it ain't laced with integrity either. Is it, Sheriff?" Pastor Jess stepped in front of me. "As you can see, Miss Worie is a bit distraught. She was tryin to make a home for them children that lost their mommas and daddies."

I pushed Pastor Jess to the side. "I can talk for myself."

"Worie, kindness is a better friend."

"Outta my way, Pastor." I went toe to toe with the sheriff. "I want two things. My brother and them little ones. And I got no intentions of leavin until I have them both." I snorted. Anger wasn't my habit, but I'd had all I could swallow. "Let's start with my brother."

The sheriff stared down at me, then commenced to pick at his teeth. "Your brother that drunk?" He wagged his finger toward the cell.

"He's a troubled soul, Sheriff." Pastor Jess tried to cover a multitude of sins.

I didn't budge, but my eyes locked with the sheriff's. "Let him out, Sheriff. I'm sure he's dry by now."

The sheriff walked to a hook by his desk and took off a large ring with four keys attached. "Justice, get your sorry rear up!"

I followed on the sheriff's heels. "I'm sure you didn't mean that the way it sounded."

Sheriff Starnes smirked. "Come on, Dressar. Your sister is here to take you home. And I better not have to haul your sorry self back in this jail again. Next time . . ."

"That'll do, Sheriff." Pastor Jess stepped in. "I feel sure Justice understands."

The lock on the steel door clicked three times as the sheriff twisted the key. A loud squeal sent chills climbin up my arms. Justice laid balled up in the corner of the cell.

I pushed my way around the sheriff. "Justice? Come on. Let's get you outta here."

"You remember what I told you." The sheriff snagged Justice by the arm. "You hear?"

Justice stared at the hand clasped around his arm. "Let go."

Trigger and Pastor Jess draped Justice's arms over their shoulders and eased him out the door.

"Much obliged," I snapped. "Now about the children."

"Them children ain't your concern."

His tone deserved a smack across the face, but if I was to be honest, my attitude wasn't any better.

"Sheriff Starnes, them youngins need their sister. They need me. Where are they?"

He walked to a wooden cabinet and pulled open a drawer. His

fingers crawled through papers like a bug workin its way through a bag of meal.

When the pages quit flippin, Sheriff Starnes pulled out an envelope and laid it on the desk. "Where is them youngins? You wanna know? Sealed shut," he said. "Their whereabouts is sealed shut."

CHAPTER

FIFTEEN

I felt my stomach turn. The thought of little T. J. being stuck in some gosh-awful place with people he didn't know broke my heart. I stood starin at the sheriff for a spell before I could spit any kind of words out.

"You mean to tell me, you know where they are but you won't tell me?" I went to grittin my teeth. How was it I'd only known these youngins a short time and they'd already dug a hole in my heart like a droopy-eyed pup?

"They ain't your children, Miss Dressar. They ain't yours to worry over."

"They don't belong to nobody else either, and since they was brought to me that oughta mean something. Their sister come to me, Sheriff! Me!"

"Don't reckon that means a thing. All you need to know is them youngins is fine. They'll be cared for." He smirked. "At least they'll have a roof over their heads."

That was a low blow and one that hit me like somebody punched me in the gut. "Just for a little, I'd slap that smirk off your face." He knew good and well I *had* a home until he helped Calvin steal it away. "Tell me somethin, Sheriff. Since when did it become the job of a lawman to steal the home from underneath a young woman? One that was housin orphans."

The sheriff squinted, then spit at my feet.

"Ain't you the gentleman?" I said.

"Miss Dressar, I suggest you take that drunk of a brother and get on outta my office before I . . ."

I stepped up to him. "Before you what, Sheriff? Take my home away from me? Seein as you done did that."

The sheriff swallowed hard.

Daddy and Momma used to always tell me, when Calvin would try to push me around, to stand my ground. "Don't take no step backward. That just shows a bully you ain't willin to fight. Boys like Calvin spend their time hopin folks will back away." Daddy would straighten my shoulders and dust my skirt straight. "You see, Worie, the trick to handlin Calvin is spreadin your feathers like a peacock."

"Like a peacock?" I edged closer to Daddy.

He bent his arms under his pits and commenced to strut around like a peacock, waggin his tail and liftin his head toward the sky. "When you stand up straight, jut out your chest, and flit your feathers, you're tellin him you ain't scared. You might not get your way, but I can promise you, he'll back down cause he don't know if you'll really come back at him." Daddy would laugh, twist me around, and pat my back. "Now go on. Take a step toward him. Flit them feathers. You'll see."

I took another step forward, pushin myself against the sheriff and forcin him to take a step back. I stared long and hard until I could see the man flinch. He took a second step back, then reached for the door.

I shoved his hand off the knob and opened the door myself. "I'll find them youngins, Sheriff, and in the meantime, I hope you find your manhood somewhere other than in bullyin women and children."

With that, I slammed the door. My hands was shakin and my heart was racin like a treein hound after a squirrel, but when I walked out of that door, I had the upper hand. Daddy was right.

Pastor Jess and Trigger stood speechless.

"Shut your mouth before you swallow a fly." I breezed past.

I had no idea what I was gonna do. Not a thought as to how I could find Farrell and T. J., but they was one thing I knew for sure. Momma was carin for them youngins for a reason, and that was passed down to me. I patted my fluffed-out shirt. It was time for this peacock to flit her feathers.

Justice had already found his way onto Sally. He scooted forward on the saddle, then stuck his hand toward me. I pulled the back tail of my skirt up between my legs and stuffed it in the waist, then took hold of his wrist. He yanked me onto the back of the saddle. Pastor Jess and Trigger still stood stunned.

I slid my arms around Justice's waist. He was two years older than me. He was mannered like Daddy and the one who carried his heart on his sleeve. Maybe that's why he'd drink like he did. Right now, it didn't matter. He was all I had left in the world, and if I could keep him dried out, we'd figure a way to get back the farm.

Pastor Jess and Trigger watched as Justice pulled the reins to one side. "Hup, girl. Come on." He clicked his lips, and Sally flipped her head from side to side. Her way of letting us know she would abide by the command but not be right happy about it.

I could tell Pastor Jess was took back at my attitude change. I've always been a bit mouthy but never pushy. Today I took to heart what Daddy taught me. They'd be no more bullyin this peacock around.

Pastor Jess hopped on his horse and tipped his hat to Trigger. He pulled his horse around and trotted to catch up. Poor Trigger still stood speechless, his mouth hung open, still unsure what just took place.

There was something freein about takin hold of that thought.

Comin to the realization that I was a grown woman, and the only one who could help me . . . was me. Least that's how I saw it. Momma was always a strong woman. I can't recall a time I ever heard her and Daddy disagree, but I can remember her respectin him, then commencing to do what she felt was best on certain matters.

Only the good Lord knew what was reelin around in Momma's head when she took her life, but they had to be more to it. Momma was not a weak woman. She was the strongest woman I'd ever known. Somethin was afoot. Somethin serious, and I aimed to find out what it was.

The weight of two on Sally's back pushed her feet deep into the mud. Every step sucked and popped as she struggled to carry us. There was nothing friendly about the red clay found this side of the mountain. It was hard as a rock when it was dry and stickier than molasses when it was wet.

"Come on, girl, just a little farther and I'll let you rest." Justice spoke real gentle to Sally. He reached one hand toward her ears and scratched. "You love that, don'tcha?"

I had to giggle. Justice was a big man. Momma always said he reminded her of her daddy. Broad through the shoulders, arms stout and firm. And handsome. Justice had girls inchin up to him all the time, but since Daddy died, the only love he had was his hooch, and that was about to end.

We was quiet for a spell, and when Sally made her way onto the path that wound through the woods, me and Justice climbed off to give her a rest. The sun was bright and warm, raisin steam from the ground as it dried the floor of the forest. Justice dropped the reins and let Sally roam into the weeds to nibble on new ferns. While she nibbled he took a stick, bendin her leg up enough to scrape some of the mud from her hooves.

"I'm much obliged, Worie." Justice brushed his face on his sleeve. "You're a good one." He wiped his hands on his trousers and tossed the stick into the woods.

"You're my brother. I love you . . ." I hesitated.

"But?" Justice leaned onto a large downed tree. "A body don't lack in their words unless there's a big 'but' comin."

"Am I that easy to read?"

"Yep. And that much like Momma. So what's the but?"

I sighed and thought a minute. My words had to be right. I wanted to shame him. Tell him if he'd been home instead of drunk, Calvin might not have been able to pull sucha stunt. I could blame him for Momma takin her life and for them youngins bein taken away, but the truth was, none of that was his fault. Despite everthing, I had to care for him first. He didn't need no more burden to carry.

"I ain't sure where to start. Except to say I need you. And I can't be sharin that need with your jug."

He stared at his feet. "I know."

"You've been dry for a spell now. I reckon you're past longin for the taste, so we just have to keep it away."

Justice patted my back. "Ain't you all grown up? Momma would be proud."

I gasped. "What do you mean, Momma *would* be proud?"

"I heard Calvin and the sheriff talkin. I know Momma is dead."

It took a minute. My mind was sortin through all that had happened and the pieces wasn't fittin. This was the second time Calvin's knowin things that he ought not know had come to mind. The first was when he busted in the cabin, lookin for Momma's jar.

"What do you mean you heard Calvin talkin to the sheriff?"

Justice snapped a twig off a dead limb. "Back at the jail. He thought I was passed out. But I wasn't."

"How could Calvin know Momma was dead? He wasn't nowhere to be found. It took me and Ely to bury her cause you two was gone."

"I reckon he saw."

"Saw what? What exactly did he see?" I felt my blood boil. Calvin had been on the farm? Did he see Momma take her life and do nothin to stop it? I squeezed my fingers into my palms, the nails burrowin into the flesh.

Justice slid down and sit on a rock. "Worie, I don't know what all he saw or didn't. You know Calvin. He ain't nothing but a liar. A body never knows what's the truth or not."

I pulled my bag from over my shoulder and untied the strings. "Look at this." I dumped my belongins onto the ground. I unrolled the wet skirt I'd rinsed at John's forge. The small jar rolled onto the ground. "This is what he wants."

Justice twisted the jar, swirling around the notes and coins. He commenced to laugh. "Why in heaven's name would he want a jar with paper and coins? That don't come close to makin sense. Even for Calvin."

I took the jar and twisted it open. The three coins and tiny satin bag dropped into Justice's hand. "He come to me right after Momma died and demanded this jar. Momma showed me where she hid it before she died, but I couldn't see no reason why it was special to her. These papers is just notes along with Scriptures from the good book. And them three coins wouldn't buy much more than a bag of flour and sugar." I slipped them back in the jar.

"What was that idiot thinkin?"

"I reckon he thought Momma had hid away money from her cannin. He wanted the money."

Justice roared. He slapped his leg. "That idiot. You shoulda just give him the jar. They ain't nothing worth anything in it."

I yanked the satin bag from his hand and opened it. A small red stone glistened in the sun. "Momma told me Mamaw give her this stone."

"Can't see it's much. You?" He eyed the tiny rock.

"It means something or Momma wouldn't have kept it hid away."

"Fact is, Worie, Calvin gets something in his mind, and betwixt the greed and selfishness, he conjures such lies that even he believes them."

I dropped the stone into the bag and added it to the jar, then twisted the lid tight.

"What's them notes?"

I loosed the lid again and pulled them out. Momma had pushed holes through the pages and tied twine through them. Unrollin them, I sat next to Justice and leaned my head on his shoulder. "She writes real purty, don't she?"

I leaned my face upward to the sun that peeked through the pines. My skin grew warm. A hawk soared in and out of the trees, callin to clouds as they passed.

Justice pressed his finger to his lips. "See that chipmunk yonder?"

I nodded.

He lifted his finger toward the sky. "Ain't that hawk a beautiful thing?"

"Uh-huh."

"Even in its beauty, it's a dangerous thing."

The bird swooped through the trees and snatched the chipmunk from the ground, lifting it high into the sky. It squealed once.

"The hawk, as beautiful as it is, does what it must to survive. And you must do the same."

CHAPTER
SIXTEEN

Me and Justice rested a spell while Sally grazed. I went to tellin him about them youngins showin up one after the other.

"It was like Momma was sending them to me. I didn't have no choice, Justice. Somebody had to give them children a reason to live."

He chewed on a teaberry leaf. "I ain't never been one on believin the dead send us signs. And you shouldn't either. Good book says, 'And beside all this, between us and you there is a great gulf fixed: so that they which would pass from hence to you cannot; neither can they pass to us, that would come from thence.'" He pointed to Momma's Bible dumped in the pile of belongins. "Momma had it marked. Look for yourself."

"Since when did you become so smart on the good book?"

"Worie, we was both raised by the same woman. Momma never hesitated teachin from the good book."

He was right. Momma held tight to the good book. She said it was the best readin book anywhere. I reached to the pile of things and took hold of it. I flipped the pages, payin attention to all her writin.

"So if you don't believe Momma was sendin me them youngins, what do you believe?"

"Well, seems to me Momma had a love for helpin those in need. Just appears to me her work caught up to you. A body can't start fillin needs and then expect the needs to stop just cause they can't do it no more."

"But . . . I . . . I . . ."

"You what, Worie? You took them children in because that's your heart. It's who you are. You coulda turned them away. Not a soul forced you to take them in."

I pulled Momma's Bible to my chest and squeezed. Tears commenced to raise.

"Them little ones come to you because Momma started carin for them. You ain't the kind of folk who would turn them away. So you do what you must." Justice put his arm around me and pulled me close. "I ain't nothin but a drunk. But you, little lady. You are Momma made over, and that ain't nothing but good."

I crawled to my feet and moseyed into the weeds. The floor of the woods was soft, covered in a spongy green rug of moss. Weeds poked out like loose hairs in a braid. Ferns jutted in bundles around the bases of elm and oak trees. When I looked up, the limbs reached across the faded path like a momma stretchin her arms to her child. Their branches intertwined like fingers. For a moment, there was a peace in my soul. The rains had left a sweet scent to take in. Things was washed clean for a time.

I twisted around. Justice sat leaned against the downed tree, his knees bent and his hands restin over them. His head bobbed like a hen pickin at the ground. A long sob poured outta him, and my heart broke into pieces. This man, this gentle man, sat wailin—grievin. I wasn't sure if I should just let him be or take him in my arms, but when a second sob seeped out, I rushed to him and pulled him close to me. I found myself pressing my palm over his cheek, just like Momma. Maybe I was like her and I didn't know it.

I'd cried over Momma, but as I stepped back to look over the last few weeks, I realized my tears was tears of selfishness. I'd grieved the loss of what I'd miss from Momma. The things I'd not have. Her teachin me to read better and better. To write. Her providin a good home despite the little we had.

But Justice, he grieved Momma. His cries was deep and broken. He suffered the pain of knowing he'd disappointed her.

I lifted his chin and looked him in the eyes. "They's so much more to you, Justice. The liquor covers what you hide deep inside. What I know is, there is a man inside you bigger and better than any man, outside of Daddy, that I know. Momma is proud of you too. And me and you . . ." I stood and pulled him to his feet. "Me and you will find a way to fix this mess."

Justice pressed his bear-sized hand against the side of my face. "Where we headin?"

"Ely and Bess's. Two of them youngins, Abeleen and Doanie, are there. There's a field to plant, a home to be made with them. Work will help us figure."

He rounded up Sally and climbed into the saddle, then lifted me up. Justice kneed the old mare, and she took to steppin right gentle over the rocks in the path.

"Don't guess you know what happened to the pastor, do you? I thought he was behind us." Justice twisted in the saddle and looked behind us.

"I saw him nod and take a turn toward the Bentons' farm. Guess he had some visits to make."

"Don't reckon you got any biscuits in that mess of stuff of yours?" Justice asked.

"Biscuit? You hungry?"

"Ain't you?"

I pressed my forehead into his back. "Reckon I am. Maybe we'll run upon a plum tree."

Justice pushed his hair back with his hat and went to singin.

Daddy used to sing like that, and Momma would whisper to me that his noise made her ears bleed. Then she'd grin a big ole grin.

"That a two-part harmony you're singin?" I asked Justice.

"Maybe. Why?"

"You can leave my part out."

Justice broke into a hearty laugh. After all them sobs, hearin his laughter was wonderful.

It only took a minute before I noticed he sat straight in the saddle. His shoulders was back and his chest was out. Ever note he sung give a newness to him. I reached my arms around my brother's waist and rested my face against his back. His shirt was damp from the rain dripping from the trees.

We passed through the forest and onto the mountain pass toward Ely's, the path slim and rocky. To the right small trees jutted from the side of the pass, and to the left, nothin but the sky lined with shadows of the mountains in the distance. A cloud passed by, coverin us in a white fog, and a soft breeze whistled by. It was like it was speakin to my soul. *You'll be alright. Trust.*

"Did you hear that?" I asked.

"Hear what? Birds, deer? Bear?"

"That whisper."

Justice shook his head. "Only whisper I hear is the breeze."

I squeezed him tight. "Yeah. That one."

That's when I got that gut feelin again. Like somebody was watchin, and the peace I had turned to fear.

The sway of Sally's steps lulled me to sleep against Justice's back. When I woke up we was just down the path from Ely's. I raised up in the saddle and saw Abeleen hunkered over a tomato plant. Ole Hooch was sittin right next to her like he was posted to guard her. He come to his feet and barreled his way toward us, howlin like nobody's brother.

Justice swung his leg over the saddle and helped me down. We'd only been gone a while, but it felt like I'd been gone for years.

Abeleen come runnin, squealin at Doanie. "Worie!" she hollered. "Ely! Miss Bess! It's Worie!" Her curls bounced in the air as she run at me. She leaped into my arms and wrapped her legs around me, sendin us both to the ground. Feelin that child in my arms was like she'd always been there. Doanie landed on top and the three of us giggled and rolled in the grass. Once we'd settled a bit I took Doanie's face in my hands and looked eye to eye with her.

"Don't say nothin, Miss Worie." She shook her head hard. "You did what you could. I didn't rightly figure you'd turn up my brother and sister." She smiled a toothless grin.

"You lost a tooth." I twisted her head from side to side, eyein her mouth.

"Yes ma'am."

"That makes you a step closer to bein a woman. Let me count how many you got left to lose."

She giggled, covering her mouth with her hand.

"The sheriff wouldn't tell me where T. J. and Farrell are. He had everthing in an envelope that he wouldn't open." I loosened my shirttail from my waist and pulled out the paper holder.

"Miss Worie! Did you take that?" Abeleen asked.

Justice went to laughin. "You're a sneaky one. That what you was doin while you was standin him down?"

I nodded.

"Why didn't you tell me on the way here?" he asked.

"I wanted to save it as a surprise."

Ely pulled me to my feet. "So you took what didn't belong to you?" His eyes poured disappointment.

"I did what I had to do to get them babies back."

"Wrong don't right wrong." He took my hand in his and pulled it to his lips.

"Ely, I thought you would be happy. This is the only way we can find them children." I waved the envelope at him.

He turned toward the barn, then threw me a backward wave as he walked away.

"Ely?" I grabbed at his arm. "Wait up."

"Me and Bess has made you a place to stay in the barn. Justice, you'll have to make your bed in the hayloft. That alright?"

"Ely! Don't walk away from me. I needed to take this to find out where T. J. and Farrell is."

"Stealin is stealin, Miss Worie. You mighta just ask an old man if he had any thoughts."

"You didn't know where they were!"

"No. I didn't. But you mighta asked. Mighta found out I had some thoughts."

I stood stunned. Ely never let on like he had any ideas where them children was taken. "Justice, what do you reckon?"

"I reckon you was pretty clever. But Ely walks the straight and narrow. I don't guess they's no bendin the rules for him."

I hugged the girls again and sent them back to their chores. Ely turned the corner toward the barn and I took to runnin to catch up, the bag over my shoulder bouncing against my side. He pulled open the barn door.

I pushed back the tears. No one had ever done nothing any kinder. It was just like Ely to try his best to make a rough time easier. Him and Miss Bess had managed to get them beds the pastor built from my barn and dragged them into their own barn. It took Bess a day or so, but she managed to sew a few of Mrs. Whitefield's quilts together and stuff them with hay so the beds was soft. Momma's quilts was folded neatly at the end of each bed. T. J.'s spot harbored them rails to keep him from fallin out, and in the corner was the hand-stitched toy his momma had made.

I walked along the beds, rubbin my hands over them. Tears

trickled. "These is wonderful, Ely. I never had nothin so nice before."

"The pastor built the beds. Me and Bess just made them something worth usin. Speakin of the pastor. Where is he?"

"Ain't right sure. I left him and Trigger standin outside the sheriff's office. The pastor followed but turned up to the Bentons' place."

"Trigger? You saw Trigger? I bet that drug up some memories."

"It was right uncomfortable, if that is what you're gettin at. But I was nice."

Ely pulled the rocker we'd took from the Whitefields next to a pile of hay. "Tell me your reasonin for becomin a thief. And do you suppose Trigger would approve of you stealin?"

His words hit like a slap in the face. As much as I tried to understand why he was so blasted upset over me takin them papers, it was hard. And his nosin about Trigger was about more than I could swallow.

"Well, first off, it don't matter what Trigger thinks, and second, I went up against that bullheaded sheriff. The fool." I felt my anger toward the sheriff rise to the surface all over again. "Ely, he taunted me. Showed me this envelope and taunted me like a schoolyard bully danglin a piece of candy over my head." I inched off the hay and sat at his feet. "You know I have always tried to do what was right. But hard times calls for harder measures. When I stood to face the sheriff, I just eased it under my shirt." I dropped the envelope at Ely's feet. "Truth is, as cocky as the man was, it was almost like he left the fruit to be picked. So I picked it."

Ely scratched his chin. The bristly sound of rough whiskers reminded me of Daddy.

"You're tellin me that the sin of Eve was really a gift from the good Lord."

I wasn't sure what to say. Ely shamed me ever time I tried to justify my actions.

Bess wandered into the barn, waggin her finger from side to side. "Ely, I heard that, and they ain't a person alive what ain't sinned. You included." She rested her hands on his shoulders. "I's remember two young black people tyin up a watchman so's they could slip out and run for the Mississippi River." Bess leaned close to Ely and kissed his cheek. "Reckon them sinners repented and the good Lord blessed them with friends like the Dressars. A home. And now the sweet voices of laughin children. Somethin we ain't never had."

Ely bowed his head. His fingers tapped on the arm of the rocker. A body could see his ponderin on Bess's words.

"The Lord ain't no more pleased with a self-righteous man than He is a thief." He smiled and picked up the envelope.

CHAPTER
SEVENTEEN

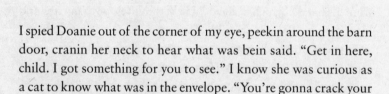

I spied Doanie out of the corner of my eye, peekin around the barn door, cranin her neck to hear what was bein said. "Get in here, child. I got something for you to see." I know she was curious as a cat to know what was in the envelope. "You're gonna crack your neck if you keep bendin it like that." I motioned her to my side.

Doanie took to runnin as hard as she could into the barn.

"I got no idea what is in this envelope, if'n they is anything. You understand?"

She nodded.

"Ely, will you cut that open with your knife?"

I could tell he still struggled with me takin the envelope, but he inched his hand into the top pocket of his overalls and pulled out a blade.

Abeleen came in and eased next to Ely. Her finger stretched toward the knife. "My daddy made that knife. I see his mark." She could hardly spit out the words, and they hung in the air.

"John was a gifted man. I reckon most folks got pieces of his work in hand." Ely reached around and hugged her. "Yep, gifted indeed." He handed Abeleen the knife.

She slowly twisted it, lookin over its cover. Her daddy had taught her how to judge work. The tips of her fingers clasped hold of the small knife and pulled the blade free from its sheath. She wrapped her hand gingerly around the blade and handed it, handle first, back to Ely.

"It's a good blade," she said. "Daddy didn't put his mark on something that wasn't good."

"That it is." And with that, Ely slipped the knife into the envelope. His pull was swift and it sliced with ease. He swiped the blade twice on the leg of his overalls and slipped it back into its cover. "Bess, can you take this for me?"

My patience was low and I wasn't willin to wait through the slow ways of an old mountain man, so I politely took the envelope from his hand. "Much obliged." I held the envelope to my lips and blew it open. The paper inside fluttered.

Justice had tried to give me some privacy to open the envelope, but he musta grown right tired of waiting outside the barn and come barrelin in like a bull. I reckon he had less patience than me.

"Aw, for Pete's sake, open the thing." He snatched the paper from my hand and unfolded it.

"Bein as they is no livin owner, the homeplace of Elbert and Rennie Whitefield shall be give to the first man to lay claim. That would be Jordan Sikes of Chattanooga, Tennessee. And all that lays on that property shall be his."

Justice handed me the paper. "That's it?"

"Seems so." I read through the paper again. "This don't say nothin about these youngins. Not a word. And who the Sam Hill is Jordan Sikes?"

Abeleen raised her hand like she was in school. "Miss Worie. That was the man that scooped up Farrell."

It come back to me. Calvin come to the homeplace with the

sheriff and another man. Sikes. "Things just ain't addin up. I got more questions than a toddler."

Ely leaned forward in the rocker and pushed a chaw of tobacco between his lip and jaw. "I got a few myself. For starters, how did this Sikes man even know the Whitefields was passed?"

I looked at Doanie. "Honey." I pulled her in front of me. "Did your daddy ever have any folks stop by before he passed? You ever remember seein a fancy-dressed man?"

"No, Miss Worie. I don't never remember no man visitin Daddy."

"You're good at cockin your head to hear talkin. Did you ever hear your daddy say something that might make a man want what he had?"

Doanie stared deep into my eyes. I could tell them wheels was turnin in her head. That's when I saw the color leave her face. She turned to walk away and I snagged her arm.

"Oh no you don't. Momma was right. When a person ain't bein honest, their eyes flit. Yours is flittin. What ain't you tellin me?"

The child stood still as a cat ready to pounce.

"Doanie, tell me what I need to know so I can find your brother and sister."

She pointed to the railed bed.

"I wish I was a mind reader, but I ain't. Spit it out, child. What about T. J.'s bed? It's new. What about it?" Then it hit me. That toy Rennie had sewed. I walked to the bed and snatched it up. "This?"

She nodded and took the toy from my hand. She held it to my ear and shook it. It clinked.

"Rocks. Your momma put a few pebbles in it for weight?"

The girl stood quiet. I could tell the words wouldn't come.

"Ely, give me that knife."

"Now, Worie, they ain't no need to destroy the youngin's toy."

"Give me the knife." I held out my hand.

Ely slowly pulled the knife from his pocket. Layin the toy on the floor, I pulled the blade through the material. A small pile of rocks dropped onto the barn floor, and inside the bunch was a small red stone. A second stone just like the one in Momma's jar.

Justice nearly leaped over Doanie to snatch it up. He spit on it and shined it on his trousers. "Look like something you've seen?" he asked.

I couldn't figure what to say. Instead, I pulled my bag from over my shoulder and dug for the jar. I pulled the satin bag out, loosened the string, and dumped the stone into Justice's hand.

Ely stretched his neck, tightenin his glasses to his face. "Them is red stones."

"Reckon, Ely. Red stones," I snapped.

"Miss Worie, them is something I seed when I was livin on the plantation and workin." He motioned to Bess.

She took one stone and held it toward the light. Tiny streams of light glistened from it. Bess laid the stone in Justice's hand. "Yep. Yep. That's what they is. My mistress on the plantation called these precious stones. Rubies."

"Rubies?" I'd heard of such a thing, but I'd never seen the likes of them before. But things went to clickin. "Doanie, where did your daddy get this?"

She shrugged.

Justice dropped both stones into the bag. "Miss Bess, you got a safe place to stash this little bag where nobody can find it?"

"Does a chicken lay eggs?" She grinned and snapped the bag away from Justice, makin her way out of the barn.

She was a dear woman. Gentle. Easy spoken. As wide as she was tall. I could tell she'd already took to the youngins. It didn't take much for Bess to take them into her heart as her own. All Ely would say was the slave masters was less than good to the black women who worked on the plantation. Despite what was behind Bess, she was a woman who chose to look ahead, and over the years I'd grown to love her like I loved Momma.

Ely and Bess were at the homeplace all the time after Daddy

died. Ely found his callin in makin sure me and Momma was alright. Bess and Momma was good, good friends, sharin their washin and clothes hangin every Wednesday mornin.

The clap of horse hooves echoed in the barn, and when they stopped, two shadows stood in the door. "There you are, Miss Worie."

"Preacher?" I said.

"Told you I knew where she'd go." Trigger?

I rushed to the door and flung my arms around Trigger's neck. He was stiff as a board. I guess shocked that I'd run to him, but in a minute he wrapped his arms around me.

The preacher smiled at my excitement. "Well, you got yourself a fine howdy do."

"Pastor Jess, I'm grateful to see you and Trigger both." I reached around his waist and give him a little hug. "I couldn't have gotten to Justice without you. I'm obliged."

"My pleasure, Worie."

"Pastor, I'm sorry. I acted right mean in the sheriff's office. But I needed—"

"No worries. Body has to do what a body has to do."

"That's right kind of you. Thank you."

"The good Lord pushed forgiveness, so I suppose if I'm to be a man of the cloth, I need to be an example of forgiveness." He laughed.

Ely picked up the paper from the floor and handed it to the pastor. "Seein as the pastor is here, Miss Worie might have a few sins to confess."

"There's always time for a come-to-the-Lord meetin." The pastor slapped his leg and laughed again. "What could you have done, Worie? You done told me you was sorry."

"Open that paper, Pastor. Take a gander. Seems Worie took something from the sheriff's office what didn't belong to her."

I'm not sure if I was embarrassed or angry with Ely. Even with

Bess's shamin him, he still saw it necessary to tattle on me. But Ely was especially mindful of a young girl that needed guidance, and I loved him like my daddy. His heart was in the right place with his callin me out to the pastor. I was just as well to hush and let him do what he felt was best.

Pastor Jess read through the paper several times. Ever time takin a stab at different words to see if it read any different. "I've knowed the Whitefields for several years, and that homestead ain't worth a pee pot. Why would Sikes want it? Or what's left of it, seein as we burned the house to the ground."

Ely commenced to tell the pastor about me stealin the letter and how I needed to bring my sins before the Lord. But when he got to the part about the stones, I butted in, gently nudgin him to hush.

"Ely is right. When I stood up to the sheriff, I sneaked that envelope with the report on them youngins under my shirt. Will the Lord forgive me? My heart was in the right place. I needed to find a way to get our youngins back."

It was easy to see my confession was less than sincere, but it seemed to satisfy Ely.

Justice heaved Doanie up on his shoulders. "We got us some plantin to do, young lady." He snagged a shovel as he carted her through the barn door. "Abeleen, you comin?"

I always knew Justice had it in him to be a good man. Seein him lug them children around made me feel safe. Still, they was work to be done if we was to find them little ones. And it needed to start with Sikes.

"Pastor?" I asked. "You know this Jordan Sikes?"

"Well, I know of him. Know where he comes from. Chatta-nooga."

"How far is Chattanooga?"

"Day's ride to Hartsboro. Two days on the train."

"Train? Preacher, I ain't got no money for a train."

"Don't need none. Railroad gives me vouchers, bein as I am clergy."

A smile tipped the edges of my mouth. "Might I ask if you'd help me out?"

The preacher tipped his hat. "We can leave tomorrow."

I run outta that barn and lifted my hands to the sky. "Lord, I ain't sorry I took that envelope, but I'm much obliged You showed me the error of my ways by the preacher. Maybe Momma was right." I dropped to my knees. "You hear the cries of Your children. And little Farrell and T. J. is cryin for their sister, and me."

Ely tapped me on the shoulder. "I don't aim to beat a dead horse, but all I's sayin, Miss Worie, is wrongs don't make a right. Them wrongs always come back to bite you. You think on that."

EIGHTEEN

I twisted and turned through the night like a rabbit on a roastin stick. Despite my best efforts to sleep, all I could think about was them children . . . and them stones. There was still more questions than answers, but a momma bird only feeds her babies a bite at a time. I reckon this was my bite.

The moon shined through the cracks in the barn door, casting streaks across our beds. Several times, I found myself slippin outta bed in the barn and sneakin to check on Doanie sleepin with Abeleen. Poor youngin was as restless as me. They was a nice breeze blowin outside and it seeped through the barn, but the child was sweatin through her clothes. That was her dreams, I guess. It did no good to cover her with a quilt to keep her from catchin a chill. She'd just kick it off.

I rubbed the plastered hair from her cheeks and she roused just a bit. "Shhh. Go back to sleep. Shhh."

I reached under the bed and pulled out my bag. My fingers walked through the bag like a spider on a web, searchin for prey. "There you are," I whispered. The jar. The metal lid was rusted and scrubbed against the glass threads as I opened it. The scrapin made me cringe.

Momma had took great pains to write her notes. I turned the first paper over and squinted to read. Moonlight don't make a good light, so I made my way to the lamp hangin by a nail on the barn wall. I took the flint hangin on the wall and clicked it together, lightin the lamp.

Beautiful loops and curls donned the words Momma wrote. Ever letter was slanted perfectly, and they crawled across the page like a line of marchin ants. I took in a deep breath and sighed. Momma. Momma. Dear Momma.

> *From the good book, James, chapter one, the twenty-seventh verse.*
>
> *Pure religion and undefiled before God and the Father is this, To visit the fatherless and widows in their affliction, and to keep himself unspotted from the world.*
>
> *Lord, I see these people dyin. I hear their babies cryin and it tears my heart in two. But even in these and their afflictions, I have my own children that I shed a river of tears over. I thought when we found . . .*

I slapped the pages against my chest. My heart skipped. I wondered what I had just read. Was my readin so bad that I didn't get it right? Momma said she'd cried rivers of tears over her children. I took the lantern off the nail and walked into the darkness. I plopped onto a rock. Runnin my finger over the words again, I took them in.

> *I shed a river of tears . . . I thought when we found . . .*

"Something wrong?"

"Good land, Justice. You scared the tar outta me."

He scooted me with his hips to sit. "I heard you talkin. Thought you was havin a bad dream. Everthing okay?"

"Lordy mercy, land's sake. I couldn't sleep, so I thought I'd read a note or two from Momma's jar. Maybe figure where them stones come from."

"And did you find out?"

"Law, no! What I got was nipped by a spider I wasn't expectin to be hidin in the pot."

Justice's lip lifted on one side. A crooked smile gleamed in the lamplight. "What spider was it?"

I handed him the note. "Look for yourself."

He leaned to one side and tilted the paper so he could see.

"Go on. Read it out loud."

Justice mumbled the words Momma had written. After a few minutes, he stopped reading. He sucked in a breath that turned to a cough. "Lord have mercy."

I balled my hands into fists. "I want this over with. I want things back to the way they was. We didn't ask for this mess. And every minute that passes just pours more manure on top of us."

"I ain't got no words. Leastways no good words." Justice rested his face in his palms. "Lawsy mercy. Momma kept *this* secret. Her and Daddy kept this secret."

"I can't say it was just a secret. It appears to me to be a lie. You an me was raised believin a lie."

"Momma never did nothing lest she had good reason. You know that. They has to be good reason." Justice slid off the rock and went to pacin. I could tell by the look on his face he wanted to find hisself a swig of liquor.

"Don't you start cravin that hooch. You hear me? This ain't nothin to make a man drink." I wasn't the drinkin sort, but if I was honest, I'd have to say the thought crossed my mind. The pastor would be by to get me in a few hours, but if this news meant leavin Justice on his own to fight off his urge for drinkin, then I'd have to wait a day. I'd not let him slip back. They was a promise made, and I intended to keep it.

I pulled the notes from his hand. Momma had shared this jar with me cause it meant something to her. I figured we'd find out soon enough what it was.

The rooster let out a crow that give me and Justice both a start, and it wasn't long before the bouncing light of a second lantern made its way toward us. Ely come tiptoein over the rocky ground. His suspenders hung to his knees and his boots wasn't tied. He was void a shirt too.

"What's goin on down here?" he said.

"Rise and shine. Looks like that old rooster is doin his job." I hid Momma's notes behind my back. "Sun's peerin over the ridge. Reckon that bird thought it was time to wake us all up."

Ely turned toward the east. "Danged old bird. Could at least give a man till the sun crested." He made his way back to his house, grumblin and slingin his hand. It seemed even sweet-natured Ely could get up on the wrong side of the bed.

I turned Justice toward me. "I ain't leavin here in the mornin if you plan on uncoverin your stash of liquor. You hear me?"

He yanked his arm away. "Two things you need to understand, Worie." Justice planted his finger close to my face. "First, you ain't Momma. I ain't your problem. And second"—his voice quivered—"if a man is to overcome something that has a hold on him, they has to be some trust."

I stood right still, not makin any effort to open my mouth.

"I ain't perfect. I'm a drunk and I ain't gonna stop bein a drunk overnight. But you have to trust me. If you can't do that, then we orta part ways now."

You coulda blowed me over. Justice was never one to raise his voice. His heart was soft, and that softness was his weakness.

"You understand, Worie, it ain't your job to fix me. It's your job to love me despite my downfalls." He ripped the notes away from me and waved them in my face. "Momma had a reason. You hear me? A reason. And it ain't our place to judge her."

They was little I could say. Justice was right. I wasn't Momma, and them youngins endin up at our homeplace was not on account of me. It was on account of her.

I had to chew a minute on his words. It was hard to muster up enough courage to trust Justice not to dig into his liquor stash. But his reasonin was well put. I couldn't hover over him and expect him to get past the drinkin. I had to . . . trust.

I picked up the jar and unscrewed the lid. "You wanna read that note again? Read it out loud so we can both take it in. Then we can shut it in its place and meet the day."

Daylight was overtakin the night and the sun was offerin some light. Justice cupped a hand around his ear and closed his eyes. "Hear them birds? Listen right tight and you almost understand what they is sayin."

We stood side by side, quiet. Listenin. Ponderin.

"I have my own children that I shed a river of tears over. I thought when we found that baby that night and brought him home, that we could save him. We give all we had to save him. Give him a name, Calvin. Give him a home. Love. Hope. But even with that, I couldn't stop his evil. It was like it was born in him."

Justice rolled the notes tight and stuffed them into the jar. I tightened the lid and put it in my bag. We was both taken back that Calvin was not our brother.

CHAPTER
NINETEEN

There was a pop and then a thud in the woodshed. "Did you hear that?" I said.

Justice grabbed a heavy stick from the ground and walked toward the shed. "Ely, that you?"

"That ain't Ely. He's up at the house," I squawked.

"Come on out. Now!" His voice was hard and demandin. "Now! Or I'll come in after you."

The shed door eased open and the pastor stumbled out.

"Pastor Jess, what are you doin in the shed?" Justice asked.

"Tryin to sleep, but I reckon they ain't no sleep to be had. Man's gotta rest where he can find shelter." He pointed toward the back of the shed. "Leastways my horse got some rest." He yawned.

"I ain't never in my life seen a body that keeps poppin up like you, Preacher." I shook my head. "Lawsy mercy."

"I just go where the good Lord sends me. Last night it was the woodshed."

This man had the heart of a saint, and though I thought it a little queer that he kept showin up like he did, he was a welcome sight.

"Sun's comin up," he said. "You ready to head to Hartsboro?"

I looked at Justice and waited for his approval.

"Trust, Worie. You have to give me some trust." He squeezed my shoulder. "Might as well go. Ain't gettin no younger."

I wasn't right with leavin Justice to fend off his hankerin for the drink, but I needed to find them babies. I never was close to Calvin. Justice was the one who tended me when Momma was away. Now he was all the family I had. I pulled him down to me and kissed his cheek. "Promise me you'll watch these girls. Promise!"

"I'll be right here with Ely. They will be fine. We'll see to it."

"Me and the preacher might be gone a few days."

"Alright." Justice made his way to the barn and brought Sally back ready to travel. He handed me my bag.

I looked toward the barn, and there was Doanie, peepin— something she was real good at doin. I squatted and motioned her to me. The child bolted from the barn, Abeleen right behind her. Them arms wrapped tight around my neck. Doanie went to cryin.

"Stop with them tears. We're gonna find them. Until then we don't waste good time bawlin. Understand me?"

Doanie nodded. Abeleen took her by the hand. "She'll be fine, Miss Worie. I'll see to it." The sun bounced off Abeleen's freckles and her teeth gleamed in the light. I cupped her cheek and kissed her head.

"I know she's in good hands." I give them one more hug, then put my foot in Justice's hand for a lift. "I might be gone a few days this time."

Justice shook Pastor Jess's hand. "Take care of my sister."

"Will do."

Ely moseyed out. He flipped the saddlebag open and dropped a bag of gun shells inside. He slid Daddy's shotgun into its scabbard while Bess added some biscuits to the bag. "You remember. Wrongs don't make a right."

"Yes sir. I'll remember."

"And you remember everthing happens in the good Lord's

timin. So if'n you don't see this workin hows you think it orta
. . . 'member that. A body should never underestimate the good
Lord's timin." Ely patted my knee. He give Sally a tap on the rump.
"Hup there, girl."

Pastor Jess took the lead, and just as we turned onto the path,
a horse and rider rounded the bend.

"Hold up. Wait! You might need an extra hand." Trigger eased
his horse between me and the pastor. "Body can't go wrong with
an extra hand."

Pastor Jess shook his head, then kneed his horse. "We got a
day's ride ahead."

I twisted in the saddle to see the girls wavin their goodbyes.
Justice tapped his heart twice and waved. All I could hear in my
head was, *Trust. They has to be some trust.*

We made the bend and the breeze carried the smell of rhodo-
dendron blooms. Lilac and mint mixed into the scents. I reckon
today was as good as any to learn trust.

They wasn't a lot said as we worked our way around the mountain toward Hartsboro. It was plain to Pastor Jess I wasn't in no
mood to jaw. They was a lot to take in. A lot to put together. I
patted my bag to be sure the jar was there. They was no doubt
Momma's Bible was there. It weighed as much as a small stuffed
turkey. But them was the two things I needed to hold tight to.

We rode the better part of the day before we stopped. The
horses was hot and the river had hit a quiet, shallow spot. Pastor
Jess climbed out of his saddle and extended his hand, but Trigger grabbed me by the waist and slid me off Sally. I know I ain't
always the sharpest nail in the pouch, but it was becomin clearer
and clearer there was an unspoken gentlemanly feud goin on.
Trigger took Sally by the harness, and I pulled his hand down
and took hold myself.

"I got her." I'd done pulled my shoes off and stepped in the icy Indian River. Water wasn't no deeper than my ankles, so me and Sally meandered across the river. They is nothin better than wadin in the river. It's one of them things that freezes your toes but calms your mind.

A school of minners splashed past my toes, and just upstream you could see trout leapin the rapids.

"Worie, you hungry?" Pastor Jess shouted across the river. "Miss Bess give me some cured ham."

I remembered the biscuits she slipped into Sally's bag, so the two of us sloshed back across the water.

"Bess give me biscuits. Oughta make a good dinner with your ham." I dropped the reins over a tree branch and flipped open my saddlebag. Bess had outdone herself. Biscuits and a small wrapped bowl of jelly. "Boys, we have a feast." I smiled as I sat on a stump between the two men.

"Good Father. Bless this food."

The pastor caught me mid-bite. I nearly choked, tryin to swallow my bite fast enough to bow my head.

"I ask, heavenly Father, for your hand of protection over us. Give us direction so we do what is right in savin them children. Bless this food to our body and give goodness to the hands that made it. In the Lord's name. Amen."

The men work their way through that cured ham like a squirrel gnawin on a walnut. "Good?" I asked. They grinned, jaws stuffed full.

I took a few bites, then wrapped the towel around my biscuit. My stomach turned at the thoughts of Momma's lie. Justice could call it a secret, but to me, it was still a lie.

It was hard to imagine Calvin anything other than my elder brother, but knowin what I did started to make a few things add up. Nothin over this jar, but things when we was kids. Like Calvin's hair so blond it was nearly white. And his skin pale. My skin, and

Justice's too, was a brown. Me and Justice could play together when we was youngins, but Calvin shied away. Justice was gentle and helpful. Calvin was never happy. I never remember him laughin or findin joy in anything. It was like he was always angry. Momma would tell him to look for the honey, not the sour grapes in life, but honey was never something Calvin considered.

I wondered if Calvin knew where he come from. Or why he was so angry, always feelin like the world owed him something.

"You're awfully quiet." Pastor Jess nudged me. "Worried about them children?"

My head nodded real easy. "Yes." I dried my feet and put my shoes on.

"Seems like they is something more on your mind. You wanna get it off your chest?"

Trigger butted in. "Pastor, give the lady her room."

I rolled my eyes. They was no lettin up from Trigger. He had to get his jab in from when the pastor called his hand at the forge.

"Come to think of it, they is something I'd like to say to you both."

The men inched closer.

"Pastor, you're a kind man and I'm much obliged by your kindness to help me. But I'm gettin the nudgin that you'd like to be closer. And Trigger. I turned you down once, and despite what my heart still feels for you, now ain't the time. So I'd be obliged if the both of you would stop this boyish banter. I got more on my mind than this." I stood and headed toward Sally. "This where you wanna cross the river to head to Hartsboro?"

The pastor nodded. So I jumped, landin on my stomach in the saddle, and pulled myself up. "Come on, Sally. Let's get a head start." I pulled her reins and inched her to the river. "I'll see you boys on the other side. Take your time."

Sally fiddled around crossin. She'd take a few steps, then bend that long, sleek neck down to suck in a taste of water, but we finally crossed. I give her a little nudge, and just as she picked up her pace, my gut give me that sick feelin. I pulled her to a halt and turned from side to side. The river rolled to one side, and the edge of the woods laid to the other. They was something watchin me. Something gnawin at my craw.

I swung my leg over the saddle and took hold of Daddy's shotgun. My feet hit the ground with a thump. I opened the chamber and saw Ely had loaded the double barrel. That was good. With one swift motion, I clicked both hammers back and walked to the woods.

"I reckon the pastor and Trigger is crossin the river right now. They'll be up with me soon. You best work your way out so I can see you."

The weeds rustled and a young girl raised her head. I squinted hard to see in the shade of the woods. "Ellie?"

The girl worked her way out of the woods.

"Ellie Olsen. Where's your brothers and sisters? Whatta you doin out here? It's been you followin me all along, ain't it?"

She held up her hand to stop me from talkin. "Miss Worie, I'm sorry about your momma."

"That's mighty kind of you, but you still ain't answered my questions."

"Can I come closer?" She pointed at the gun.

I let the hammers down and hung the gun under my arm. She walked straight to me and laid her head on my shoulder. The girl cried for a spell. My arm inched up and around her neck.

"Where's your brothers and sisters? They was a passel of you youngins."

She snubbed and swiped at her nose. "The twins, Joshua and Mark, died. So did Eliza, the least one. They took sick not long after Momma died. They was nothin I could do but herd the rest of the youngins into the barn away from the sick ones. Matthew and Robert loaded the wagon and I sent them toward the gap. Told

136

them boys to stop at homeplaces and ask if they could work for food while they tried to make their way to one of Daddy's people in Saunder's Gap." Her shoulders shook from the sobs. "Worie, I didn't know what else to do except to find you. I couldn't take no chance of the rest of them growin sick."

"It's alright. I know what it means to do what you have to do. Why didn't you just come to me instead of hidin away?"

"You had them other children. I couldn't ask."

"Ellie, what are you, fourteen, fifteen?"

"I'm fifteen."

"You're a woman. Stand up straight and act like one."

She took a step back, shocked that I called her out.

"Body can't take care of theirself if they're wallerin in pity. You did what you had to do. That's that. Now you step up."

"But I don't know what to do. Where to go."

"You'll stay with me. I got things to work out. We'll figure something out to help you find your siblins. That alright with you?"

She hugged me again. "Thank you."

"No need for thanks. I got the pastor and Trigger comin up behind me. We gotta make them see a reason for you to go to Chattanooga."

"Miss Worie?"

I clasped my fingers together so I could boost her up on Sally. Her foot pressed into my hand and she bounced, one, two, three. "Up you go." I climbed in front of her and tapped Sally. "What's you want to say?"

"I've been lookin for Calvin."

I turned. "What? Why do you want Calvin?"

"I'm with child."

137

TWENTY

I leaned forward and rested my head on Sally's neck. Her wiry mane brushed against my lashes ever time I blinked. The wind was sucked outta me a second time in one day. My stomach was already churnin and this was like addin fuel to the fire, and it didn't seem like this fire was gonna go out anytime soon.

"Miss Worie?" Ellie rubbed the middle of my back. "Miss Worie, you alright?"

I couldn't get no words out without the bile crawlin into my mouth, so I reached one hand back and patted her knee. All the girl knew to do was scratch my back, and for what it was worth, the chills the scratchin made calmed my need to vomit.

It took me a minute before I could speak, and in the meantime the girl went to snubbin and whimperin. I'd just told her to act like a woman. Seemed I needed to take my own advice. I swallowed hard and raised up. They was no lookin at her. Instead I give Sal a little tap and we headed down the path along the river.

"Worie? You gonna be silent for long?" Ellie asked. "I didn't mean to make you mad at me. I can go away. Not cause you no trouble. I understand."

"Oh, stop that whinin. I just needed to catch my breath. They's been one shock after the next today. Sometimes a body just has to get their wits about them. And I ain't mad at you. I'm upset *for* you."

If the girl only knew all the bull I'd been through.

I gasped. There it was again. My own selfishness risin to the surface. This young girl had been through so much. She was forced to make decisions nobody should have to make. Here I was, comparing my own sorry self to her. I was ashamed. Ashamed that I could let myself be as bad as if not worse than Calvin.

Daddy would sit on the porch at night and chew a twig. He'd tell us what he expected of us. Momma'd pull out the good book and read. Funny what a body remembers, but I remember her quotin the Lord. "'He hath shewed thee, O man, what is good; and what doth the LORD require of thee, but to do justly, and to love mercy, and to walk humbly with thy God?'" Momma and Daddy might not have been right in all they did, but they was never a question about what they expected of us. Calvin heard them same words over and over. But even as a boy, he never took heed. Momma worried too. She'd plead with him to do right by folks. I reckon some of us ain't cut out to do right.

"I'm sorry, Worie. I reckon I've upset you." Ellie pulled a cloth from her pouch and blew her nose.

"When did you lay with Calvin?"

Ellie went to snubbin again, and finally she spit out the words. "It wasn't by choice. My brothers and sisters was sick and starvin. They was dyin."

"That ain't no reason to lay with a man," I snapped.

"They was more to it than that. See, Calvin promised he had a bottle of medicine that could make Eliza better. He said he would give it to me if I would do one thing."

"I reckon that one thing was to lay with him?"

"No, it wasn't."

One more time I was dumbfounded. I couldn't fault the girl too much, she was just a young woman. When I come of age, Momma told me, "Worie, your body can harbor babies now. Don't listen to them young boys after you like a dog in heat. They'll tell you anything to lay with you."

"Law help me. What did he want from you?" I asked Ellie.

"A rock. A little red rock."

I reared my head up and took notice. "I need you to do some explainin. I ain't following you."

They was no question what the rock was, but what wasn't comin together was how the Olsens woulda had one. And how Calvin would have knowed. This would make three stones. Three.

"Go on. Keep talkin," I said.

"It was when the twins and Eliza was so sick. I'd done moved the other youngins into the barn and Matthew kept a fire blazin in the house. Eliza was bad with fever and chillin."

"Go on." I tried to be patient as she fumbled through the story. What was important to her wasn't bearin no nevermind on me.

"Calvin showed up with this bottle of medicine. He told me to look in Momma's things, her private things, and see if they was a red rock. He pulled a pouch from his pocket and opened it. There in plain sight was one. Right purty too."

"You're tellin me Calvin had a stone?"

"Yes ma'am. He did. I'd never seen sucha thing and I told him so. But he kept on at me, tellin me Momma had to have a box or a jar or a bag where she kept things that was precious to her."

"Did your momma have anything?"

"Well, I went to lookin. All the time he was breathin down my neck, naggin at me to find it. Said they wasn't a woman alive that didn't have trinkets hid away. I crawled up on the table and reached up to Momma's butter jar on the top of the pantry. When I opened it, they was a nickel, a writin pencil, and that little rock stuck to the bottom of the jar. I'd have never noticed it if I'd not been lookin specific for it."

"Calvin took your momma's jar?"

"No, he set it down, then whisked me off the table. He told me the medicine wouldn't work unless I give of myself. I needed that medicine for the twins and for Eliza. I remember Momma tellin Miss Louise she did whatever she had to to care for her youngins. Layin with Calvin was a small price to pay if I could save my siblins.

"Next thing I knew, he was done with me. He busted Momma's butter jar and took the rock. 'What about the bottle of medicine? You told me I could have that medicine if I give myself to you. Now give it over!' Miss Worie, I shouted at him loud. But he went to laughin an awful laugh, then he threw the bottle on the ground and it shattered. I won't never forget his laughin at me. Callin me a fool."

I felt my anger come to a boil. I knew Calvin was slick, but this was more than I thought even he was capable of. I couldn't hold my stomach no longer. I slipped off my horse and run to the edge of the woods to gag. What little bit I'd eat of that biscuit come back on me. They was anger and shame all balled together. To think Calvin would do sucha thing. To a young girl . . . a new woman. I felt my stomach roll again, but all I could do was retch. They was nothin left in me to vomit.

I wiped my mouth and stumbled back to Sally. "Sweet child. Lordy mercy." I pushed my hand against Ellie's stomach. "How long ago?"

"Just after Momma died. Goin on a couple of months now."

The girl wasn't no bigger than a splinter, and though her belly didn't pooch out, it had rounded. Martha Olsen died close to two weeks before Momma took her life, so the timin fit. Calvin was already doin his evil.

"Ellie, do you know how your momma got that rock?"

She shrugged. "I never knew she even had it, and like I said, if I twernt lookin for it, I'd never have saw it."

My heart ached for this girl. She was no different than Abeleen and Doanie, 'cept they'd come to me before Calvin could prey on them like a wolf. Ellie did what she thought would save her siblins, at her own sacrifice.

I remember Momma talkin about the good Lord sendin His Son and about how He give all He had to save us. I wasn't right sure it was the same thing, seein as Ellie didn't die, but she sure as the dickens did sacrifice herself. My words might hurt her but the girl needed to know the truth so she didn't live with no guilt. Why is it the truth hurts?

I took in a big gulp of air and commenced to talk. "Ellie, honey, we need to get some things straight."

"Alright. I promise I won't be no trouble, Miss Worie."

"No, darlin, you ain't no trouble. This is about your decisions."

She fingered Sally's mane.

"First of all, you did right loadin up your siblins and sending them away. That was exactly the right thing to do. I know it was harder than an elm root, but it was right."

Tears dripped off her nose.

"Second, Calvin is a liar. A swindler. Always has been. He's bad to the core. They ain't nothing he'd stop at to get what he wants, includin tellin you that that medicine wouldn't work unless you give yourself." I reached up and swiped a tear away. "This ain't your fault." I laid my hand on her belly. "But it is what it is and so we'll manage together. You understand what I'm tellin you, Ellie? They is no reason for you to feel guilty about any of this. The lot in life we is given ain't always one we choose."

A smile edged her lips. "A child is a wonderful gift from the good Lord, and we don't spend our time frettin over how it got here, just how we're goin to love this special gift," she said as she wrapped her arms around her belly.

"You're gonna be a good momma. Good like Miss Martha. And you know how wonderful she was, don't you?"

"Uh-huh. She was good like your momma. We'd have starved if'n it wasn't for Miss Louise."

Momma did good by a lot of folks, but then there was them secrets. I was still tryin to take them in.

"And one other thing," I said. "That bottle wasn't no medicine. More than likely it was a little hooch. Calvin ain't truthful about nothin. And if they was a medicine that would stop folks from dyin on the mountain from this fever, don't you think somebody would have figured out how to get it to everone?"

"I reckon."

I pulled myself into the saddle. The echo of hooves clopped behind us. I wasn't sure how I was gonna explain this to the pastor. Tellin him about them stones wasn't something I'd planned on. But, one more time, it appeared the truth would hurt.

"There comes the pastor and Trigger. I reckon we got us some explainin to do, don't we?"

CHAPTER
TWENTY-ONE

"You had some time to yourself? Enough to ponder on things?" Pastor Jess rested his arms on his saddle horn. "Who's this young woman?"

Trigger kicked his horse and bumped him into a trot, gettin to me before the pastor. "Everthing alright, Worie? Pastor here said you had something weighin heavy on your mind. I didn't realize when I—"

I shushed Trigger. "I done told you. Now ain't the time. They ain't nary a thing for you to jut your chest out and prance around like a rooster when it comes to the pastor. Leave things alone."

Trigger twisted his mouth. I could tell he was bitin his tongue to keep from sayin anything. But he was kind not to spar with me.

Pastor Jess jumped from his horse and walked to my side. "I feel like I know this young lady, Miss Worie." He cocked his head, then squinted. I could see he was tryin to place Ellie.

"This here is . . ." I hardly got a word out before the pastor slapped his leg and butted in.

"Olsen. Emmie. No. El . . . Ellie. Ellie Olsen. I knew it'd come to me." He seemed right proud he'd recalled her name. "What's

Miss Ellie doin on your horse?" Pastor Jess reached his hand up to shake.

"I . . . I . . . uh . . ." Ellie stuttered like a youngin with her mouth full of mush.

"Pastor Jess," I said. "We got some talkin to do. And I'd trust you to give Ellie here a little room to take in everthing."

He lowered his hand. The smile left his face. "This here sounds serious."

"It's right serious. But you need to trust me." Them words come back at me like a shovel full of rocks. Justice's request all of a sudden made good sense. I needed the pastor to trust me the same way Justice needed me to trust him. Still, they was a lot of things I needed to sort through before tellin him.

I sighed. I done figured trust is a funny thing. It's one of them words a body throws around like seedin a field, but when it comes to puttin it into practice . . . well, then they's a real skill to that.

"How long till we reach Hartsboro?" I asked.

The pastor peered up at the sun and then stared hard at where we was. "Oh, best guess is a couple of hours if we don't make no stops. Train hits Hartsboro just before dusk."

"Then come up beside me, Pastor. Trigger, you take the other side. And I'd oblige you both to just be quiet whilst I tell you about this mess we are about to face."

Sally took a step and stumbled.

"Whoa there, girl. You okay?" I patted her neck.

"She's old, Worie. Puttin two on her is a little much for the distance we are travelin." Pastor Jess walked his horse to my side, then reached out to Ellie. "Miss Ellie, might I lift you onto my horse?"

Ellie put her hands on the pastor's shoulders, and he lifted her from Sally to his horse, then climbed up. "That oughta give ole Sally some rest. Let's get goin. You got some talkin to do and we got some listenin to do."

The pastor was a young man but wise for his youth. I reckon

when the good Lord picked a soul to be His workman, He'd gift them with the right ways to handle things. They was times I thought Pastor Jess was clumsy and right slow, and then they was times like now that I could see the goodness of his heart.

"Miss Ellie, you feel free to rest against me if you get tired." He took Sal by the harness and give her a tug. "Start talkin. I'm listenin."

Despite hisself, Trigger never uttered a word the rest of the trip to Hartsboro. I took my time givin the pastor and him what I knew to be true, from Momma's death to the jar, the letters, and the stones. And when all was said and done they wasn't no need to even mention Ellie's predicament. I ain't sure how he managed, but the pastor done figured it out. Ever time Ellie would sniffle, Pastor Jess would gently reach his hand back and pat her.

It took the better part of the time to weave this story into a web that would hold a bug, and as we turned the last bend before Hartsboro, the pastor finally spoke. "This is a quandary, ain't it?" He took his hat off and rested it on his knee. "I knew your momma, Worie. I knew her heart. She was the most givin woman I've ever met. That's why it was no surprise to me them youngins started showin up on your porch. But them stones. That don't make no sense."

"Four of them, Pastor. Four. And all them who owned them is dead."

"That's something to ponder on. But leastways we know what Calvin is after. He wants them stones. So I'd not be surprised what he tries next."

The horses lumbered into Hartsboro, and when the sheriff's office come into view I knew they was something I needed to do. But first things first. We had to see if Sikes had an office.

We rested the horses in the forge. Trigger unsaddled and fed them, then latched them into a stall. They'd be safe there until we got back from Chattanooga. Ellie was tired, and Trigger offered to let her rest in his room whilst we hunted down this Sikes.

"Ellie," I said as I covered her with a blanket, "just rest. Trigger will fix you a bite to eat. Try to eat if you can keep something down. I'll be back in a bit."

She didn't have to say a word. Her eyes said it all. She was both scared and grateful. Just knowin someone cared to help her.

"I'm guessin if we see Calvin, we keep Ellie's state to ourselves," Pastor Jess said.

I couldn't argue. Calvin wouldn't care what chaos he caused.

Me and the pastor made our way down the town's bumpy road. Across from the forge was a general store and a boardin house. I figured that was where Calvin spent his nights when he wasn't wreakin havoc. Just across from the boardin house and down from the forge was the sheriff's office and the bank.

I pointed at the bank. "Reckon that's where we'll find Sikes?"

"Good a place as any."

We made our way over. A short and stocky man, wearin a black coat and white shirt, met us at the bank's door.

Pastor Jess stuck out his hand. "Sir, I'm Pastor Jess. This here is my friend Worie Dressar. We're hopin you might help us."

The man eyed us up one side and down the other before he stepped aside and motioned to a desk and a couple of chairs. "How can I help you?"

Pastor Jess kept on. "We're lookin for some information on a gentleman named Jordan Sikes. Wondered if you might tell us where we could find him."

The man went to squirmin in his seat, clearin his throat, coughin. It was plain to see he knew something but didn't want to talk. I waited patiently while the pastor hemhawed around, tryin to ease the tension, until I finally come to my feet.

"Listen, this Sikes took my youngins. I want to know where they are and I want to know now. Spit it out." The man stood and I shoved him back into his seat. "Don't you act like you ain't got no idea either. The papers to take my homeplace was from this here bank. The sheriff, my brother, and this Sikes come flashin them in my face. Before I knew it, Sikes had one of my least ones under his arm. Him and the sheriff loaded them up and took them. So, unless you have somebody you answer to, I reckon you orta start talkin."

"Those children are orphans!" the banker said as he jumped to his feet. He pressed his hand over his mouth. He'd let the cat outta the bag. "I don't know a thing. I just stamped the papers. They was all legal and all."

"Who said they was legal? Who?" I snapped. "And they ain't no takin back what come outta your mouth. You know where them youngins is and I want them back." I leaned further across the desk and pushed my finger into his chest.

The pastor stepped between me and the desk and pressed me into a chair. "Worie, this here man looks to be tellin the truth."

"Truth?" I shouted.

Pastor Jess turned and stepped around the desk. "I know he must be tellin the truth because the good Lord knows a man's heart. Even the parts we can't see. He can see the sin that we can't speak. Ain't that right, Mr. . . . ?"

"Barker. Mr. Barker." The man whispered his name.

"Mr. Barker here wouldn't lie to a man of the cloth, especially knowin the good Lord is on his side. Now would you, Mr. Barker."

Barker pulled his collar, trying to loosen it so he could swallow his lie, then pulled open a desk drawer and took out a ledger. He thumbed through the pages and scribbled something on a sheet of paper. "Here. I'd thank you kindly to leave my bank now."

Pastor Jess took the paper and smiled. He thanked Barker, then offered me his arm. I stood and slipped my hand through the crook. "We'll be leavin now," he said.

All I could do was spit and sputter, tryin to figure out what had just happened. But once we was outside and across the road, Pastor Jess held up the paper. "This is the address."

"Address for what? Sikes?"

"Nope. Them children." He grinned like a bear scrapin honey from a beehive.

I snagged the paper and read it. "'Charles and Mable Holtsclaw, 1 Riding Road, Chattanooga. Home for Lost Children.' But you didn't even ask where them youngins was?"

Pastor Jess folded the paper and tucked it in his coat pocket. "Didn't need to. Guilt can be your worst enemy. And this man was guilty. You learn after a spell when folks is caught in a lie they'll do two things. Keep lyin or try to amend the wrong." Pastor Jess was right proud of hisself. "This man aimed to amend a wrong."

"How long till the train?"

He eyed the sun again. "Anytime now."

We reached the forge and I eyed poor Ellie. It was right easy to see the girl was spent. She was in no mind to make a long trip. She was tore all to pieces. As hard as it was to admit it, I didn't need to be responsible for her right now. The longer I stared at Ellie, the better a plan formed in my head.

We walked toward the train, and the thud of our steps on the walkway seemed to ring through the town. People wandered in and out of the general store, and horses clopped through the dryin mud.

"Pastor Jess, I might want your opinion here."

"What's eaten at your mind?" He patted my hand graspin his arm.

"It's Ellie. She ain't up to this trip. Reckon you could do some fast talkin and get Trigger to take her back to Ely and Bess? The girl needs rest and she needs someone to guide her with this baby." I sighed. "Bess can give her that. This whole mess is about more than the girl can manage."

The preacher scrubbed his chin with his finger. "Less is better. That's a right good idea."

I knew Trigger would never listen to me, but the preacher could plead a good case for Ellie's best interest. And that he did. He headed the few steps back to the forge and motioned Trigger over. Them heads was bobbing whilst they conversed, and before I knew it Trigger was leading Ellie away. He looked over his shoulder and winked. What a sweet soul he was. I coulda battled it out with him, but I had a hunch Pastor Jess could convince Trigger without a struggle.

I pressed my fingers against my lips and gently blew Trigger a kiss. You'd have thought somebody opened a fresh jar of apple butter, his grin was so big. This was best. They wasn't no need for too many hands in the pot.

This trip would be enough with just me and Pastor Jess. Totin around a pregnant woman and a well-meanin friend was too much. Me and Pastor Jess had some hard work to do and not much time.

I pulled the envelope I'd took from my bag. Wastin no time, I run across the road and peeked into the sheriff's window. The room was dark and I was glad. I called that an act of God in and of itself. Real easy like, I slipped the envelope under the door and give it a shove, hoping I could land it next to the desk so it looked like it just fell off. Then I took toward the pastor. He grabbed my arm and pulled me toward the train platform.

The train's whistle echoed through the valley as it rounded the curve. Its brakes squawked as metal rubbed hard against metal, bringing the iron horse to a rough halt. In minutes the pastor talked his way onto the train with an extra person in tow.

We planted ourselves on a seat in the back of the car. The train jolted and cried as its wheels spun, tryin to grab hold of the rails. It lunged forward and pulled away from the platform. There on the platform stood the sheriff, arms crossed, and I wondered . . . did he know?

CHAPTER
TWENTY-TWO

I slid deep into my seat, hopin the sheriff didn't get a glance of me. I'd give back the envelope I took, but standin eye to eye with him was not what I wanted. I wasn't right sure the sheriff was as forgivin as Ely or the pastor. Still, he had his envelope back and I'd pushed it hard under the door. I could only hope for the best. Either way, I was glad to be pullin away from that platform.

My fingers grasped the metal edge around the window. At least a live horse had reins to hold to.

"You look to be on the nervous side?" the pastor asked.

"Reckon what give you that idea, Preacher?"

"Might be, just sayin now . . . that your knuckles is white." He went to chucklin. "Ain't you never rode a train before?"

"Well, ain't you just smart and all?"

"Don't get your hackles up. I'm teasin. It seems you need a bit of laughter about now." Pastor Jess sat in the seat that faced me. He leaned forward and rested his elbows on his knees. "I understand you're bein worried." He took my hand. "Seems like one broke pot leads to another."

I pulled my hand away and slipped it into my skirt pocket. I could tell the pastor was tryin to comfort me, but they didn't seem to be no comfort found. Momma always told me not to be a whiner, and even though I'd cried a passel of tears over all that happened, my heart just wasn't healin. Would it ever?

My mind slipped back to a time when things seemed easier. A little girl playin under fresh hung sheets on the clothesline. A puppy nippin at my feet. Momma smilin as I played. I couldn't imagine my life without Momma then, and to tell the truth, I still can't. But it is what it is, and I'd keep tryin to understand why Momma would break my heart like she did.

Ever time I think about findin Momma dead, my chest goes so tight I can't breathe and my heart aches so bad I can't move from the pain. I shook my head, tryin to put the thoughts outta my mind.

I wiggled my finger toward the preacher, then leaned to whisper, "Pastor Jess, I had enough to worry with over them little ones. I feel real bad about sendin Ellie away."

"You did right by that girl. She's old enough to learn the ways of a momma. This trip woulda been too much for her in her state." He crossed his legs and bounced his foot to the rhythm of the train. "No offense here, but you don't need Trigger dotin over you either."

I tilted my head to one side. "Dotin?" I tried to not get riled. "Look, Preacher. What Trigger is or ain't to me ain't got nothin to do with you."

"I wasn't tryin to say nothin bad. Just that you have your work cut out for you. Trigger ain't workin in your favor. He's tryin to protect you. That ain't helpin."

I pushed my head into the seat. My mind wasn't made up about the pastor's intentions. One minute he was funny and kind, the next a bit snide. I couldn't make no sense of him all the time. Albeit good, I think, he did tend to rile me. I pushed his remark to the back of my head.

"Ellie is a sweet girl," I said. "Love her heart, she did everthing she could to fill her own momma's shoes after she died."

"I'm sure she did, Worie." Pastor Jess took his hat and placed it over his eyes, partially to keep out the light, but mostly to keep out the soot and cinders from the engine. He crossed his arms and settled into his seat. "Try to rest. We got a long road to work our way through."

Ever time I thought about Calvin usin Ellie, it burned my britches. I ain't the brightest thing they is, but I had enough life under me to see when I was bein hornswoggled. That girl was a young woman with nothin. She stepped right into that manure without seein it hidin in the weeds.

It was startin to make sense what Calvin was after. Them red stones had some value, and he'd be the first one in line with his hand out if he thought they was a dollar to be made. Momma tried so hard to soften his heart, but they was no softenin. And he was never kind to Justice. I still think a good part of Justice's drinkin is Calvin's fault.

The train bumped and jarred as it climbed the steep hill toward Chattanooga. The pastor said what would be a four-day ride on horseback would be two days on the iron beast.

I closed my eyes as the sway of the train drawed me into sleep. I wrapped the strings of my bag tight around my wrist, my hand clutchin the small Mason jar inside. Them words I read from Momma's Bible crawled around my mind like a mouse huntin for corn kernels.

But Jesus said, Suffer little children, and forbid them not, to come unto me: for of such is the kingdom of heaven.

I reckon what did the good Lord mean by that? Suffer? Why?

The train squalled like a trapped coon as it bumped and banged to a stop. I guessed it was just reflex, but I come outta that seat like I'd been prodded with a hot iron.

"Ain't nothin, Worie," the pastor said. "The train stops at

ever station, and they's a lot of them from Hartsboro to Chat-tanooga."

I eased against the side of the train to peer out. The whistle squalled, and ash and cinder rushed inside the car. When the train come to a rest, a dozen or so children stepped in. Ever child that passed got my eye over them. Could one of them be Farrell? T. J.?

"Pastor, where's these children headin?" I asked.

He took his hat and rested it on his chest. I could tell by the look on his face he didn't want to tell me nothin. He hesitated a spell before he spoke. Like he was ponderin just what to say.

"Worie, these children are orphans. More than likely headed toward St. Louis to catch a train out west and find a home."

St. Louis. I'd never heard of sucha place, and who in their right mind would load a bunch of children onto a train to fend for themselves? My heart bled as them children, dirty and bro-ken, lined past me and set on the benches in the back. I saw right then and there that the pastor was respected since we was able to sit in one of the leather seats and not the bench that stretched across the car.

They was nothin I could do for them children. Not a thing. So I got up from my seat and walked to one of the benches. A boy, reckon to be about eleven or so, held a small girl on his lap. Her face was streaked with tear trails, her fingers nasty. The dirt under her nails didn't stop her from shoving them fingers into her mouth. I squeezed my eyes tight to keep the wellin tears from fallin. Them youngins was pitiful.

I dug into my bag, searchin for the last of the biscuit Bess give me. The train whistle howled, and once again the cars shifted and knocked against each other. I took a few steps and the car jolted, sendin me off balance, but I caught myself.

"Scooch over," I said.

The boy inched to one side, his sister clingin tight to his neck. I broke a bite of biscuit loose and gently pulled the girl's hand from her mouth. "Here, honey, chew this over them fingers. At least it has some taste."

The girl stared hard at the bread, then easy as a mouse stealin corn, she wrapped them wet fingers around it.

"Say thank ye, Delta." The boy pointed toward me.

"Wanna sit on my lap?" I held out my hands. She eyed me for a minute, then reached. She didn't weigh nothin. Tiny as could be. When she settled into my lap, she leaned her head against my chest.

"Oh Lord. I don't understand this. I just don't understand."

Another boy wiggled into the small space between me and the side of the car. Then one come to my feet and inched closer. And another. The train picked up speed and locked into its rhythm. Ever child that could got close enough to touch me. And at that moment, I understood what Momma meant when she said she was called by the good Lord. It was clear to me, even in my doubtin Him, even sparrin or cussin Him, what my plight would be. I didn't feel like we was on good speakin terms yet, the good Lord and me, but now I understood what Momma meant, and the tug on my own mind.

I looked around at the passel of children around me, and my heart bled just like the blood that poured from Momma. I knew their pain. I understood the sufferin. Their snubbin stopped and a quiet fell over them. I knew how they felt cause I was one of 'em. Right there on that train, I took ahold of what I really was—and I took my place with the orphans.

CHAPTER
TWENTY-THREE

It seemed ever time that train caught up some speed, it turned right around and slowed for the next station. Climbing its way around them steep mountains didn't help the trip pass any faster. As we chugged into one more station, a man come round and roused them youngins. He herded them like sheep toward the door in the car, then come back for the little one on my lap. I wrapped my arms tighter around her and shook my head, but that didn't stop him from tuggin her.

The pastor gently loosened my grip. "Worie, let her go. Come on. Let her go so she don't get separated from her brother."

My fingers was clasped tight together as I pulled her closer. "They can't do this, Pastor. They can't. Don't let them take all these babies."

Pastor Jess worked the child out of my arms and handed her to the man. He wasn't ugly to the children, instead he was right kind. "Come on, baby girl, let's find your brother," the man whispered, and kissed her head. He took a few steps and looked over his shoulder. "Thank ye kindly, miss. These youngins will remember your goodness."

The girl's brother stepped from the group and took his sister. When I went to my knees sobbin, Pastor Jess just rubbed my shoulder.

The train halted and the man ushered the children off. Just as her brother stepped onto the platform, the girl shouted, "Thank ye, lady." She pressed her palm to her lips and kissed it.

I couldn't contain my grief no more, wonderin if Farrell and T. J. was alright. Had they kept them little ones together or tore them apart again? They was no guessin that Farrell couldn't stand one more loss. And little T. J. All I could think of was the youngin didn't have no clean britches and had he stopped messin in what he had.

"Lord have mercy, I feel like my chest is gonna split wide open." I let out a wail that beat all.

They was no explainin why these children Momma had been carin for had grown into my heart. I'd only knowed them for a short time, but they was mine. They was ever one mine. Just like I'd birthed them myself.

"Worie. It'll be fine. Them youngins is safe. They're goin to find homes."

Despite the pastor's words, I reckon I just had pain inside that needed to pour free. "But Farrell and T. J. have a home. They got a home with me, Abeleen, Ely and Bess . . . and Doanie. Lordy, lordy, that little Doanie is heartbroke."

"You got to trust me, Worie. We'll find them youngins. Trust me."

I looked right quick like at the pastor. There was that word again. The same one Justice had give me. *Trust.* I thought trust was something you could find, but I'm seein it ain't found—it's gived.

The pastor helped me to my feet and guided me toward our seats. I pulled back toward the bench where I set holding that child.

"Pastor Jess, I'll set on the bench if it's all the same to you." And I did. I slid down and laid my arms in the window, pressin my face into the bend of my elbow. The wind rushed over me like a stream runnin down the summit, and night commenced to close in around us.

Ely's words swarmed my head like a bunch of angry bees. "Good Lord don't turn His back on little ones. Lordy no. He knows them babies has suffered and He wants them brung to Him for peace, Miss Worie. Don't you understand?"

I'd be lyin if I uttered a yes to Ely, cause lettin any person suffer didn't seem right. I just knew they was something I needed to do and I aimed to do it. "I don't understand little children sufferin!"

"Oh, Miss Worie, you got it all wrong. It ain't that the good Lord *makes* them youngins suffer, it's that He wants them sufferin little ones brung to Him. I done said it once. Let it sink in."

The memory of my talk with Ely faded into the darkness.

I moped a bit, then I took a handkerchief from my bag and blew my nose. I remembered how Momma used to say when things was pushin you down, the best way to plow through was to stand up and straighten your shoulders. She'd take me by the shoulders and lift me from a chair, press her hand betwixt my shoulder blades, and lift my chin. "There, you see!" she'd say. "When you stand tall and hold your head up you pull strength from your gut. Strength that you need to get things done."

I rubbed my hand on the bench where them children set. Splinters jutted up here and there. Then I did what Momma said. I stood and shoved my chest out, lifted my chin, and took in a good breath. "Pastor, how much longer to Chattanooga?"

"Early mornin. You're gonna want to rest a bit."

"You know, Pastor Jess, you keep naggin that I need to rest. Well, they ain't no rest to be had. I might sleep a bit, but I don't rest. And I won't till Farrell and T. J. is back with me and Doanie." I commenced to walk the aisle, pacin like a mountain lion. "They ain't no rest to be had."

Pastor Jess lowered his head like he was ponderin something

right hard. And when he lifted it, he stood, jutted out his chest, and went to pacin too.

"Whatta ya doin?" I asked.

"I figure a man that needs to out a plan does it better if he does a little pacin."

I smiled. Reckon he was doin his best to help, and if he was willin to pace, I was willin to rest—or try anyway.

Pastor Jess stuck out his hand. "Can we shake on this? Pace awhile, rest awhile?"

His grip was strong. Daddy used to say you could tell a man's character by his handshake. "You want somebody to take you serious, then you shake their hand tight. None of this wishy-washy stuff. You take their hand and shake it good." So I clamped his hand tight and shook it like I meant it.

He motioned to the leather seat. "Rest?"

"Alright. For a spell. But I need to figure a plan. I'm bringin them youngins home even if I have to steal them."

Pastor Jess raised a brow. "Ain't sure the Lord would approve of stealin a youngin, but I think even in His eyes He might call this savin over stealin."

"Reckon we'll find them?"

"Dunno. But we'll start with the Holtsclaws." He took the scribbled paper from his coat pocket and unfolded it. "Yeah, we'll start here." He tapped the paper with his finger.

"What about Sikes?"

Pastor Jess pulled a quilt from a bar that hung behind the seat. He gingerly unfolded it and laid it over me, then tucked the sides around my arms. "These open cars get chilly at night. You'll need a quilt." He lifted my feet and wrapped the end of the blanket around them, and when he stepped back he looked right proud of his tuckin.

"I ask you again . . ."

"What about Sikes? I know. I heard you the first time." He yanked another quilt from the bar and went to wrappin it around hisself. He set with a plop into the seat. "I've known Justice for several years. He's a good man. Calvin, though . . . I only met him a handful of times, and I can't say he ever once seemed to know the difference between truth and his lies. All that to say . . ."

"Oh fiddle. Just say what's on your mind. Quit draggin a dead dog through the mud." My impatience seeped out.

"All that to say, if a man never told the truth, what is they to say he's tellin the truth about Sikes bein a uppity lawyer from Chattanooga."

The pastor had a fish on the line. My mind went to churnin. "You're sayin Sikes probably ain't no lawyer?"

"It would make sense. Don't you think? See, I went to putting things together when that banker give me this here name instead of information on Sikes. He was so shamed about them children, that's the name he give us from the ledger."

My mind went to spinnin like a waterwheel. "That banker said he stamped the papers and they was legal."

"But legal for what? The land and your cabin, them children? What?"

"The sheriff read that paper to me." I scratched my knees whilst I pondered. Then it hit me. "Pastor Jess, that paper never said what property. Or who." I come to my feet. The quilt dropped to the floor, and when I went to speak my voice climbed higher. "Best I remember, it said the land went to family." I clapped my hands. "Family! Lands a goshin! It said family. It didn't name no one single person."

Pastor Jess went to grinnin. "See, Calvin don't know the truth, and this time the truth has set *you* free."

I went to whirlin around in circles on that train car, trippin and stumblin as the train moved. "I got the paper, Pastor. I still got the paper. I keep it right here with me." I smacked my bag.

For the first time in weeks, my heart had a taste of joy. *Family. The paper said family.* The breeze comin through the train windows was nippy, so I grabbed up that quilt and wrapped tight in it.

"I might just be able to rest, Pastor. I might just."

All them times Calvin lied through the years led him to never know who he told the truth to. Momma always said ever spider's web gets tore down, and I reckon she was right. Calvin's web of lies was thick. It had caught a bunch of insects up in it, but I was comin with a broom.

I took in a deep breath and filled my lungs. Even the smell of smoke from the engine was pleasant.

"You know what else, Pastor?"

"What's that?"

"You're right. Nothin Calvin has ever said was truth. That means this Sikes was more than likely a wolf in sheep's clothin."

Pastor Jess eased his hat over his face again. "Ever now and again, the Lord speaks to my heart. When He does, I tend to listen."

I eased back and rested my head against the window rail. The outline of the mountains raised high on one side of the tracks, and the dark sky harbored so many stars it was like lanterns lightin the night. We rounded a bend and the whistle eased out three quick notes. Over the noise of the steel wheels, I could hear the rush of the river as we passed by. A doe and her fawn perked their ears and inched deeper into the darkness.

Daddy was right about these mountains. Even in the hardest of times their beauty speaks to you. Life is hard here. A body only has the simple things to keep them goin. A man closes his eyes at night and just prays to open them when the rooster crows.

My eyes grew heavy, but in the midst of this mess I suddenly had a peace. I pulled my bag close to my body and hugged it. They was hope. I couldn't remember the last time I'd felt sucha thing. My thoughts jumped to them early days on the farm when things was happier. As sleep edged in, I felt the edges of my mouth turnin up toward the heavens. Yes sir, they was hope.

CHAPTER
TWENTY-FOUR

I had no mind how many times that train stopped and started through the night, but when I woke up the sun had painted the sky the colors of posies in a field. They was nothin I could do to ward off the stiffness from sittin on that train all night. The crick in my neck ached like whiz when I turned my head.

My mouth felt like something had crawled inside it and died, so I took the edge of my sleeve and rubbed my teeth and tongue, hopin to wipe away some of the smell. The pastor was standin at the window, arm raised above his head, forehead on his wrist.

"Pastor Jess?" I rolled my head, tryin to work out the crick. "Where we at?"

He dropped his arm and turned. "Chattanooga."

"What?" I rushed to the window and leaned out. It was bigger than Hartsboro and even busier at the crack of dawn. The train slowed as it crossed a river wider than our Indian River. The water run quiet but deep. They was no wadin across this water like our river at home. Long flatboats loaded with crates floated alongside the river, tied to rails along the bank. I'd never seen the likes. Some was bein unloaded. Lines of small houses crawled up the bank to the level road, and horses pulled wagons through the town.

My heart raced. The sight of such things took my breath, and I edged behind the pastor. I'd be lyin if I said my knees wasn't shakin. The noise alone made me think twice before I ever hollered again at the frogs and crickets singin in the night.

He looked over his shoulder. "Worie, welcome to the big city. Ain't it something?"

They was no words for what I was takin in, other than my mountains was laid in the distance and I could tell I was a long way from home. I'd never seen the glory of the mountains from a way off. It didn't take much to figure I didn't belong here. I knew, though life was hard on the ridge, most folks scraped to get all they had. These folks here, they seemed to have everthing. On the mountain, a person was who they was, be it good or bad. Folks knew that, and though sometimes we was fooled, for the most part a body knew the heart of their neighbors.

I glanced once more at the city in front of me, then back to the view of mountains that stretched as far as the eye could see. My innards was screamin, "Go back," but my heart was sayin, "Find them youngins."

"I ain't right impressed, Pastor. They ain't no mountain river singin a sweet song, and I ain't heard a bird yet, much less seen one."

He went to laughin. "There's a whole different world off the mountain."

"I'll thank you kindly to take me home as soon as we get our business done. This ain't no place for me."

"Keep in mind what we're here to do."

"I know, 1 Riding Road. Home for Lost Children. I reckon it's burned in my mind, Pastor."

The train brakes squealed and it stopped. The pastor motioned me to the door and I stepped down onto the platform. A passel of folks passed around me to get on the iron beast, and I stepped to one side. That's when I lost the pastor in the crowd.

"Pastor. Pastor Jess?" I wheeled around in circles, my eyes scanning the platform. "Pastor Jess!" Panic edged into my soul. "Paaastoor!"

"Worie, over here." He waved his hand for me to come, and I edged my way through the crowd to where he stood. He shoved his hand into his pocket and pulled out the paper to show the address to a man decked out in fancy clothes.

I stepped closer to the pastor, and the man eyed me. He inched away like he thought I was filthy.

"Wondered if you could direct me toward this road?" The pastor took me by the hand and pulled me close to him.

The man pointed toward a row of buildins. "Top of the hill and turn left. Pass the general store and dress shop. You'll see the church. That's the road."

"Dress shop? What's that?" I had a hunch I knew, but this was a strange place.

"In the city, most women pay to have their dresses sewed." Pastor Jess gently nudged me ahead. "Maybe we can stop in for you to look at the dresses later."

I looked at him right strange. "Pastor, I'm a mountain girl. I ain't never seen the likes of this, and if the truth be knowed, I don't want to. I just want to find Farrell and T. J., get back on that train, and go back to the mountains where I belong."

He smiled and motioned me ahead.

We walked up a steep hill lined with long, thin houses, then, like the man said, the pastor turned toward the church. People dodged piles of horse manure as they crossed from one side of the road to the other, while wagons just sloshed right through.

"Pastor Jess?"

He took my arm and led me to the boardwalk. "I'm sure we ain't far. What's on your mind?"

I stopped and faced him. "I'm scared. What if Calvin has done something terrible with them children? What if I can't find them?

And what about Doanie? She'll be brokenhearted the rest of her life. What if—"

"Worie, stop. What-ifs can't never be answered, and once you start askin about them they're like rabbits. They just keep multiplyin." He bent enough to look me in the eye. "The good Lord tells us it ain't for us to worry over. He knows ever hair on your head, and if that ain't enough, He reminds us that even the birds are fed. He knows exactly what He will do. Don't worry."

Them sounded like nice words, but as Momma used to say, "That's easier said than done."

Pastor Jess stepped around me to eye the buildins down the way, but I leaned in front of him. "I ain't never been real close to the good Lord. Momma was. Ever day she went to her knees by her bed. And I sure don't aim to say I appreciate what He has allowed to happen—with Momma, these children . . . and all. But I know one thing. I felt like I found my direction on that train, and that was enough to make me sit up and take mind."

"That's a good thing. The Lord makes Hisself known to us."

"I ain't sure how, but I heard Him clear as could be. So you need to know, I took a minute to speak my mind to Him."

Pastor Jess laughed as he slipped my arm through his. "I'm sure you did."

I think Pastor Jess knew they was no point in preachin to a hardheaded woman, so he didn't commence to tell me how to behave or insist I pray more. Guess the good Lord give him the wits enough to know He'd done the work that needed to be done in my heart. Pastor Jess knew then to just keep his mouth shut. And he did.

Pastor Jess's steps grew longer, and he pulled me along. His arm went up as he pointed. "There! There it is."

I yanked his arm down. "Where? Do you see the youngins? Where? I don't see where."

"There. The painted red house."

I broke into a run, shovin folks outta my way, Pastor Jess right behind me. I worked my way through the hordes of people to the house where a sign hung over a huge white door.

1 Riding Road
Home for Lost Children
All Who Enter Are Loved

A bell hung from a metal holder, waitin for me to yank the rope. I wheeled around and stared at Pastor Jess. "Preacher, my hand won't reach up there."

It had nothin to do with my bein able to grab the rope. My hands was froze in place. Behind this door was the children.

"Would you?" I asked.

Pastor Jess tugged the rope and it rung loud for its size. My mind spun in circles. What would I say? How would the children act? Had they missed me, Doanie? I felt my gut churn and my stomach retch.

The knob wiggled and a woman pulled the door open just enough to peer through. "Yes? Who calls?"

Pastor Jess tipped his hat and introduced himself. "We're in search of two children. Siblins. Was hopin we might find them here."

The woman made no effort to open the door, and her ponderin was takin way too long. I laid my shoulder against the door and pushed. She didn't weigh nothin, for I shoved her right easy outta the way.

"My name is Worie Dressar. They was a man, Calvin Dressar, my brother, that took two children from me . . . from their sister. One was a little girl about five years old, maybe six, and a little boy, three or four years old. I need these children to come home. Their sister is a mess worryin over them. They here?"

Pastor Jess gently nudged me to the side. "What she says is true.

The children were taken without permission. The girl's name is Farrell and the boy is T. J."

She went to ponderin again, and whilst I waited for the old woman to decide if we was truthful or not, I looked over the house. A large stairway climbed its way upward, and fancy crocheted doilies covered shiny wood tables with dishes I feared would shatter if a body breathed too hard. The house was quiet. No sounds of children. No signs that young ones lived there.

The woman pointed to a long chair. "Have a seat. I'll get Master Holtsclaw."

"Master?" I snapped. "On the mountain we have slaves that was freed."

Pastor Jess bumped my arm. "Shhh! It ain't what you think."

But Ely and Bess had told me stories of their master and how he made them work and live in filth. And how they attacked him and tied him up to get away. What else could "master" mean? I was sure, nothin good.

We waited a spell before a tall, handsome man come around the corner. A lean, well-dressed woman followed. He extended his hand. "Charles Holtsclaw. This is Mable, my wife. She tells me you're looking for two children."

I leaped up. "They was took from me. Took from their sister. I want them back. Where are they?"

Pastor Jess faced me. "Worie, sit down and hush. Now."

I could tell he was riled. I eyed him a minute, then found my seat. That's when I heard that voice in my head. *Rest in Me. Trust.* A chill climbed my spine, for I heard them words as clear as day. Momma always said a body's conscience would speak to them, but I wasn't bettin on my conscience. Not this time.

I watched as Pastor Jess and Mr. Holtsclaw talked, and then I heard words that took my heart right outta my chest. Surely I wasn't hearin the man right. The words "train," "orphan," and "west" burned my soul, and I come off that chair in a rage.

"Are you tellin me you put my little Farrell on a train and sent her away from her family? Is that what you are tellin me?"

The man took a step back. "Families pay good money to find children they can love."

The rage inside me let loose like a flood after a heavy rain. I went to slappin the man on his chest, screamin. They was nothing I could do to stop my anger. It raged. Words belted outta my mouth that I can't even recall. The man took hold of my arms and held them tight against my sides while Pastor Jess tried to talk sense to me. And when it finally passed, I dropped to my knees and sobbed.

"Lordy mercy. You sold my youngin. You took Doanie's baby sister and sold her." Sobs, wails, fell from the deepest part of me.

Pastor Jess knelt beside me. They was not a word he could say. Nothin.

"You sold my little Farrell." That was when I felt that voice again. *Trust Me.*

I stood and pushed Pastor Jess to one side. Straightenin my shoulders and raisin my chin, I swiped the tears. "What a man will do for money," I said. "What a man will do for money."

I opened the door and walked out. The sign on the door hung by a small chain and a nail. I pulled it down, threw it on the ground, and stomped it. The man stood dumbfounded.

"All who enter are loved! Hogwash! Like I said, what a man will do for money." And I walked away.

CHAPTER
TWENTY-FIVE

Pastor Jess followed behind me, hollerin, "Worie, wait. Wait."

I didn't know where I'd go or what I'd do. I just know a rollin hate bubbled outta me.

I stopped and wheeled around. "Leave me be!" I screamed. "Leave me be!" Folks walking by eased past, afraid I was speakin to them. "They ain't nothin you can say, Pastor Jess. Nothin. They is no excuse for a man to sell a little youngin. None." Rage rose, and I put my hands on my head and screamed long and hard. Tears poured out.

Pastor Jess just stood at my side. His lips moved, but nothin come out. I figured he was prayin for the good Lord to strike me down. Lord knows that was what I was prayin.

When I simmered down, Pastor Jess gently pulled me close. "I know your heart is broken," he whispered.

Them was the right words, cause if he'd said, "I know how you feel," I'd have slapped him.

"Let's find a place to rest. Let you get your wits back."

We walked to a square covered in grass. A pretty wooden porch stood to one side. Flowers lined a stone walkway, and birdhouses stood on poles nestled inside the beds of flowers.

"It's called a gazebo." Pastor Jess pulled me tighter under his arm. "Isn't it beautiful?"

It was beautiful. Green vines crawled up the sides, and clusters of purple flowers hung. Bees hummed about, happy to have flowers to sip from. We climbed the stairs to a bench. Pastor Jess pulled a handkerchief from his pocket and dangled it in front of me.

"What will I tell Doanie?" The words oozed from me with the same agony I felt when I found Momma dead. "Oh Lordy, what will I tell that youngin? 'A man sold your sister to a stranger'?"

"We can't change what is. We don't forget Farrell, but we trust she has found a family that will love her. It's all we can do."

"But . . ."

"No buts, Worie. We know she has a home. We can't change that. We look to find T. J. and hope there is still something we can do for him."

"We didn't ask about T. J.," I whimpered.

"Before you lost your temper—"

"I had reason to lose my temper!" I snapped.

Pastor Jess swallowed and let his chin drop to his chest. I could tell his patience was wearin thin, but bein a man of the cloth, he worked right hard to not grow angry. "Before you lost your temper, once you hushed up talkin and set down, I was able to talk to Holtsclaw. No one offered him a boy."

"What?" I pulled myself up straight. "That must mean Calvin still has him."

"That would be my guess."

"But Calvin ain't a patient man, and that boy ain't learned to use the hole yet. I ain't seein Calvin changin that youngin's pants."

Pastor Jess smiled. "Well, I hadn't thought of that, but it is a good thought."

"You reckon he plans to do the same with T. J.? Sell him? You know if there is a dollar to be made, Calvin will stoop to hell to grab it."

"Well, farmers need boys to raise so they can shoulder the hard work in the fields."

I could have swore my heart quit beatin. I could see life in the city was easier than in the peaks of the mountains. Folks had more. It wasn't hard to see that the more a body has, the more they want. At least in the hills, we take care of our own. Momma helped them orphaned children, and she never once offered to sell one.

I slung my head from side to side, tryin to shake the horrible thoughts out, but all that come to mind was Ely and Bess tellin me about bein whipped with a bridle strap. "They better not a soul lay a hand on them youngins to hurt them. I will hunt them down." I buried my face in my hands and cried. "They'll be no peace until I have them back in my arms."

It took all my strength to muster up the courage and *trust* to offer a prayer. But I did. "Reckon everbody says You know best. But bein sold ain't best for a three-year-old boy. Oh Lord, have mercy." I whispered the words into my palms. "Can't You just one time show me You're real?"

I stood and paced the large rounded porch, and when I stopped and looked across the deep green grass my eye caught on a man. I grabbed the pastor's sleeve and pulled him toward me. "Look yonder. Is that . . . Oh Lordy . . . is that . . . ?"

"Calvin?" Pastor Jess slapped his forehead. "I can't believe my eyes."

I slowly pulled the tail of my skirt between my legs and tucked it in at the waist. One tug and I'd pulled the string of my bag tight around my arm. You didn't have to be right bright to figure I was ready to take after him, so Pastor Jess pressed his arm in front of me.

"We ain't seen the boy. Wait!"

It seemed ever turn I made somebody was tellin me to wait or trust, and I was up to my gullet in hearin them words, but the pastor was right. We hadn't seen T. J., and runnin Calvin down now might ruin my findin the youngin. We waited and watched.

Two men walked to Calvin and shook his hand. I could see them heads bobbin up and down as they laughed and talked. Calvin eased around a wagon and pulled up a cover. Then it happened. Me and the pastor saw a little blond head pop up like a mole in a hole.

"That's him!" I shouted. I cocked my head toward the heavens and lifted my hand. "Alright, You've proved Yourself, Lord." And with that, I took out across the grassy square. I couldn't muster no words to holler, I just run as hard as I could. Pastor Jess strode beside me.

When I got within earshot of Calvin, I commenced to shout, "Give me my boy!"

I hadn't much more than got the words out when I lowered my head and rammed Calvin with my shoulder, knockin him to the ground. It was like when we was kids roughhousin, and this time I hit low and hard first. Pastor Jess landed on top of us both, and while he managed Calvin, I climbed to my feet and reached for T. J.

"Hey there, baby boy. Miss Worie's come to get you." Them little arms stretched out and wrapped tight around my neck. I closed my eyes and squeezed. "It's alright, baby. We gonna get you home. Doanie cries after you ever day."

I wasn't sure where I would go, but everthing in me told me to run. And I did. I run as hard as I could toward that train platform.

Pastor Jess was hollerin, "Worie, don't run! Don't run!"

Despite his yellin, I did what I had to do. T. J.'s legs wrapped tight around my waist, and his head pressed hard into my neck. With ever step, I felt the air push from my lungs. I could run and do it real good. I'd done it enough as a youngin when Calvin would take after me.

The train whistle squalled and the steam hissed from its sides. Just a little farther and I'd be on my way home. My legs felt like they had logs tied to them. *Just a little farther. Just a little more.*

Suddenly it felt like somebody hit me in the back with a branch. I grabbed the back of T. J.'s head as I fell forward. Arms wrapped tight around my knees, stoppin me from kickin, and when I rolled over, there stood a man huffin and puffin.

They was no way I was turnin T. J. loose, no matter how they pried my fingers.

"Get up, young lady. I'm takin you to jail."

Pastor Jess finally made his way to my side, his chest heavin. "Wait, Sheriff. Let me explain."

"Let go of the child."

"No!" I shouted. "Calvin stole him once. He ain't stealin him again."

"That's my boy." Calvin heaved the words out.

"He ain't neither. Don't you touch him." I swung to one side to keep Calvin from touchin T. J. "Pastor, tell them. Don't just stand there. Make them listen." I squeezed T. J. tighter. "Baby boy, you hang on to Miss Worie with all your worth. You hear me?" I felt his head nod.

Calvin ranted to the sheriff about how the boy was his fair and square.

"Fair and square!" I hollered. "This here is a youngin, not a bet. You don't win a little youngin fair and square. You idiot." T. J. held so tight around my neck that I commenced to cough. "You ain't takin this boy away from me again. Get away from us."

By this time a crowd of people circled us, and I felt an idea come over me. They wasn't nobody in their right mind who would let a person yank a child from his momma's arms. So I used that to help me and T. J.

"T. J., listen to me," I whispered in his ear. "You can talk plenty good enough. Miss Worie needs you to start screamin and callin me your momma. Can you do that?"

And the little one did just that. "Mommmmaaa! Mommm-maaa!" he screamed as loud as he could.

I looked at the crowd. "Don't let them take my boy. Please don't stand there and let them take my boy!"

Ever time Calvin tried to touch T. J. he screamed, "Momm-mmaaa!" And it was only minutes before the crowd took hold, pressuring the sheriff to leave the boy in my arms.

"Ain't you the sly one?" the sheriff said.

"I done told you, you ain't takin my boy again."

Pastor Jess stood between Calvin and me, keepin him from tryin to take T. J. "This wasn't how I figured we'd get T. J. back," he uttered.

"You just figure how to sweet-talk that sheriff," I snapped.

The sheriff pointed toward a building just down the way. "Alright. You hold that boy, but we're walkin to the jail. You understand?"

I nodded.

"Worie, what are you tryin to do, takin the boy back?" Calvin kept grabbin at T. J. and cussin ever other word.

"Them ain't words that the good Lord will find favor on," Pastor Jess said as he kept shovin Calvin's arms away.

"You ain't sellin this boy. I'm takin him home to his sister," I said.

It didn't take us but a few minutes to get to the buildin. That crowd of people followed, shoutin at the sheriff to let a momma have her youngin. I wasn't always sneaky, but I was right proud of rilin that bunch of folks.

Once inside the jail, the sheriff unlocked the bars and nudged me inside. "You takin that boy inside the cell?"

I held T. J. snug. "Pastor?" I cocked my head, lookin to Pastor Jess for help. "You gotta tell them what happened."

"I will. Let me have the boy." Pastor Jess held out his hands. I pressed my face into T. J. and kissed his cheek. I wanted to cry, but cryin would be what Calvin wanted. He'd done took T. J. once, and they was nothin gonna let me give him the pleasure of seein my tears.

"Sheriff, promise me you won't let this youngin outside this building?" I was stern when I spoke. Determined.

"I don't make promises."

"Then I don't turn the youngin loose and he'll keep right on screamin." I nodded toward the door. "And that's an awful lot of people outside there who think I'm right."

The sheriff eyed the crowd that had followed us to the jail, then he stared at Calvin and the pastor. "I reckon the pastor can take the child—keep him in here."

I kissed T. J. again and whispered, "Go with Pastor Jess. And make Miss Worie a promise. If Calvin gets ahold of you"—I winked and grinned—"mess your pants. Mess them real big."

TWENTY-SIX

T. J. was like a baby possum clingin to my neck, but he finally slid from my arms into the pastor's.

"You remember your promise, Sheriff. You hear?" I stepped back inside the cell and the door shut behind me.

Calvin grasped hold of the bars and squeezed his face against them. "Right where you need to be! Right where you need to be."

It took everthing in me not to poke his eyes out as he stared at me through the bars, but it wouldn't have done no good.

"You're finally in jail. All we need is Justice and the both of you could rot together." Calvin stuck his arm through the bars and smacked at me.

Momma used to say they is times when your gut tells you to lash out, beat the tar outta somebody. But don't never listen. That's the devil pushin at you to do wrong. Right now I felt like I needed to grab that flappin arm of Calvin's and snap it in half. I didn't though. There was no explainin why, but a great sorrow come over me and I grasped his hand and pulled it to my lips. It was a tender kiss on his knuckles. Wasn't no words spoke. Calvin stood there, lookin me in the eye. It was like a soft breeze passed over him. His eyes softened and his chin quivered. For a minute, he saw I loved him.

It didn't last. He jerked his hand away and commenced to cuss, but for the time it took to take in a breath, I knew I'd touched his soul. That was something else Momma would say. Even the baddest of bad people has a tender spot. It's up to us to keep huntin for it. Plant a seed of goodness if we can. I was as surprised as Calvin when that breath of goodness seeped out of me. Maybe, just maybe, Momma was right. Maybe I planted a seed. They was something that turned Calvin the way he was. It was as big a mystery as them red stones, and now I felt as much a need to figure that out as I did to figure out Calvin's plan.

I listened to Pastor Jess plead my reason for stealin T. J. Ever time he tried to say something, Calvin would trample over his words.

The sheriff soon grew weary of Calvin's buttin in. "If you don't hush, I'm gonna toss you in that cell too." Despite the sheriff's threats, Calvin was always one to get the last word.

Still Pastor Jess kept on talkin, spillin the whole story from Momma takin her life to the children comin to me, all the way down to Calvin takin the homestead. I crossed my arms and leaned against the cold wall, keepin a close watch on T. J. The little feller wrapped around the pastor like a turtle in a shell. My fingers tapped against the skin on my wrist, tinkerin with the string on my bag.

"My bag!" I said. "I got the paper in my bag! Pastor, I got the paper." I reckon they was a reason I got it outta that box at Ely's. Somethin told me I might need proof about the farm.

I fumbled to untie the bag and dug around for the paper the man at the bank had signed. "Sheriff, I got proof about my home. Proof Calvin is lyin about it belongin to only him. You can see for yourself." I brought out the paper.

Calvin reached for the page, tryin to take it, but the sheriff stepped up and moved him away.

"Sheriff, if you see the pastor and me is tellin you the truth about the cabin, and Calvin makin me take them youngins and move, then you have to believe he stole this boy and his sister." I felt them tears crawlin into the corners of my eyes, and I blinked to get them away. "Sheriff, Calvin sold little T. J.'s sister, and the Holtsclaws put her on a train and sent her out west. He was gettin ready to do the same with T. J."

"Ain't true!" Calvin squawked. "She ain't got no paper. I own that land fair and square."

There that was again. Fair and square. It was like Calvin was a youngin fightin for first dibs at the fishin hole.

Pastor Jess tried to turn loose of T. J. The child stuck to his chest like molasses. If he was anything, he was well behaved, doin just what I'd told him. I reckon it didn't help that child was scared to death.

I handed the paper to Pastor Jess. He opened it. Calvin went to cussin again. Rantin about how I was lyin, and then Pastor Jess read the line.

This document certifies, that the land be left to the family.

I remembered as me and Ely buried Momma, askin, "I don't understand why Momma did this horrible thing. I just wanna know the truth."

Ely had tossed another shovel of dirt on Momma's body, then pulled his handkerchief from his pocket and wiped his face. "Yes ma'am. The truth shall set you free."

For a minute, this paper did just that. It set me free.

The sheriff pushed his glasses tight against his nose. Despite them, he still squinted. His arm went in and out, pullin that paper close then takin it back, and I wanted to scream. I motioned to the pastor to move closer to the bars so I could brush T. J.'s hair away from his eyes. I wasn't no momma, but this little one felt like he'd come from my own loins.

Pastor Jess inched closer, and T. J.'s arms and legs come through the bars, wrappin around me. Even in the seriousness of the moment, a body couldn't help but chuckle as that youngin hung on to me through them bars. He had the grip of ten men.

"T. J., listen to Miss Worie. I know you're scared. I know they's a lot of mess goin on that you can't figure. But baby boy, you're gonna have to be a little man for a time."

He snuffed and whimpered.

"Can you do that for Miss Worie? Can you be a little man?"

His face pressed betwixt the bars and his lips pooched out. I twisted my head to the side and let the little feller kiss me on the cheek. "That's about the sweetest kiss I've ever had."

Pastor Jess pried the boy loose and pulled him away from the bars. "Rest your head on my shoulder. I ain't gonna let nothin happen to you."

I nodded and T. J. snuffed again. "T. J.," I said. "Trust me. Trust Pastor Jess."

Them words hit me right between the eyes again. If the good Lord wasn't doin nothin else other than teachin me what it meant to trust, then I was the better for listenin.

The room was quiet while the sheriff read that paper over again, and when he called his deputy over then sent him out the door, I wondered if this jail would become my home.

Ever time Calvin tried to open his mouth, the sheriff would shush him. Truth be knowed, it was the first time I'd ever seen a soul shut Calvin up.

The sheriff took Calvin by the arm and led him out the door.

"Sheriff, please don't let him go," I said. "Please don't. You don't know what you're askin for if you do. As sure as I stand here, he'll kill me, and more than likely the pastor here too."

They was not a word uttered by the sheriff. He just dragged Calvin outside. The crowd still held close. I wasn't sure if they was just nosey or if they thought they was gonna be a lynchin—my lynchin.

Minutes passed, but it felt like hours before the sheriff come

179

leadin Calvin back in. "Miss Dressar, Calvin here insists that homestead is his. So I sent my deputy here over to the bank."

Had he found Sikes? Was they gonna find somethin else to take from me?

"Mr. Ellison from the bank looked over this here paper, and he agrees fully that the homestead belongs to you and Calvin."

Daddy would have took his strap to Calvin's backside for them words that fell outta his mouth. He ranted and raved like a madman until T. J. put his hands over his ears and went to cryin.

"That's enough. Hush up now." The sheriff pulled Calvin's arms together and snugged them with a rope. Then he opened the bars and set me free. "Now here's what's gonna happen. We're gonna all take a train ride to Hartsboro, and when we get there we're gonna talk to the banker that signed this here paper."

A sigh hissed from my lungs. Maybe I had a fightin chance.

"Miss Worie, I ain't gonna tie your hands. Somebody has to tend this youngin. But if you make one effort to take that boy and run, I will shoot you. Do you understand?"

I took T. J. from Pastor Jess and nodded. "I understand."

Pastor Jess took to smilin. I supposed he knew if we could get to Hartsboro, that banker would fess up again.

We walked out of the jail, and when the crowd saw me holdin T. J. they went to cheerin. I'd never seen the likes before, but I felt like I'd just won a pie-eatin contest.

The deputy pulled a wagon around and we all crawled in, Calvin still cussin. Pastor Jess tried to squeeze between me and Calvin, but the sheriff made him move, forcin us to sit close like when we was kids. If they was a fight, Momma would tie our hands together with a rag and make us stay hooked to each other. She'd say, "When the words are kind and forgiveness has been had, I'll untie you. Not a minute sooner."

There I set snugged next to my brother. My bro . . . ther. A memory of Momma's note seeped in. It was a long ride to Hartsboro. I planned to make ever second count. What was comin out of me wasn't kind. I was an angry, downtrodden woman, and I had things to tell Calvin that would wear the hide off his rear. As Momma used to say, "Ain't nothin worse than a woman with an axe to grind."

I had an axe to grind. And it went back years. Back to the day we buried Daddy. Calvin had some questions to answer, and I aimed to get answers.

T. J.'s eyes fluttered as we boarded the train. The youngin was done spent. We filed onto the bench seats, Calvin first, then me and Pastor Jess. Once we was set down I stretched T. J. across our laps so his head rested on Pastor Jess's arm and his feet dangled over my knees. The youngin didn't even flinch when the train whistle let loose and the cars jolted.

I pulled my bag close to my chest and untied the string. Real slow like, I pulled out the note Momma had wrote. The one that had brought me and Justice to our feet. My insides was battlin back and forth. It was like they was a devil on one side and the good Lord on the other, both of them tuggin at me, tryin to get their way.

Calvin stared out the window, the wind blowin his blond hair away from his face. Handsome as he was, it didn't take but a minute for my heart to harden and remember he was meaner than a rattler.

"Calvin." I nudged him with my elbow.

He never uttered a word. His eyes just burned holes in me.

"You know that Mason jar of Momma's?"

I could see him grit his teeth.

I lifted the paper from my bag and held it up. "Momma wrote this and left it in the jar."

He didn't have to say a word for me to see his anger bubblin up.

"Me and Justice was right surprised at what Momma wrote."

The angry red from his face grew brighter.

*"I have my own children that I shed a river of tears over.
I thought when we found that baby that night and brought
him home, that we could save him. We give all we had to
save him. Give him a name, Calvin . . ."*

That red face of Calvin's turned white. I shoulda stopped right
then. Hushed. But there was a fire in me that wanted to get even. I
wanted Calvin, for once in his life, to feel somethin. I didn't rightly
care if it was hurtful or not. Just so he felt the sting. Lord knows
he'd hurt Momma, Justice. Me.

Right as I was ready to finish the words, Calvin's elbow reared
up like a snake and struck me square in the mouth. My feet come
up over my head, and I landed flat on my back between the benches.

The sheriff grabbed Calvin and tied his wrists to the bench.
Pastor Jess had grabbed T. J. to keep him from hittin the floor
when I went sailin backward.

T. J. I crawled to my knees, blood seepin from my lip.

"Worie," the pastor said, holdin T. J. under one arm and strug-
gling to lift me to the seat behind Calvin. "You alright?" He pulled
his handkerchief from his pocket.

"I'm fine, Pastor." I blotted my lip. "I reckon that was the good
Lord's way of tellin a hardheaded woman to hush." I'd hit a soft
spot on Calvin, but I couldn't tell if he already knew he was found
or if he was thunderstruck.

Calvin craned his neck to see me. "Next time I'll break your
neck."

I reckon that threat answered my question. Calvin knew.

TWENTY-SEVEN

My lip swelled like a plum stuffed in a squirrel's jaw. I knew Calvin meant to do more than bust my lip. If he could have hit me hard enough to break my neck, he woulda been all the happier. Still, he was quiet the entire day.

When the train stopped to load that black rock, the sheriff stood Calvin and wrapped a rope tight around his chest and arms. He untied his hands and turned to the deputy. "Ralston, you sit here with Miss Worie and the pastor whilst Johnson and me take ole Calvin here to the outhouse. It's been a long ride, everbody needs some relief." The sheriff took hold of the ropes and led Calvin past me, then paused at the train stairs. "You remember what I said. You try to take that boy and run, I'll shoot you. Or leastways, Ralston here will. Understood?"

I nodded.

T. J. roused and sat straight as a stick. He wiggled his finger and I leaned down. I took in a big gulp of air, then laughed.

"Pastor, T. J. here has done growed up on us. He needs to use the hole."

Pastor Jess went to praisin T. J. like it was a church service. He took him by the hand and led him off the train, leavin me with Ralston.

Ralston wasn't a big man. He was broad but not tall. They wasn't a hair on his head, but a beard covered his face. It was like all his hair slid off his head and onto his chin.

I felt a smile edge up. "Mr. Ralston?" I crossed my arms. "You look like a good man. You got a family?"

He nodded. "A wife and two boys."

"I hope them boys got their hair in the right spot."

Ralston chuckled and rubbed his bald head. "I reckon they do. They got their momma's red hair."

"Ain't that nice. Can I ask you a question?"

"Ask away."

"Has you and your wife thought about what would happen to your youngins if you was to die?"

The smile left his face, and he commenced to draw on the bench with his finger. "I can't say as we have."

"Little T. J. is the leftover of a momma and daddy who died from the fever. He's got two sisters. One just a couple of years older than him and the other about ten."

Ralston shook his head. "Right sad."

"Right sad is right. That ten-year-old come to me lookin for food. Them three youngins was starvin. They was starving, Mr. Ralston. They was orphans that was starvin."

Ralston stuffed a wad of tobacco between his lip and gum.

"Would your boys be orphans if you and the Mrs. died today? Would they be left to starve?" I pointed my finger in his face. "You best be makin plans for them youngins. Make you some plans."

I could see Ralston start to wiggle in his seat. I'd done give him some hard things to think on. If he could see why I was so dead set on these children, maybe, just maybe, he'd lean to help me. Whether I managed that or not, I'd still give him some meat to chew on with his own family.

"You need to relieve yourself?" Ralston asked.

"I do."

184

"Quick as the sheriff gets back, I'll walk you to the outhouse." He turned his head and stared toward the train's platform.

I couldn't tell what made him more uneasy, my puttin him on the spot about his youngins or the fact he'd have to walk me to the outhouse. Either way, I had planted them seeds Momma talked about. If nothin more come from our talkin than I made him go to thinkin about his boys, then I'd done alright.

My lip kept drippin blood. Calvin had split it right good. Ralston took my handkerchief and walked to the front of the train car. A small bucket of water hung from a hook. He dipped a ladle of water and poured it into the cloth, then squeezed the bloody water out.

"This oughta help." He handed me the cloth. "Press on that lip and see if you can stop the bleedin."

Ralston seemed to be a kind man. I had hoped my plantin them seeds in him would get him to askin me questions. And he did.

When the sheriff come back to the train with Calvin, he retied his hands, then unwrapped the ropes from around his chest and arms. "It ain't that I don't trust you, Calvin. But I don't trust you." He secured the ropes around Calvin's hands and feet. It was like watchin Daddy hog-tie a pig. "I can't have no more foolishness outta you."

Ralston took me by the arm and motioned for me to walk with him. We made our way down the train steps and over a small rock pathway. He walked me clean up to the outhouse. "I'll wait right here in front of the door. Let me know when you're done."

I walked into the outhouse. A lantern glowed from a hook on the wall. Oddly enough, someone had set a bowl filled with flowers to one corner. I reckon it was the first outhouse I'd been in that had light and flowers. I did my business, then just as I started to peck on the door for Ralston, I felt my legs grow weak. I remembered askin Pastor Jess to put T. J. on the hole. All that worry boiled to the surface and I leaned hard against the door. I pressed my back against the boards and rested my hands on my knees, tryin to keep standin. My heart went to achin as I thought about poor Farrell alone on a train. The child was just five or six. I pounded my hands on the floor, and sobs come outta me like vomit.

Oh Lord, the pastor has told me You have mercy. Please have mercy on that poor youngin.

It didn't take but a minute for Ralston to figure somethin was wrong, and he flung open the door to find me layin on the floor. "Miss Worie, are you sick?" He pulled me to my feet.

"I am sick, Mr. Ralston. Sick to death that Calvin broke a family apart. Sick to death he has busted our family up. And sicker still that his greed shows no mercy."

"Let's get you outta here." He put his arm around my waist and took hold of my wrist. We walked to the edge of the train, where I went to sobbin tears that wouldn't cease.

"Lordy mercy. What will that little girl do? What will happen to her?"

Doanie come to mind, and I knew I was gonna have to find the words to tell her that her sister was gone. I couldn't ration tellin her the truth. Would it be easier to tell her Farrell was dead, or leave her to wonder the rest of her life what happened? They didn't seem to be no good answer.

I walked down the platform to the window where Calvin set, tears streamin like a rollin flood. "Calvin, what will I tell Doanie? You give Farrell to a man who sold her? What will I tell that little girl about her sister?"

Calvin stared past me, his eyes coal black. They wasn't an ounce of regret in him.

Ralston led me toward the door. "Come on, Miss Worie. Things will be alright. You have little T. J. here that needs you."

I know Mr. Ralston was doin his best to comfort me, but it was like when a body went to a wake. Sometimes you kept your mouth shut despite your good intentions. Words don't help.

Calvin leaned his head outta the window and spit, then swiped his mouth on his sleeve. "Ain't you pitiful?" He snarled when he spoke.

This time Ralston set between me and Calvin. Pastor Jess and T. J. set across from me and the sheriff stood, hand restin on his gun.

I never figured myself to be strong. Momma would say, "Strength comes from deep in your belly." She would pat my stomach. "It rises when you need it most." I hoped this gnawin in my gut was the strength Momma talked about. Calvin was like a hungry wolf, starved by bitterness. That is what filled his belly when he was hungry. That bitterness only served to make him angry and weak. Was this the edge I needed over him?

I decided right that minute to make my peace with the devil. They was this calm in my gut. The train jerked to a start.

"Pastor Jess, what does it feel like when the good Lord nudges you?"

The pastor stammered around, searchin for the right words. He shook his head and let out a sigh. "I suppose it's different for ever person. It depends on if the person is willin to listen or if the good Lord has to thump them on the head." He smiled.

"What about peace, Pastor? Does a body have peace and calm when the good Lord nudges?"

Pastor Jess sat starin at me. I know I sent him for a flip by askin such questions, but I watched as he mustered his wits and put on his preachin hat.

"Worie, the good Lord has a plan for ever man and woman." He patted T. J. on the back. "Ever child." Pastor Jess went to bouncing his knee, givin T. J. a little ride. "We don't always know what the plan is, but they is one thing for sure. The good Lord does. And they ain't been nary a time that His work has gone undone." He stood and swung T. J. to his hip. "Ever nudge ain't one of peace. Speakin for myself, ever one I've had never give me peace. It give me determination to do somethin I wouldn't choose to do. Like go to fight for a young woman who found herself carin for a bunch of orphans."

I stood, and the sheriff stepped toward me. "I ain't gonna do nothin. I'm gonna talk to my brother." Brother . . . Despite Momma's notes, I didn't know no different. Calvin was still my brother.

I took T. J. and set down in the pastor's place. Calvin wouldn't look at me.

"It's fine that you don't look at me. I still got things to say to you."

T. J. climbed off my lap and grabbed the pastor's legs. I pulled open my bag and brought out the notes Momma had wrote.

"Calvin, I shouldn't have broke that news to you about bein found like I did. I was angry. That was wrong of me."

Refusin to look at me, he stared at the passin trees. Daddy used to say that talkin to Calvin was like talkin to a rock. His eyes was fixed like a dead man and his jaw flinched as he gritted his teeth. He had no intentions of listenin or of softenin up.

"All you wanted was Momma's jar." I held up the roll of notes. "This is what was in the jar. Notes from Momma. It was like she was writin her every thought for us to read."

Calvin glanced toward me.

"Why would you take them youngins, Calvin? Why them little youngins? When Momma and Daddy took you in and raised you. They loved you with all they had. Never treated you no different. You, better than anyone, knowed what it was like to be an orphan."

He never uttered a word.

"Calvin, they's somethin else you need to know."

That caught his attention and he turned toward me.

"Ellie Olsen. You remember Ellie?"

A snide smile crossed his face.

"You told her you had medicine that could save her sick siblins. But you didn't."

Calvin's smile never cracked.

"You promised Ellie if she found that stone, you'd give her the medicine. You promised that girl hope, but you took her flesh instead."

Calvin went to laughin. "She was a tender one."

I felt my anger rise, but that voice inside my gut calmed me. *The wolf feeds on bitterness.*

"Just spit it out, Worie. I'm tired of listenin to you yackin," Calvin snapped.

They was no bein kind to Calvin, and when Pastor Jess realized what I was about to spill out, he nodded in approval. Calvin needed to know.

"You had a red stone. Ely said it was a ruby. Valuable. And I ain't sure how Mrs. Olsen come upon one or how you knew she'd have it, but you waltzed into that Olsen house when them youngins was sick, and you promised Ellie false hope and healin for that stone."

They was nothin meaner than the laugh that seeped outta Calvin. It grated against me. He was right proud of hisself. Right pleased at what he'd done.

"Foolish girl," he uttered. "Foolhearted. Stupid."

I come to my feet and pressed my finger toward Calvin's face.

The sheriff pushed me back onto the seat. "I ain't aimin for no more fightin on this train. You stay on that bench."

The sheriff meant business, but I was past bein nice. I leaned forward. "Look at me, Calvin."

He moved closer. "You think you can make me flinch?"

One more time, the child come outta Calvin. Anything I had to say was just a game to him. So I did what I needed to do and blurted it out.

"Was that stone worth the seed you left behind? Cause Ellie is full with your youngin."

Calvin cocked his head. I could see he was surprised, but then he shrugged. "What about that. I get to make an orphan of my own."

189

TWENTY-EIGHT

I had little left to say to Calvin the rest of the trip. Every bend in the tracks brought us closer to home. I pulled T. J. onto my hip and leaned against the train window. "Don't that wind feel fine, little man?"

T. J. lifted his arms into the air and giggled.

I rested my hand behind his head and pulled him close to kiss his forehead. "Miss Worie is so, so glad to have you back. I feel the need to squeeze the stuffin outta you." I tickled his tummy and then twisted from side to side, squeezin the little feller close.

We pointed at everthing we could along the track. Birds, a bear fishin by the river, men on horses.

"Look how big them trees is gettin," I said. "Turn your nose up and smell the air." Despite the train's smoke that hit us in the face as we rounded the bends in the mountain, a body could catch a whiff of the river and the pine waftin through the pass.

Pastor Jess come close and took T. J. "This is a right sweet child, ain't he?"

"He is, Pastor. And Farrell is too. It just breaks my heart to think of that baby girl all alone."

"I done told you. She's goin to a good home. The Holtsclaws

don't sell children for slaves." He bent forward and dangled T. J., makin the youngin bust out laughing.

"Pastor, them people took money for a youngin. A youngin that wasn't theirs to take or give. It ain't no use tryin to justify evil."

"I can't rightly argue with that. But we have to hope for the best. Believe things will be good for Farrell. They ain't nothing we can do for that child now. Nothin but pray."

"At least you see things my way." I smiled and scratched T. J.'s back. "You know, Pastor Jess, something ain't settin just right."

"What's eatin at you?"

"It ain't like Calvin to be quiet. I ain't never knowed him to hold his tongue more than a few minutes. He ain't hardly uttered a word."

Pastor Jess glanced toward Calvin. "He looks pretty solemn."

"That's what I'm sayin. This ain't right for Calvin." I searched for the sheriff, and when I caught his attention I motioned him over.

"Is they a problem?" The sheriff rested his hands on his waist and stretched. "Train seats ain't good on the back."

"Look, Sheriff, I know I've give you some fight, but for the most part I've done everthing you asked me to do."

"You have. Once I got you and Calvin to hush, things has been good."

"That's the problem. Things is too good. Calvin is my brother. I've been raised at his feet, and that ought to carry some weight when I tell you somethin ain't right. I ain't never knowed Calvin to sit quiet for this long."

The sheriff leaned back and roared laughin. "Well, he is hog-tied. That tends to quiet anybody."

"No! It don't. Not Calvin. Just because he can't move around don't stop him from runnin his mouth. I'm tellin you. My gut is tellin me somethin is wrong."

The sheriff eyed me, then walked real calm like to Calvin. He bent over and tested the ropes to see they was tight, then made his way back. "You need to sit down and follow your brother's example."

I could feel my stomach rumble and fear inch its way up my throat. "Please, Sheriff. Please listen to me."

The sheriff had no intention of listenin to me any more than he'd listen to Calvin. But I knew Calvin and he was a swindler. "Pastor Jess. Take T. J. all the way to the back of the train car. Put him on the floor against the wall and set tight in front of him. You hear?"

"Worie, don't you think you're—"

"I ain't. No, I ain't. Please, Pastor. Please. Outta sight, outta mind. Please."

Pastor Jess took the boy by the hand and led him to the rear of the car. If anything he could sense my fear. I sat on the bench behind Calvin and never opened my mouth. The deeper the train chugged through the mountain passes, the more my gut churned.

I tried to rest my head against the window, but they was no rest to be had. T. J. was quiet, and when I looked over my shoulder he was stretched out on the floor against the wall. Pastor Jess pressed his finger against his lips to let me know the boy was asleep.

The train groaned, and I felt the steel wheels slip on the rails as we climbed the mountain. To my right, I could stretch out my arm and let my fingers drag against the side of the bluff. To my left, a long, steep drop into the gorge below. The echo of a wild river made it hard to hear what a body was sayin.

Calvin craned his neck and peered over the gorge. "Long way down, ain't it?" He hauled off and spit, and the saliva flew back and hit me in the face.

I wanted to vomit, but I just wiped my face and never said a thing. Calvin had done got the last rise from me he was gonna get.

Steam hissed from the sides of the train as it topped the ridge and started down the other side. It put me in the mind of an old man huffin and puffin to climb a hill and then sighin in relief as he headed down.

The mountains quickly turned into open meadows filled with deer nibblin on buttercups, and the river soon run even with the tracks. A body can't never beat the beauty of a field of wildflowers. Me an Momma used to cut flowers ever day when they was in bloom. Our little cabin smelled as sweet as lilac and honeysuckle.

Calvin went to wigglin, and before I could holler at the sheriff, five men come tearin out of the woods on horseback, makin their way to the train.

I moved to set in front of Calvin. It was easy to see he was up to something. I tried to shout at the sheriff, but Calvin leaned back and lifted his feet, landin his boot heels in my gut. He fell backward onto the floor and I went sailin over the benches. It all happened so fast.

"Watch the boy!" I squalled at the pastor. "Don't you let him outta your sight."

Mr. Ralston and the sheriff wrestled two of the men, but a third grabbed hold of the train window and pulled hisself on board. He pulled a knife from his boot and sliced the ropes loose from Calvin's hands.

As I tried to stand and catch a breath, Calvin hit me again. Him and his friend dragged me across the car. Pastor Jess come to his feet.

I screamed, "Keep T. J.! Keep T. J.!" Then I felt a boot in the middle of my back.

I soared like a bird, hit the ground, and rolled to the edge of the river. My eyes was blurry, and all I saw was Calvin ride deep into the woods. I crawled to my knees, my arm danglin like a wet rag. Pastor Jess hung out the window of the train, T. J. on his hip. I fell, took a deep breath, and watched as the river went black.

TWENTY-NINE

I come to layin in a small cabin. A woman dabbed my face. My arm was braced between two strong sticks, and white strips of cloth tied them tight. They was no openin one eye, and ever breath I took felt like Calvin's boot heel kickin me again.

"Where am I?" My mouth was so swelled I could hardly speak.

"You're safe."

The voice sounded familiar, but I struggled to figure things. My one good eye was blurry, and the light caused it to water like a well pump.

A soft whisper tickled my ear. "Worie, honey. It's Bess."

"Who?"

"Ely and the pastor got you home. You're safe. Pretty tore up, but you're safe." She patted the shotgun settin next to her. "I'm a pretty good shot. Ain't no reason for you to worry."

"T. J.?" It was comin to me. "Where's my boy?" I tried to raise myself off the pallet, but this lady would have nothin of it.

"No, no! You lay right back down. I told you everthing is fine. The pastor, the youngin, even that sheriff, they all here. Don't you know me, baby girl? Come on now. Try hard."

She squeezed the water from the rag and dabbed my lips. I felt myself lift from the bed.

"Am I dyin?"

"Lord have mercy, I hope to goodness not. You're sure a mess though." She patted my forehead with the rag. "Come on, honey, it's Miss Bess. I changed your diapers when you was born."

I shook my head, tryin to clear the cobwebs. "Bess? Ely?"

"Yessss. Oh yes, baby girl." She come to her feet and run to the door. "Ely, she's awake. And she knows me."

The sound of boots across the slat floor reminded me of herdin cows. A man kneeled next to me. "Worie, it's me. Justice. You 'member me?"

I lifted my hand to his cheek and nodded.

Tears filled his eyes, but as quick as they come, fury dried them. "I'll kill him when I find him. You hear me? I'll kill him for doin this to you."

Ely touched his shoulder. "Come on, son, this ain't helpin your sister. Help me tend to the sheriff." He gently lifted Justice from his knees and led him out the door. "Bess, I'll manage him. Spend your time on our girl. Hear me?" He brushed her cheek as he passed. She leaned her head into his touch.

"Lawsy, Miss Worie, you's a mess." Bess lifted my head and poured a spoonful of something nasty into my mouth. I twisted my lips. "Don't you spit that out. That's castor oil and alum root. It'll numb the pain."

She was right. My mouth drawed tight as I swallowed.

"Where's T. J.?" I grimaced to open my mouth.

"He's as cute as a cherry on a tree. Doanie has him down at the creek. They'll be along in a minute. That youngin was beside herself when the pastor carried that boy in."

I tried to smile, but my mouth and cheeks was numb.

"Lordy, yes. That girl fell flat on her knees and went to bawlin like a whipped animal when she saw her little brother. She ain't turned him loose since."

I laid back. Ever bone in my body hurt. Things started to come to me, and I remembered Calvin and his thug shoving me off the train. I tried to take a deep breath, but it hurt too much. I groaned.

"Then we done good." I spit some blood. "We got the boy."

Bess tenderly wiped my mouth. "Yes, you did right good. Now take a sip of spring water. It's right cold. Oughta feel good on that swolled lip." She slipped her hand under my head and gently lifted me enough to drink. The water stung hard on my cut lip.

I tried to smile. Tried to nod. But anything I did to show my gratitude hurt too bad.

Bess lifted my arm and checked the ties. I could see the wheels in her head turnin as she looked over the sticks. "I believe Ely is gonna have to get me two bigger sticks. Your arm is swellin over these." She made her way to the door. "Ely! Ely!" she shouted. "Bring in two more sticks for this youngin's arm. These is too small."

Her voice gnawed into my head. *Just don't squall no more. Please don't squall no more.* I'd never been drunk on shine, but Justice told me when the burn wears off, your head feels like it's been hit with a coal bucket. My head hurt just like that.

I motioned Bess over. "Where's the pastor?"

"Oh. He said he was goin after your brother."

They was no movin. My body couldn't hold its own weight. Justice was here, so all I could do was pray. Pastor Jess had gone after Calvin. Lord have mercy. This was not what I wanted.

"My bag. Where's my bag?"

Bess shuffled across the floor to a shelf. "I stuck it away for safe keepin. I know what you carry is important."

I mouthed, "Thank you."

The sound of horse hooves echoed through the cabin. "Looka there. It's the pastor."

I heard voices, and before I could turn to look, there stood Pastor Jess and Ely. "Where's Calvin?" I asked.

"Hard to say. He took off. But I daresay he couldn't have got too far off." Ely's dark hand wrapped around my fingers. Tears filled his eyes. "Oh, Miss Worie, I's so sorry. So sorry." He gently run his knuckle over my cheek. "Don't you worry none. We're here, and we brought someone to see you."

I was took back when the sheriff from Hartsboro stood in front of me. He come close and bent down to my side.

"Miss Dressar, we meet again, but this time on your terms. I know talkin ain't easy, so you do your best to just listen." He took my hand. "I done talked to the sheriff from Chattanooga. He was about as banged up as you. He ain't holdin nothing against you. Not after what happened on the train. He's give me full authority to do what I need to to bring Calvin back to Chattanooga."

I strained to talk. "Little Farrell?"

The sheriff squirmed. "Ain't much I can do 'bout that. The pastor here is gonna contact some of his friends up north and see if they is any hope of findin her. But right now, Calvin is the briar. I've posted some men around Ely's place here. If he comes around we'll catch him."

I tried to say "thank you," but the sheriff shushed me, then went to laughin. "That was right nice of you, Miss Dressar, to slide them papers back under the door for me, but they wasn't no need to give me them back. I couldn't officially say what was in them. But I could leave them on my desk and hope you'd do what any momma would do. Miss Dressar, you'll be well cared for here." He squeezed my hand. "I best get to doin my job." He patted my hand. "When I helped Calvin get the homestead, I meant no harm to you or them youngins. I was doin my job. He had them papers." He set his hat and turned. "Even lawmen get the wool pulled over their eyes ever once in a while. We'll make this right." With that, he whispered a few things to Bess, then tipped his hat and was gone.

I'd never wanted to be dead in the ground any more than I did layin in that bed. Ever part of me ached, but nothing as much as my heart. It was broke for little Farrell. Would that youngin be alright? Was she even still alive? There was an emptiness in my chest. I rolled my head to the side. Tears dripped.

Momma was the one that did the prayin, teachin. I just never saw no need to talk to a body I couldn't lay eyes on. Still, all them times Momma quoted the good word . . . stuck. There wasn't no searchin for the understandin. It just come to me. *Pray.* And at that moment, I could have sworn I heard Momma's voice . . . Somehow, I just knew we'd find a way to get through this mess. I wasn't sure, but I figured Momma was somehow smilin down from heaven, seein my heart change.

The cabin door flew open, and in come T. J. followed by Doanie. The two rushed to my side and T. J. climbed onto me. Though pain shot me through, I wasn't about to shun that little one. I squeezed him as best as I could. Doanie took hold of him and pulled him onto her hip.

"We come to see you, Miss Worie. Come to say we're much obliged." Doanie beamed as she kissed her brother. "Mr. Ely told me not to worry no more about Farrell. She is safe in the good Lord's arms, and I believe him. I have to believe him, leastways I couldn't sleep at night."

"I . . . tried . . ." The words barely inched out.

"Shhh. You rest. That's what Farrell would want."

I knew all along the child was wise for her years. Her and Abeleen both. I wondered if that's what happens when you become an orphan—get forced to do things you ain't rightly ready to take on. A body either gets desperate or wise. Seemed as though the good Lord had give Abeleen an extra portion of wisdom. She would be the shoulders I could stand on while I healed.

If this was the good Lord's way of provin His presence, then I guess He managed to make a hard heart soft.

"Let's go, T. J. Let Miss Worie rest." Doanie kissed his cheek again. The boy pressed his fingers to his lips and blew me a kiss.

I knew somethin had been wrong on that train. Maybe it was a nudge from the good Lord to be ready. They was somethin to be said for havin Ely and Justice at hand. The fear was easier to take. And with Pastor Jess, there was a comfort. A peace.

But there was more to come. This was just the beginnin. Calvin wouldn't give up easy. He'd be back, and he'd be bringin the wrath of hell with him.

THIRTY

I wasn't right sure how many days I slipped in and out of sleep. When the pain would grow hard, I found myself fadin. There was only bits and pieces of memories about the train. Chattanooga. It all seemed to run together, but when I opened my eyes today, things was clear as the mornin sky.

I glanced around the room. Bess sat slumped in the pine rocker, one hand restin on her stomach, the other proppin her head. Her mouth hung open and her breathin put me in the mind of Daddy sawin a tree stump. She'd been so faithful to care for me, I didn't dare rouse her.

I pulled myself up and dropped my feet over the edge of the bed. A long groan seeped outta me. My legs was weak, but I managed to get my feet under me and work my way to the door. It was a trick to figure how to get around my broke arm, but I finally got the door open. The mornin air kissed my cheek, and I closed my eyes and took in a deep breath, lettin the sweet smell of honeysuckle fill my lungs.

The mountain air brings a newness, seeps down deep, and clears out the things that weigh heavy on a body's soul. Despite how hard things are, it's like the mountain is forgivin. It demands a man's hard work to survive, but then it wraps its soul and spirit around you, claimin you as its own child.

I shaded my eyes as the morning sun peeked above the crest of the mountain. Purples, blues, streaks of pink, and then that big yellow ball peerin down. A soft breeze caressed my cheek. I was home. Or as close to home as I could be for now. There was no desire to return to the city, and short of findin T. J. the rest was nothing but regret.

My legs ached and my arm throbbed, but even with those ailin me, my feelins was tore between joy and brokenheartedness. I had some inklin of peace.

I rubbed my cheek, my fingertips gingerly touchin scabs still raw from healin. Memories of seein the happiness on Doanie's face filled me with joy, but knowin little Farrell was still lost took what joy I had and tossed it over the bluff.

"You're lucky your arm was all that was broke. Coulda been your neck," a voice whispered from behind me.

"Pastor Jess," I said. "You just put the fear of God in me."

"It's always a pastor's hope to sway a heathen, but I never put that name on you." He laughed. "I'd hug you, but I'm afraid it would just cause you more pain."

"Much obliged." I inched to one side of the porch rail so he could lean. "I owe you, Pastor. Doanie wouldn't have her brother back if it wasn't for you."

"Sometimes bein a pastor has some advantages. But if it wasn't for the good Lord's mercy, if it wasn't for Him, I'd be nothin. Have nothin."

"Sounds like there's a story behind that." I gently bumped against the pastor. "Like you wasn't always a good-hearted man?"

Pastor Jess scrubbed his fingers along his jaw, scratchin at his poor excuse for a beard. "Don't reckon I know a soul who was perfect from the beginnin. We're all folk with hardship and learnin behind us."

I supposed the pastor was right, but I stopped to think, what had I done wrong to deserve this path? I was a good youngin growin up. Never give Momma or Daddy no trouble. Did what I was told, and when. There was no bad things I could think of. Nothin that I'd done that was so horrible. Then like a hard rain washin over me, I commenced to see the bad in my soul. And it hurt.

"Pastor, I ain't never been a body like Calvin. I thought I was a good person." I twisted to ease the pressure on that broke arm. "But I'm beginnin to see it ain't always the things we do that makes us bad. Sometimes it's the things in our heart and our head that makes us worse than the bad."

Pastor Jess patted my shoulder. "This sounds like a confession."

"Yeah, I'm sure you're all ears now, ain't ya?"

He cupped his hands around his ears.

"Bein a smart aleck ain't right becomin, Pastor."

"It is what it is. I done told you, we all got our skeletons."

Skeletons was a right good word. What haunted me was my lack of compassion. Why did I not see Momma was sufferin? All I had on my mind was what she could teach me so I could learn to be a teacher. That's all I wanted. It never hit me to think about her.

I felt tears rise. "I've been mighty selfish, Pastor. Maybe if I'd been less about myself and thought more about Momma, I'd have seen she was sufferin. Maybe I coulda stopped her from takin her life."

"A body never knows the darkness a soul has to fight through. Sometimes that soul just can't fight no more. In their eyes, death makes life easier for those still livin."

"But Momma wasn't a problem. She was happy. Or I thought she was."

"Worie, you can wish and wonder till your days end, and you'll never understand what clawed away in your momma's head. Best you can do is stop blamin and start livin."

"Them's powerful words, Pastor."

"Well, it's truth. And truth ain't promised to be easy, but it is promised to always be right."

I hobbled to the edge of the porch. Ely's rooster pranced across the rail fence, huntin for just the right place to let out his bellow.

"Reckon Ely is right? I have to believe Farrell is safe in God's arms and hope them arms is long enough to hold her wherever she is." My voice quivered. "I still see the fear in her eyes when Sikes yanked her away. There wasn't a thing I could do. Nothin. And I know I keep sayin it over and over, but Pastor Jess . . . it haunts me."

"Mr. Holtsclaw ain't a bad man. Him and his wife try hard to find homes for lost children. Their heart is right. Their ways just ain't ours."

"You'd be right on that one. I'd take them little ones under my wing. I don't take money and toss them on a train to who knows where!" I felt the anger rise in my heart. "I can't believe you'd defend such a thing."

"Worie, I don't defend Mr. Holtsclaw's way. All I'm sayin is folks manage things different. There's more than one way to skin a cat."

"Well, sending a five-year-old child on a train ain't what I call lovin. It's right cold, Pastor."

Pastor Jess leaned across the porch rail and sighed.

"What?" I asked. "What ain't you sayin?"

The look on his face spoke loud. "Maybe we need to back up and talk about that confession."

Them words hit me like a rock. My heart opened up and bled hurt. The pastor had just slapped me square betwixt the eyes with my own misgivins. Was I wrong to be angry at Holtsclaw? The thought wallowed around in my head.

I wasn't wrong to be angry at Holtsclaw. I was wrong to judge his intentions before I knew his plan.

There it was—laid out on the mornin breeze. I was selfish and judgmental. I was angry, stubborn, a tad hateful.

"Pastor Jess, I'm grateful for what you've done for me. Grateful for your part in bringin home T. J. and for savin me. But right now, I need to be left alone."

"Good Lord likes it when you wanna be left alone." Pastor Jess gently squeezed my shoulder.

"Why's that?"

"He likes bustin in on your heart when you're alone and cleanin out the muck when you're alone. Besides, folks listen better then." He shrugged and turned.

The mist that hid the ground commenced to lift. I watched the pastor walk down the steps and toward the creek. He seemed gulped up in the fog. Just like that, he vanished, and *alone* crept up the porch, wrappin tight around me.

My heart ached as I dug deep into my soul, seekin peace. Seekin understandin. Seekin forgiveness.

I had a lot of forgivin to do. There was forgiveness for Momma takin her life. I didn't understand why, but it wasn't my fault and it wasn't my place to condemn her for things I didn't know about. There was Calvin. I had no idea how to begin to forgive him. I'd never tried to figure him or his ways out. I just hated him for his meanness, never takin to heart he was filled with a reason that made sense to him. He was an orphan too.

The web of anger kept spreadin.

Momma and Daddy kept Calvin's past a secret. They was no explanation why, but if we'd known, maybe me and Justice could have made a change in him. And Justice. That man carried a secret all his own. I needed to truly forgive him. I blamed him for not bein there when Momma took her life. It wasn't his fault. He couldn't have stopped her any more than me. His drinkin was somethin inside his heart. He needed forgiveness of his own.

A cloud passed over the sun, dimming its morning light. It was like a heaviness covered me. My soul hurt worse than any part of the bruises and broken bones of my flesh. I felt like my chest would rip open.

I wasn't sure what the good Lord wanted from me or why He'd picked me. The deeper I looked into my heart, the more of a mess I saw. Why on earth would the good Lord want a mess to deal with? And why me? Why did these little youngins bore so deep into my bein?

I remembered one of them papers Momma wrote on.

> But I have trusted in thy mercy; my heart shall rejoice in thy salvation.
> I don't know Your ways, good Father, but I trust mercy and I rejoice despite my misgivins. Help me to forgive others so I can be forgiven.

Right then, in that moment, Momma made things right clear. I understood that forgiveness wasn't for the other person. It was for me. It was what the good Lord would use to set me free and help me make my way. Right then I understood that the things that happened in the past was not who I was. They helped to etch notches in me, like Daddy when he whittled on a stick, but them things wasn't who I was. What would make me, shape me, grow me, would be the decisions I'd make from here on out. Them things was up to me. One more time, things pointed to trust.

A peace seeped over me again. I couldn't see my way clear just yet, but I felt like the good Lord had done just what Pastor Jess said. He butted in to my *alone* and cleaned out some of the mess.

"Worie Dressar, you ain't got one iota of business outta that bed."
Bess had roused from her sleep and come huntin me down. "You
get yourself back in that cabin. You understand me?"

I tried to soothe her frustration by showin my gratitude. "I
didn't wanna wake you. I know you was tired. You've been so kind
to care for me."

Bess pressed both hands to her hips and tapped her foot against
the hard wooden slats. She let me know right quick she wasn't happy.

"Miss Bess, maybe I can sit out here on the porch. I'm feelin
much better this morning," I said.

She was like a bull ponderin a charge. Her foot kept right on
tappin while she waited for me to move.

Ely pushed open the door to the cabin. "Lordy mercy, look at
you. Standin and all." He pulled a pine chair close and motioned
for me to sit.

"Much obliged," I said. "Miss Bess was just fussin at me for
bein outside."

Ely whirled around to face his wife. His finger wagged in her
face. "This here is a blessin. I didn't think she'd be able to walk
for weeks. Let the girl alone, Bessy. Sunshine is good for healin."

Bess snorted and headed inside, grumbling under her breath that Ely wasn't no business questionin her doctorin.

"That was right kind of you, Ely. I know Miss Bess is worried over me."

"She means well. She'd have been a good momma, given a chance. She mommas anything that needs help, be it a bird, a pup, or a person."

I wiggled to get comfortable in the chair. "She's been good to me, Ely. You both have."

"We do what we do for you because we love you. We owe that to Miss Louise."

My heart was warmed. I could tell Ely was truthful. Him and Bess had always been in my life.

"Ely, can I ask you somethin?"

"Surely."

"You and Bess has been around Momma all my life. Did you ever figure she was takin care of them orphans?"

"Louise was a generous woman. She come from down near Atlanta. They wasn't a mountain bone in her body. She loved with the heart of the mountain."

I was stunned. Momma never seemed anything but a mountain girl. She sure never mentioned it.

"I reckon it ain't gonna do no harm to tell you now."

"Tell me what?" I couldn't imagine what other secrets Momma kept.

"Louise met your daddy when he was tradin furs. She was teachin at a school close to Chattanooga."

"Momma was a teacher?"

"She was. Me and Bess served her in the house she lived in. We was took in by her daddy after we run from the plantation."

"You've always known Momma? Even before me?"

I didn't know what to say. Momma's secrets just kept getting deeper and deeper. So did Ely's. Seemed him and Momma was tied pretty tight.

I tried to push it back, but anger twisted my stomach. "Everthing I know about Momma is a lie! You lied!"

Ely put his finger in my face. "You listen here. Louise was a good woman. The secrets she kept was to protect you'ins. Don't you be givin me no whinin about truthfulness. They was never a better woman than your momma."

I turned my head and sniffed away the tears. "What else do I need to know?"

"I ain't sure I'm gonna tell you with that snitty attitude."

I took in a breath to calm myself. "All I want is the truth. That's all, Ely. Justice keeps whinin I need to trust, but that's hard to do when they ain't no truth to be had. Try and understand, Ely. Try." I struggled to stand.

He slipped his knife from his boot sheath and cut a small branch that jutted from an oak limb onto the porch. I could see him chewin on his words as he picked off the leaves and let them float to the ground.

"Ely. Please. I need the truth. I can't figure things right if I ain't got the truth. What else was Momma hidin?" There had to be more.

The door squeaked as Bess pushed it open with her elbow. "Here. Leastways you both have some coffee." She run the hot brew under my nose so I could get a good sniff.

The smell sent chills down my arms as it tickled ever bud on my tongue. "Don't you think so, Bess?"

She handed Ely his cup. "Thinkin is somethin I try to do ever step I take." She snickered at her own joke. "So guess you best tell me what I should be thinkin over?"

"Lawsy mercy. Here it comes." Ely shook his head. Askin Bess for an opinion was like stickin your hand in the honey tree. It might just get stung.

"Truth, Miss Bess. I asked Ely to tell me the truth about Momma. All of it. I'm tired of tryin to piece these lies together."

I'd struck a nerve, cause Bess's smile dropped. She glanced at Ely and then back at me, never utterin a word.

"You know too, don't you?"

Bess sighed. She patted Ely's hand and nodded. "Truth comes in all sorts of shapes. Sometimes it's hard to take in. Other times it becomes the light that guides us." She leaned into Ely and kissed his cheek. "Even if it's hard to swaller . . . it's always right. Ain't that so, Ely?" She walked inside.

"Ely? You're scarin me. Did Momma do somethin bad?"

"Louise was a wonderful soul. She saved me and Bess."

"I know that, you've told me."

Ely paced the porch before he stopped. "Miss Worie, the truth is, your momma loved children, and it just killed her she could never have her own babies."

"What?" I felt my knees buckle. Ely took my good arm and set me in the rocker. "What do you mean, Momma couldn't have no babies of her own? There's me and Justice."

"Miss Worie, this is a can of worms I never wanted to open."

My voice raised a notch. "It's open, Ely. Ain't no closin it now."

Ely went to his knees. "Your momma never could have babies. No matter how she tried, she couldn't never have no youngins. One day she run upon a woman tryin to give birth—your momma—and bein the woman she was, stepped in to help."

There was no words. I couldn't get my thoughts together. My whole life, Justice's whole life. We was both just like Calvin. Orphans. I couldn't breathe.

Ely took my hand. "You listen to me, Miss Worie. That woman died havin you. She didn't have no family. And when your momma looked around and saw little Justice toddlin around, and when she held you, brand new in this world, she wasn't gonna let either of you die."

My chest ached like somebody had stabbed me.

"Your momma and daddy brought all you youngins into their home. Calvin. You and Justice. In her eyes you was all hers. Ever one of you. She never looked no different at you youngins. Never one time."

"You knew all this time?" I asked.

Ely stared at the porch slats. He run his finger along the cracks between the boards. "I knew. We knew. Me and Bess. Whether you never knew your real momma died never mattered. You'd never know her. She was dead. They was no point in raisin you to wonder. Your momma and daddy never wanted you to have no void. They loved you youngins with everthing they had. That's the kinda folks they was. That's the kinda friends they was."

I thought hard for a minute. My heart was tore. I loved my momma and daddy. Ely was right. They was the kinda folks any child would want. Momma was tender, gentle, lovin. Daddy was stern, but his love was nothin I ever questioned. Still, it was seventeen years of lies. Lies. How could I forget that?

I was angry. Hurt. And at the same time, I never felt so loved. Then it hit me.

"Justice," I whispered. What about Justice? He'd been tryin so hard to stop drinkin the hooch. Betwixt me nearly gettin killed and now this, stayin away from his crutch would be hard.

Ely stood. "I reckon this is my job to give him this news. You ain't in no frame of mind to do it."

"Poor Justice," I whispered. Would this ache not end?

"Worie, that boy is a man. When is you gonna learn you ain't his momma?"

I shouted back at Ely, "I reckon he ain't got no momma, now does he? Never had one!"

Ely eyed me straight on. I'd done crossed the line between hurt and anger. The vein in his neck raised. He was bitin back his anger. "Justice is grown. He's got to learn to take hard news like a man.

You best learn that you can't do it for him. He'll be fine." Ely rubbed his neck and his nose flared. "But you. You gotta let loose of this anger. They comes a time in a body's life when they need to accept the blessins the good Lord lays on them. His ways ain't ours. That's in the good book." He dusted his trousers and gently squeezed my knee. "I ain't sorry for keepin this from you. It wasn't no sin. It was love. You need to learn love does what it must. If you question that, then read the good book."

"That ain't fair, Ely. That ain't fair!" I shouted.

Ely come right to my face. "What ain't fair? It ain't fair that your real momma died birthin you. It ain't fair you was took in by a momma who loved you with ever part of her soul. Raised you good. Taught you what you know. I reckon I ain't too good at understandin what fair is."

"But . . ."

"But what, Worie? I don't supposed I've ever raised my voice to you. I's just an old slave been set free in more ways than you know, but you need to stop blamin and start lovin." Ely stomped through the door, and after a minute he come back. He slammed a book on my lap. "You want truth, Miss Worie. Look for it. You'll find it right here."

I eyed the book. Momma's Bible. I felt like I had just been beat with a horse whip.

Ely swiped at his eyes. "Miss Worie, you're a good woman. You got your momma's heart. But you got an anger that takes the good and does away with it."

"I what? I got anger?"

"Anger! And till you figure the world don't spin to suit you, you ain't gonna never have no peace." Ely tapped his fingers on the book, then walked away.

I rubbed my fingers across Momma's Bible. They wasn't no reason why I couldn't believe in the good Lord like Momma did. But once I started takin heed to Him, it seemed like nothin but trouble

211

followed. I shook my head. No matter what I did, I couldn't push away the tug at my heart. Is this how the good Lord shoves His way on people? Puttin them in places where they couldn't say no?

My fingers dug into the weathered leather, and I pulled it close to my heart. I'd done come face-to-face with my own misgivins, and I supposed they was still misgivins to have. Bess knew what she was talkin about. Truth can be hard to swaller, and right now I was chokin.

Momma raised us good. They was no reason for Calvin's hate or Justice's drinkin. It come to me that Momma did the best she could. She couldn't make our decisions. The paths we took as grown-ups was our own doin. Momma couldn't fix them. I guessed that's why she wrote them papers. Maybe them was her hopes for us. One last effort to guide us in a different direction.

I strained to stand and make my way to the porch rail. The morning fog had lifted and the outline of the mountains was drawed across the sky. Memories of the city brushed through my mind. It wasn't a place for me. There was no desire to ever go back, just the desire to make things right for these youngins.

Doanie and T. J. come outta the outhouse. She was praisin him to high heaven for usin the hole. In the midst of this mess, I had to laugh. She was like a little momma herself. Abeleen carried a basket into the henhouse. She stopped and petted the hound that stayed at her heels. What a strong child. She'd grow into a fine woman.

All I could do for these youngins was love them, guide them. They'd come a day, just like Momma, I couldn't change their paths.

I looked at them youngins, and I could see they had happiness in the horror of what they'd survived. Despite all them children had lost . . . there was laughter. It was a lesson I needed to learn.

Out by the garden, Ely stood, hands in his pockets, talkin to Justice. I watched as Justice bent forward and rested his hands on his knees. Ely had told him. Justice picked up a rock and tossed it hard across the garden. But what touched me most was seein Ely wrap his arms around Justice. They was no doubt Ely and Bess had loved Momma and Daddy. Loved us.

I tried to hold the reins on everthing that happened. It had to be my way. I knew best . . . or did I? I was always hardheaded, even stubborn. It was hard to imagine somebody else might have a better way of doin things.

Ely come back to the cabin. He took my good hand and kissed it. "I love you, Miss Worie. Always have."

His voice was hard, and when it quivered, I thought it was just that he was old, but it wasn't. I saw somethin in Ely's eyes I'd never seen . . . His eyes was filled with hurt. Hurt I'd brought on.

THIRTY-TWO

Since things had been quiet for a few weeks, I thought it would bring me peace, but it didn't. Daddy always talked about the quiet before the storm. I remember him standin on the porch, watchin the lightnin in the distance. Hours passed and the lightnin never come no closer.

Daddy said, "Louise, the storm . . . it's growin. Night's comin. I hate it when I can't see the evil crawlin through the dark." He paced the path by the house. "They ain't no sound. Not even a bird. It's the quiet before the storm. You know that means all hell is about to break loose."

Daddy was never wrong when it come to readin Mother Nature, so Momma herded us youngins into the house. I remember he hadn't much more than got them words outta his mouth when the wind kicked up and the thunder went to shakin the mountain. It was a storm like none we'd seen. Trees twisted and their roots was tore outta the ground. Balls of ice fell from the heavens, slammin the wooden roof of the cabin, knockin out the thatch. As that storm roared through the gap, I remember the five of us huddled in a circle, arms wrapped tight around one another. And Momma prayed through the noise of the wind, "Good Father, if You save nothin, save my babies."

Save my babies. It come to me how selfless Momma was. She'd have died for us . . . died in our place.

There was no comfort not hearin from Calvin. Lookin over my shoulder wasn't any way to live. Even on days when things seemed alright, they really wasn't. I was just waiting for the storm.

I'd got outta that bed and to my feet as quick as I could force my legs to hold me steady. Work was the best healin—despite how hard it was. The guilt of not pullin my weight worried me. I'd washed eggs, pulled weeds from the garden. Anything I could do to help. My arm ached, but Bess was good to keep after me to hold it steady. I couldn't do much without her dotin over me, tyin it tight to my chest so I couldn't move it.

"Missy, that arm ain't gonna heal if you don't hold it still," Bess snapped. I kissed her forehead. She waved her hand at me. "Don't you be tryin to butter me up. I know what needs to be done to heal that wing. Your scootin close to my heart ain't gonna change that." She grumbled and made her way toward the house.

Trigger come up the path from the barn. He was haulin two baskets of eggs Abeleen had took from the henhouse. I watched as he climbed the rocky path to the porch.

"Looky there. Good to see you gettin up and about." He kissed my cheek.

A chill went down my spine and I smiled. "What brings you up here?" I asked.

"I've been back and forth from Hartsboro. Checkin in on things. Waitin on you to heal. Gotta keep that forge runnin. Wondered if Abeleen might let me buy that forge. If you think that is a good idea."

Trigger hadn't changed in the years we was apart. He still waited. Momma would say he was a patient man. I said he never had no backbone. He couldn't make a decision—waited for somebody to always tell him what he was doin was right. He tugged at my heart and made me mad all at the same time.

"Trigger, why are you waitin on me? What is they to wait on?"

He looked at me right strange like.

"What's on your mind?" I didn't mean for my words to seem harsh, but he befuddled me. As much as I cared for Trigger, as much as he sent chills down my back, I can't say I loved him. He was sweet, genuine, and it took me some time to figure that. Maybe that's why it was so easy to choose to stay and help Momma manage the homestead rather than to marry Trigger. My heart wasn't in it.

The more I thought about it, the more I realized it wasn't Trigger that was missin backbone. It was me. I didn't have the umph to just tell him he was a good man but not one that took my heart. It was easier to blame my givin up marryin him on Momma. Truth was, I couldn't be honest with myself.

My askin what he was waitin on seemed to sting him like a bumblebee. Trigger cleared his throat. "I need to get these eggs to Miss Bess. We can talk when you're feelin stronger. Ain't nothin pressin."

"No, Trigger. We can talk now."

He froze in his steps.

"Set them eggs down and talk to me."

He eased the baskets to the ground. I sat on the porch step and motioned for him to sit too.

"Like I said, I'm glad to see you up and about." Trigger gently tapped my knee with his hand.

"Trigger, what are you waitin for? What's on your mind?"

He squirmed next to me, hemmin and hawin, tryin to find the words.

"Oh, for Pete's sake," I snapped. "Can't you just one time say what's on your mind?"

"Alright. If that's what you want. I didn't want to cause you no more hurt."

"I reckon that's needless worry. Look at me. I'm about as hurt as a woman can be. Come on, spit out your words." I sounded right hateful.

Trigger stood and took my good hand. "They was a time I pined after you. And when we run upon each other in Hartsboro, I felt them same feelins rise up in my heart. But the truth is . . ."

I couldn't imagine what he was achin to say, but I kept my mouth shut and give him the time he needed to spit out the words.

"I don't want you to think I still have them feelins."

I stared Trigger in the eye, tryin to decide whether to laugh out loud.

"Truth is, I've been spendin a good amount of time with Miss Ellie."

"Ellie?" I tried to be polite. It was obvious Trigger was worried he'd set me into a rage. "Well, ain't that somethin."

"Now, don't go gettin all bent outta shape. I know she's carryin a child. But I've growed attached to her."

I caught sight of someone peekin around the edge of the barn. "That Ellie eyein us from the barn?"

Trigger spit and sputtered, tryin to find good words. "You was good to take her in. Just like you took in them other youngins. But she's a woman carryin a child."

I stood and returned the kiss he'd placed on my cheek. "Trig, they was a time you filled a space in my heart too, but I got these youngins to care for. Right now, managin them, seein to Justice, and doin my part best as I can to help Ely and Bess takes up what heart I got."

Trigger was silent.

I couldn't tell if he was tore from hurt or just relieved. "Ellie is a good person. She's been done wrong by Calvin, and if you're willin to take her in, care for her and her youngin, then I'd say you're a better person than I could ever be."

"I'm took back, Worie. I figured I'd be eggin a fight."

Another slap in the face. Did ever person that come my way expect a fight? "You go bring Ellie up here. Let me talk to her."

Trigger tore down to the barn, hollerin for Ellie like a little boy that just killed his first squirrel.

It wasn't long before she peeked around the edge of the porch. "You called for me?"

I looked at the girl, her belly rounded with a new life, and all I could do was take her in my arms. "They ain't enough words to tell you how sorry I am for what you have been put through." I stepped back, then took her face in my hands. "Trigger is a good man. He'll make a good husband." I touched her tummy. "And a good daddy."

Her eyes brightened as she pressed my hand tight against her child. She nodded, then walked away.

"That was right kind of you."

I jumped, startled like a pup stealin a sliver of meat from the hook. Pastor Jess stepped outta the cabin, a cup of coffee steaming in his hand.

"Can't say they was anything nice to be done."

"I see a couple of things I call good. The first bein you set a young man free."

"Pastor, I didn't have no chains on Trigger. He's been free of me for a couple of years."

"Maybe not chains you could see. But you freed him from an obligation. Give him permission to follow his heart."

I took the coffee from the pastor's hand and took a swig. "You talk like I got some kind of power over people."

"No. But love is a funny thing. It makes its own chains that bind us to one another. Sometimes a body just needs to know it's alright to move on."

Move on. Them was words that sounded right nice, but they was no movin for me. Not until Calvin was caught.

"Pastor Jess, you've been with Justice. How's he doin?"

"Ain't for me to say. He's your brother. And it seems you both got some things you need to get used to. Ely told me about your momma."

"Mine and Justice's life is a lie." I glanced right quick at the pastor. There it was again. My anger.

"Worie, ain't a person alive can change the past. You might not ever understand why your momma decided not to tell you ever-thing. But what you got to focus on ain't what's behind that you can't change. A body has to look at the good that come from the past. Learn to be grateful for bein given a chance at a better life."

I couldn't argue with Pastor Jess. That sorty ticked me off. He was doin his best to help make me understand.

"Your momma and daddy could have left you and Justice. They could have left Calvin—to die. But they chose to protect you from that life and give you one filled with love. Best I can see, you're doin the same thing your momma did with these youngins. Ain't you?"

I was never good at bein wrong. It eat at me. But Pastor Jess just cleared a puddle of muddy water, and I saw he was right.

He leaned against the porch rail and took in a deep breath. "You ain't your momma. What you're doin for these youngins ain't because of what your momma did. You're doin it cause your heart was pricked. Make sense?" He took his coffee back and emptied the cup.

The ache was so deep, it was like ever bit of the air was bein sucked outta me. I made my way off the porch. "Pastor Jess, could you . . ."

His hand went up. "I can't talk to Justice for you. This is be-tween you'ins. You'll work through the hurt together. Now go on. Justice is out at the garden."

When I finally made my way around to the garden, Justice was squatted down, pickin at weeds. I watched as he fingered the green shoots. He was tryin to take in Ely's news.

I eased up behind him. "Justice."

He twisted and went to his knees. Wrapped his arms around my legs and went to sobbin. I dug my fingers into his hair. This was the second time I'd seen his heart bleed, and I wondered why mine wouldn't.

THIRTY-THREE

Me and Justice walked the length of the garden before my legs commenced to give. He scooped me up and carried me to the barn. I looked over them beds the pastor built, and things started to sink in.

"What are we gonna do, Justice? First we find out Calvin was an orphan Momma picked up, and now we find out we're just as bad."

"Bad?" Justice scratched his head. He raised a brow. "Worie, we is just folks. We ain't no better or no worse than anybody else on the mountain."

"How can you say that? You know what Calvin has done, and all for his greed."

"Worie, don't be mixin Calvin's greed with the fact we are orphans. The two don't meet."

"But . . ."

Justice hung his head. He shoved his hand into his pocket and pulled out the satin bag that held Momma's stones. He'd took it from Bess. "Tell me somethin, Worie." He opened my hand and dropped the bag in it. "What does this bag mean to you?"

"What do you mean, what does it mean to me?"

"Well, you was determined to keep it from Calvin. We had Bess hide it once Ely told us these stones was worth somethin."

"What are you sayin?" My heart raced. "What are you gettin at?"

Justice stood quiet, ponderin his words. "What do you reckon woulda happened if you'd just give this bag to Calvin when he busted in Momma's cabin early on?"

Bile crawled up my throat, burnin like a hard swig of moonshine. "Are you sayin this whole thing is my fault?"

"No, I ain't sayin that. But I am sayin you mighta been able to prevent it. Ain't no way to know what Calvin would do, but I ain't no better than him." Justice kicked at the dirt floor. "I can't tell you the times I've snuck and had me some liquor even after I promised you I wouldn't. We all got our demons."

"Momma told me to keep the jar a secret."

"Momma is dead," he come back at me.

I took a step back. Justice's words tore through me like a hot prod. I went to pacin the barn, thoughts runnin fast through my mind. "I promised her."

"Yes you did. But tell me somethin. Does Momma care now? Right this minute, do you think Momma cares who has this bag? Wrapped in that blanket, buried in the ground . . . all them rocks on top of her. Do you think Momma cares about a jar or a bag, or papers she wrote on?"

I'd never known Justice to be so hard. "Have you been drinkin? Cause that's the only thing that would make you talk like this. You asked me to trust you. And I did. Is this how you repay me?"

"When Ely told me about our real momma dyin, my heart broke. But it never broke because I felt like Momma lied to us. It broke cause I was plumb awful. Never thankin Momma for the love she give me. Never thankin her for the times she forgive me. I was never honest with her. Never grateful for her worryin over me. I let Calvin bully me into never tellin Momma the truth. Or why that lie drove me to drown my pain. Worie, I was ashamed."

"I ain't bad. I always did what Momma told me," I shouted. "It wasn't my fault I was never good enough to keep Momma from takin her life."

All the hurt I felt while Momma laid dyin in my arms bubbled up. I fell to the floor, and sobs heaped outta me like vomit.

"Momma, I'm sorry." I laid my face in the hay. "I'm so sorry. I was just tryin to do right by you."

Ely must have heard me and Justice arguin and wasted no time runnin to the barn. "What's goin on here?" He took me by the shoulders to help me stand.

Justice stood toe to toe with Ely. "This is between me and Worie. My sister had ever chance in the world to let go of her selfishness. If she ain't gonna let go on her own, then I'm gonna straighten her out."

I was growin weary of folks tellin me I was angry, holdin on to bitterness. But I reckon Justice made his point. This time things sunk into my hard head.

It was never my fault them youngins lost their folks. And it sure wasn't my fault Momma took her life. But this wrath from Calvin . . . that was my fault. That was me bein stubborn. That stubbornness caused Doanie to lose Farrell and caused us to lose the homestead. All that I could have prevented by not bein so . . . so . . . self-righteous.

Justice picked up a shovel and whaled the tar outta the side of the barn. His anger flared like I'd never seen. "Let me get the rest of this nightmare out in the open." He come straight to my face. "Me, Daddy, and Calvin went huntin. Them two got into it over Daddy's shotgun. They was tuggin back and forth on that gun till Calvin kicked Daddy's legs out from under him. He fell hard. His head landed on a rock. Daddy never moved again."

I stood shakin my head. Momma and me believed Daddy growed sick when they was huntin. "We thought he died from the fever," I said.

"Well, he didn't. And Calvin swore if I opened my mouth, he'd kill you and Momma."

There was nothin left in me. I was spent. For the first time, I thought I might understand why Momma pulled that trigger. A body can only take so much before they can't swaller no more. Dyin sounded right invitin.

Things went to fallin into place. Justice had lived in fear of Calvin, and I accused him of bein weak.

Ely tried to comfort me, but they was no comfort to be found. I took that shovel outta Justice's hand and flung it across the barn. I draped my arms over his shoulders and pressed my forehead against his.

"Ely! Bess is right." I kissed my brother's cheek, then took hold of his hand. "Yes sirree. She's right. The truth ain't always easy to swaller, but it is always right."

I'd done gone a few rounds with the good Lord. I supposed He'd finally got my attention.

This mess wasn't about them youngins. It wasn't about Justice. Or Calvin. It wasn't even about Momma's lies. It was about me and just how broke I was and how I was gonna fix it.

I couldn't turn loose of Justice. I was afraid if I did, I'd lose him too.

Betwixt all the hollerin and wailin, everbody had made their way to the barn to see what the commotion was about. They circled around me and Justice. I reckon it was time we had a family talk. Pastor Jess pulled a barrel close so I could sit. I took hold of Justice's hand, mine shakin.

I glanced around the barn. Abeleen and the pastor. Trigger and Ellie. Bess and Ely. Doanie and T. J. It appeared what I had was a family. Only one of them was blood family. The rest was stragglers.

Bess pulled some papers from her pocket and went to sortin

through them. "Miss Worie, your momma taught me to read. And that opened up a whole new freedom for me. So it's best you know, while you was sleepin all them days, I commenced to read through these. Not to be nosey, but to see if they was something else we needed to know."

Them papers was no secret, but to Bess, she'd broke my trust by readin them. I smiled at her. "And was they anything?"

"Yes ma'am. They was. And you need to read this."

Bess's eyes carried a look of concern. I wasn't sure if I needed to ready myself for one more blow or not. She flipped through the pages until she found the one she wanted, then she handed it to me. Justice squatted next to me. I laid the paper on my lap and smoothed down the edges.

"Read them words out loud, Miss Worie," Bess said. "They need to be said so everbody hears."

From the book of Proverbs, the seventeenth chapter, verse eight, I write the words of the good Lord.

A gift is as a precious stone in the eyes of him that hath it: whithersoever it turneth, it prospereth.

I don't suppose you will rightly understand why I have to do what I do. I'm burnin with fever and my bones is growin weak. It's hard to keep goin like they ain't nothin wrong, so this decision, hard as it is, is one I've wrestled with the good Lord over.

That bag has some stones. Rubies from my necklace. My momma give it to me when I left to marry your daddy. "If you ever need a way out, this will get you home. And you can always come home with open arms."

My momma . . . she is a good woman. She never approved of Daddy's tryin to keep me away from the man I loved, but she knew when I left, she'd never see me again. Still, she made a way for me to come home. They was four stones. I give two away. I give them to people who I thought could make a difference. After all, the good Lord wants us to make more of what we have. My hope was they would use them when the time was right. I never expected them to die before they could do good with them.

Their youngins burned in my heart. Just like Calvin, Justice, and you burned in my heart. So I'm leavin you a way to make a difference. I know it will take some time to figure that road, but when you do, I have great faith you will change things.

I can't let this fever be passed on to the ones I love. The only way I can save you from this is to take away what carries it. This ain't your fault. It ain't nobody's fault but bad luck. What I do, I do to save you.

I hope someday you will understand the gift I am givin you is like a precious stone. Turn it and prosper.

I love you all. They is no hard feelins over our rough times. All I have done has been outta love.

THIRTY-FOUR

T. J. climbed on my lap. The words Momma had wrote wrapped around us both like a warm quilt. I pulled him close. "You know Miss Worie is so glad you are home. She loves you." He took my face in his hands and rubbed my cheeks, swipin the tears that streamed. "Sweet boy."

Pastor Jess squeezed my shoulder. "He knows. They all know."

Abeleen made her way to my feet and laid her head in my lap. "When Ely dragged me to your farm, I knew as soon as I saw you that you would take care of me. I ain't doubted it since. This is where Daddy would want me to be."

Them youngins gathered tight against me, and I knew Momma was right. It didn't matter that we wasn't blood. Just that we was family.

The moment was nice, and I coulda set there all day takin in ever one of them, but things needed to move ahead. "Now that we all know we was meant to be family, there is chores that need to be done. Get with it." I give T. J. a little peck on the cheek. "Ain't you got some chickens to feed?"

Ely pressed his face to my cheek, then took Bess's hand. "I

reckon he does. Doanie, you go with Miss Bess and finish hangin them clothes on the line. And Abeleen, them horses need let out."

"Yes sir, Mr. Ely. I can do that." Abeleen was up like a shot and headed to the pen.

"That girl's got a way with them horses." Ely chuckled.

He was barkin commands one after the other, and youngins was scatterin. I was grateful. Grateful him and Bess was with me.

Daddy used to talk about the cornerstone when him and the boys was buildin the barn. "Gotta get this rock in level. Sturdy it up. It's what holds the whole barn up."

Ely was that rock, holdin me up even when I was swayin in the wind.

It wasn't long before there was just me and Justice sittin in the quiet of the barn. I couldn't think of nothin to say that could hold up to Momma's paper. I took the crumpled paper from my lap and handed it to Justice.

He folded it and pushed it into his pocket. "Looks like T. J. managed to wad it up a little." He rested his arm across my lap. "We ain't done answerin that question I asked earlier. The one about just givin that bag to Calvin." He raised a brow.

"I don't want to fight, Justice."

"Fightin stopped when you read Momma's note. Me and you got to decide what we need to do." Justice wiped his face with his handkerchief.

"I'm sorry," I said. "I know when you get your hackles up it makes you want to drink."

Justice stared at me. "I ain't sure you're gonna ever learn how to soften your words. Are you?"

"I . . . I . . . didn't mean . . ."

"Truth is, Worie, I don't feel no need to get my hooch. Tellin you the truth about Daddy seemed to kill the taste."

"So what do we do from here?"

"We know what them stones was for and that they have some

wealth to them. For now, we think on what to do with them. If I was to say what I thought we really needed to do . . ."

"Say it." I nudged him.

"I say we load up and go back to the house. Take back what's ours. Leave the youngins here with Ely and Bess until we get things worked out." He stuck his hand out and I took hold, lettin him stand me up. "Whatta you think?"

I slipped my hand over the crook of his elbow. It was like something took hold of me and strengthened me. I swallowed hard. All this time I'd not been afraid of Calvin, but somehow bein throwed off a train by him give me something to fear.

"You think he's at the cabin?" I asked.

"Nope."

"But you think he's . . ."

"Watchin? Oh, you bet your bootstraps he's watchin."

"What do we do?"

"We go home, Worie. We go home."

A voice come from the door of the barn. "Not that a soul asked me, but I believe Justice is right. Go home. Take what is yours." Pastor Jess stood leanin just outside the door.

"I believe you are the nosiest soul alive. Always hearin ever conversation whether it belongs to you or not." I waved my hand at him.

"It's a gift!" He went to heehawin. "A gift from the good Lord. But either way, Justice is right. It's time you both stood your ground."

"Pastor's right, Worie. We done know Calvin ain't got no legal hold on that land. And I don't know about you, but I'm up for a good fight."

I walked to the barn door and looked over the mountains that stair-stepped their way to heaven. The blue of the sky bounced off the ridges, leavin a soft, warm color.

I sighed. "Feel that sun? It's like it sucks the rotten out of us."

The men walked to either side of me. "What's it gonna be, Worie?" Justice asked. "We gonna hunker down and let Calvin hover over us like a animal huntin prey, or are we gonna run him off?"

I never had trouble fightin before, but this was different. I wasn't goin after a brother that stole my supper. I was facin down one that killed our Daddy, broke Momma's heart, and stole a child away.

"It ain't about the farm, you know." My eyes met Justice's.

"Nope. It ain't."

"It's about Farrell. And Momma."

Pastor Jess chimed in. "It's about becomin who you both was meant to be. That's what your momma would have wanted. That's what the good Lord wants for His children."

"Becomin who I was meant to be. Hummm." I couldn't rightly say I knew what that was except that I loved them children. I loved my brother, Ely, and Bess. I wanted what was best for them. "Pastor Jess."

"Yes ma'am."

"Reckon you would make your way to Hartsboro and get the sheriff? Let him know there's about to be a fight on the mountain."

The pastor nodded. "I'd be happy to. Just give me time to get him up here before you start throwin rocks."

"Oh Pastor, I ain't gonna be throwin no rocks." I pulled my shoulders back. "I'm gonna be throwin words. Powerful words. Momma's words."

Pastor Jess had the biggest smile plastered across his face. Bigger than I'd ever seen. He walked toward the pen and hollered for Abeleen to bring his horse. He tipped his hat and headed out.

Justice and me stood starin out at the mountains.

"They are beautiful, ain't they?" I said.

"They are." Justice scratched his head and set his hat. "Daddy used to say the mountains could talk."

"I remember. And Momma would tell him it wasn't the mountains he heard, but the voice of the good Lord." I took a few steps into the sunlight, lifted my hand, and shaded my eyes. The howl of a coyote echoed across the valley. And I heard the mountains whisper.

Home. Go home.

THIRTY-FIVE

Ely was good enough to tell the youngins me and Justice was leavin. I'm not sure I could have looked them in the eyes and told them myself I was leavin again. They was no tellin when I'd be back to get them—or even if. Knowin Calvin, anything could happen. He could kill us both. At this point, it wouldn't be as easy as just givin him Momma's stones. It was a matter of pride for him now.

Justice suited up the wagon, and Bess and the girls added a few provisions. Ely handed me Daddy's shotgun and a bag of shells while Justice spun the chamber on his gun. I hated the thought that we'd face Calvin on these terms, but he'd done gone over the edge. He was a cocked gun ready to be fired.

"Hup there, Sally. Hup." Justice gently tapped the mare with the reins.

Sally groaned and leaned into the yoke. The wagon wheels turned and we headed up the rocky path to Momma's house. Every stick that broke, every rock that slipped and fell, put us both on edge.

"You as jumpy as me?" I asked.

"Jumpier than a toad on a hot rock."

"This is the right thing to do, ain't it?"

Justice leaned his elbows on his knees and let the reins droop between his hands. "It's the right thing."

"Calvin ain't gonna make this easy, is he?"

Justice bumped against me. "Ever knowed him to do anything easy?"

I chuckled. "No, I reckon not."

Bess had put my things in my bag. The jar with the notes, the satin bag. She'd laid Momma's Bible beside me on the wagon bench. I traced the edge of the worn leather with my fingers. "I feel like this is all the possessions I have in the world."

Justice glanced over, then back to the path. "Uh-huh. But it ain't. You got me. You got them youngins. You got what counts. So do I."

"I reckon so." I eased my hand into the bag and pulled out the satin pouch that held the stones. "I've decided we need to give this to Calvin. I didn't give you no say-so."

"Don't need none. Been penniless all my life. Ain't got no plans of changin that now."

I stared at Justice. He never give me no back talk at all. Lookin at him, just one more time, reminded me of Daddy. How could he? Still he did. I remembered lookin in that mirror at the forge and thinkin I was lookin at Momma. I couldn't understand how. How could either of us remind me of Momma and Daddy when we wasn't their blood children?

The wagon bumped and bounced along the trail. It had been a spell since we'd been home, and the trail proved that. Weeds growed in the furrows where the wagon wheels rolled, and tree limbs hung low over the path. Had Calvin even been back here? After kickin me and them youngins out, had he just left the place empty?

I'd said before, Calvin only wanted what he couldn't have. He was like a mountain lion that played with its prey then walked away, leavin it half dead and wallerin in the dirt.

Justice took his hat and rested it on his knee. His hands harbored long, slim fingers. Fingers just like Daddy's. How? How on earth?

"I was gonna say you reminded me of Daddy, sittin there like that."

Justice laughed. "Kinda funny, ain't it? How we can look like somebody who ain't our blood?"

I cocked my head and shrugged. "But you do look like Daddy. I can't explain it. But you do."

Then it come to me. The folks we are around are the folks we imitate. Me and Justice looked like Momma and Daddy because we took on their expressions, their movements. We didn't have to be blood children to take on the things about Momma and Daddy that stayed with us.

The cabin come into view as we rounded the bend. The cows wandered in the field and the chickens picked at the grass. I was glad it was the warm part of the year. The animals could forage the land and make do.

To the left of the cabin stood two crosses. Momma and Daddy's final restin place. The dirt we'd mounded on top of Momma had settled to a smooth, flat place where a thick of grass grew. Mornin glories strung their way around the two crosses like we had planted them there. Their blooms dangled and moved gently in the breeze. Daisies lifted their heads toward the sky around the foot of their graves. Momma would have liked that.

Justice pulled the wagon to a halt and helped me down. I stepped over the ashes left from the mattress I'd burned, and Justice picked up what was left of the frame from the screen door Calvin had ripped off the house.

Outside of the cold quietness, nothin had changed. I knelt down and memories flooded back. The stench of blood rooted deep in that mattress burned in my memory. I twisted my palm up, and in my mind I could see Momma's blood puddled between my fingers and under my nails. I cringed.

"You alright?" Justice draped his arm over my shoulders.

"I'm fine. It's just . . ."

"Memories?"

"Memories." I could see by his face, Justice ached.

"Worie, I'm sorry I wasn't here. I'm so sorry."

"They was nothin you could have done, Justice. You heard what Momma wrote. She had a reason for doin what she did. Nothin would have stopped her. And if she thought for a minute one of us would grow sick from the fever, she'd have never been able to live with herself."

Justice pushed open the heavy wooden door into the cabin. What little things we had was strewed all over everwhere. Calvin had done just as he promised. Tore the place apart.

Momma's rocker was broke, and the drawers in her hutch was yanked out and throwed on the floor. It wasn't enough for Calvin to just tear through and look. He had to make his point clear.

I stared at the fireplace. Momma's hidin place was closed tight. Calvin would have never found the jar. As I gazed around the cabin, lookin at the chaos and destruction, it come home to me that Justice was right. I could have prevented this.

"It's my fault. All of it." I buried my head in the bend of my arm. "Lord have mercy, this is my fault."

"Stop it, Worie."

"But I could have. You said it yourself. I could have prevented this by just giving the bag to Calvin."

"Stop it. You hear me? We both said things in the heat of anger. You couldn't have stopped Calvin. This ain't your doin." Justice took my shoulders and twisted me toward him.

"All he wanted was the jar. I could have give it to him and he'd have left." My voice quivered.

"And Worie, he'd have been back for something else. You know better than the next person, Calvin's got a greedy hunger ain't never satisfied. Givin him that bag would have just put him off for a spell. He'd have been back lookin for somethin else. That's who Calvin is."

I sat on the edge of the hearth and pulled Momma's notes from the jar.

> *From the book of Philippians, the fourth chapter and the seventh verse, the good Lord spoke these words.*
> *And the peace of God, which passeth all understanding, shall keep your hearts and minds through Christ Jesus.*
> *Good Father, I long for your peace. I long to understand why people is dyin and why, oh why, is their children starving. I can't keep up with the loss, and now I'm findin my own self waverin. There is all them youngins hidin in the side of the mountain. Last I counted they was seven. Oh Lord, have mercy on them wee ones. Help me understand.*

"Oh Lordy mercy!" I shouted. "Oh Lordy."

"What in tarnation are you yelling about?" I reckon I scared Justice outta his skin. "You purt near give me heart failure."

"Look at this!" I shoved the note in his face and come to my feet. "We have to get up to that cave by the river."

Justice read the note. "Worie, you don't reckon there's still children up there? It's been months. They'd be starved by now."

"Not if Momma was Momma. She'd have taught them to forage. We have to go. We have to try."

Justice helped me into the wagon, and we headed up the windy trail to a small cave where we played when we was children. The boys had built a ladder to the openin, and just inside the mouth of the cave, a small stream of fresh water had seeped from the rock wall. The water was clear as a mornin sky. All we could do was hope, and right now, hope was a lot.

It took us a spell to make our way up the side of the mountain in a wagon. The path was made for walkin, not for wagons, but

Sally proved her worth when we reached the summit. The ground was wet from the stream in the cave, and wherever we stepped water seeped into our prints, forming small puddles.

"Here, Sally." Justice bent over and scooped a handful of water. "Drink up, gal." She lapped at his hand, then lowered her head to the puddle. "You're a good ole girl." Justice gently slapped her neck. "Good girl."

"Help me," I said. "Is that ladder you boys built still here?"

We hunted around until we found it. Odd as it was, it looked just like it did when we was youngins.

Justice and me worked our way up the rungs to the cave openin. It was quiet as Momma's house. To one side was three heaped-up piles of rocks. I didn't have to guess that them rocks covered three bodies.

I hollered into the cave, "Come on out. Momma sent me to get you. Come on." My voice shook.

Nothin. Silence.

"Please come out. Please." I commenced to sob ever word I spoke.

After a minute or two, Justice turned me around. "They ain't here, Worie. Let's go."

It was like I had give birth myself and the infants died one by one. The pain was tormenting, and all I could do was wail, "Lord, Momma asked for help. I'm askin now."

We eased down the steep and rickety ladder. The times we'd played in that cave as children faded into sadness. Me and Justice both shed tears.

When we reached the wagon, we couldn't believe our eyes. I covered my mouth and gasped. Four children, three boys and a little girl, stood peerin over its edge.

THIRTY-SIX

We got them youngins down to the cabin. Justice rounded the boys up and took them to the river to scrub them down. I took the girl. Her little face was scratched and her fingers and toes raw from climbin on rough rocks. She had one braid that run down her back and looked like a nest of mice lived there.

I pumped some fresh water from the well and set her on Momma's table. I'd managed to find a few bowls Calvin hadn't busted and a rag or two, so I give her a drink and then started to wash her down. The child was skinny from hunger, and it was hard to tell her age. Maybe eleven or twelve.

I took the extra shirt Bess had tucked in my bag and shook it straight. "You can wear this until I get your dress cleaned."

She never uttered a word. And I didn't force none. Instead, I just went to tellin her about Abeleen and Doanie. I told her about T. J. messin his pants, and it dragged a smile outta her. It took a minute or two to get that braid loose, but when I did, long brownish-blonde locks spread across her back. I dipped water over her head and scrubbed her clean, all the time singin and talkin to her. My fingers was the best I could do to brush through her hair, but once it was clean not a piece hung on my knuckles.

She was a beautiful child. Blue eyes the color of the sky and a dark tint to her skin.

I slipped my shirt over her head, ripped a strip of cloth from the rag, and tied it around her waist. "There! Don't you look pretty?"

She run her hand down the material, then pulled it out from her body. "Much obliged," she whispered.

I felt all my emotions rush to my face. "Oh honey, you are welcome. So, so welcome." I pulled her close and kissed her head. "You got a name?"

"Tilda."

I took her chin between my fingers and held her face close. "Well, Miss Tilda, my name is Worie. Worie Dressar."

"Momma Dressar?"

Her words took me back. I cocked my head and smiled. "No, Momma Dressar was my momma. She's passed on."

"That's why she quit comin with beans?" Tilda asked.

Momma had cared for these children too. How many more that I wouldn't know about?

Justice hollered inside the cabin, "Can we come in? You girls decent?"

I had to laugh. He made it sound like we was both just little youngins. "Come on in."

Justice led the boys inside. He stopped and knelt in front of Tilda. "My, my, what a lovely young woman."

Her face turned crimson as a sunset, and she pushed him away, takin her place with the boys.

"Worie, this here is Elden, Rocky, and Titus. And before we come back to the house we checked the springhouse. They was plenty of smoked meat." He laid a slice of pork the size of a rock on the table. "What do you say we eat a bite?"

I stood there starin. Justice looked like a different man. Maybe I was just seein him through new eyes, but he was different.

"And the barn is filled with hay. I'm sure we can rustle up enough blankets to sleep on tonight. I done started a fire in the pit in the barn."

I let out a guffaw. "Ain't you just handier than butter on bread?" I pulled my knife from my boot and commenced to cut the meat. "You reckon you youngins could come up with some plates that ain't broke?"

They scurried around like a passel of squirrels.

"Justice," I said, "thank you for trustin me to go up to the cave."

"Right is right. Momma ain't led us wrong yet."

The sun was dippin fast behind the knoll, so we eat and made our way to the barn. Justice had done good. His fire was blazin right nice, and he'd started a pot of coffee. Miss Bess would never let us go without coffee. I felt peace settle over the little ones as we bedded them down for the night. They'd managed alone for months. Strong, that is what they was. Strong.

Justice pushed the barn door closed and slipped a shovel through the rope pulls to hold it shut. "It ain't a bar, but it'll keep out the critters."

The fire cracked and popped, and the smell of fresh-burned hickory filled the barn. Momma loved the smell of hickory. She swore by it when it come to smokin pork. For what it was worth, her smoked pork beat anybody's on this side of the mountain.

I poured Justice a second cup of coffee and set beside him. I rested my head on his shoulder. "Did you ever think this could happen?"

He pondered before he spoke. That was Justice. One who always thought on his words before they spilled outta his mouth. "I've been dragged through the mud so much, by my own doin, that nothin really surprises me anymore."

"I'm glad you're here with me."

"Little sister, we got us a new family. Don't reckon I'll be goin anyplace."

Them words was a comfort to me. I'd allowed myself to feel

alone for so long that it was right nice to know Justice was stayin with me.

An owl hooted in the loft, takin me back a little. It hooted again and then there was a swoosh. The bird dropped from the loft, run plumb through with an arrow.

"Looks like the gates of hell just opened." Justice picked up the bird and tossed it to the side of the barn. "Wake them youngins up. Get 'em back behind them haystacks and dare them to make a sound."

I knew I'd felt Calvin's eyes on me more times than I could count. There was just no catchin him.

I roused the children and hid them behind the haystacks. "Shhh. You do Miss Worie a favor and be quiet as a mouse. Lay down and cover up with this blanket. I'm gonna lay some hay on you so you won't be seen. Alright?"

They nodded.

"Lay on your belly and rest your head on your arms. That way you can breathe good. And if me or Justice tells you to run, you run outta here as hard and fast as you can run. Hear me?"

Tilda squeezed my hand. "We're right good at hidin."

I rubbed her cheek. "Yes you are. Now, roll over and be quiet." I covered them, then shook handfuls of hay over them.

Justice climbed to the loft and was peerin out the door when I heard another swoosh. An arrow breezed past him, stickin in the wall behind him. "Dang coward. He can't come out in the open."

"Right now that coward is whizzin arrows through the loft. Don't you reckon you oughta come down?" I hadn't hardly got the words out before another arrow flew past, this time nickin Justice's arm.

I'd never seen rage like that on Justice before. He was a peacemaker. Never the one who dished out the mess. But it was like his body blowed up with air. His shoulders hunched and his arms hung away from his body. Ever step he took down that loft ladder was hard, and when I tried to touch him, he pushed me away.

241

"Worie, this ends tonight. You hear me? Stay outta the way." He took me by the good arm and pulled me away from the door. He pointed his finger in my face. "Stay outta the way. Now ain't the time to be stubborn."

With that, he stormed to the barn door, yanked the shovel out of the rope loops, and swung open the door. "Come on, Calvin. You always was a coward. Lettin other people fight your battles. Hung over folks like a buzzard, threatenin them. Come on, brother. Be a man."

That was when I heard laughin. Hard laughin. Calvin was howlin like an idiot. Laughin like he was drunk. He stepped outta the shadows and walked toward Justice. "Lookie at you, all rough and tough. You ain't never one time had the guts to stand your ground." He walked straight up to Justice.

Justice never uttered a word, but he stepped one more step, nearly touchin toes with Calvin.

"What's a matter? Can't you talk? Missin your hooch? She's a mighty fine lady, ain't she?"

Justice towered over Calvin, a full head taller. He stared down at him, darin him to lift a hand. I lit a lantern and took out from the barn. Never in my days had I seen this look on Justice. He was ready to let loose.

"Justice, he ain't worth this. Look, Calvin, I got Momma's pouch." He cocked his head toward me. "You had it all along?"

I dangled the pouch in the air. "They is two stones in here. Ely says they are rubies. I didn't know what they was. I thought you was lookin for money, not stones."

Calvin took a step to his left, and Justice stepped too.

"Don't do this, Justice. Please. Calvin, here's what you wanted. Take it. Leave. Don't never come back." I tossed the bag at his feet. I could see Justice's fists balled tight. "Go on, Calvin. Take it. Just take it and leave," I squalled.

Just like Justice said, Calvin couldn't be satisfied. He grabbed up the bag and loosened the strings. "There's the treasure I was lookin for." He counted them stones. "Ain't they more? I thought they was six."

I come closer. Thought I could reason with him, but like always, there was no reasonin. "Two is all we have. Momma only had four. That's what she wrote in her notes. They was only four. And you got the one you took from Ellie."

"There's more than that. You're keepin the rest."

And that was the last word he got outta his mouth before Justice took a swing. A bear-sized fist caught Calvin under the chin and sent his feet over his head. There was nothin I could do. Justice was on Calvin like a buzzard on a dead animal. One, two, three more whacks and Justice had tore a hole in Calvin's cheek.

Calvin rolled to his knees and grabbed his knife from his belt. He jabbed, catchin Justice in the side. Justice groaned, then he dropped to his knees. Calvin staggered to him and kicked him in the stomach.

I felt my stomach turn. I remembered Ely talkin about when him and Bess was runnin from the plantation, and how his anger turned to fear. I felt my heart take to racin as my anger turned to fear. I couldn't stand to lose Justice—not now. They was nothin worth my losin him.

"Stop it," I said. "You have the stones. That's all they was. Just go, Calvin."

Calvin dragged hisself to me. "I ain't got no place to go, baby sister. You took my home." He wiped his bloody mouth on his sleeve.

"I did no sucha thing. You lied about them papers. Momma and Daddy left this place to all of us. Problem is, you can't get along or do your part."

He grabbed me by the throat and lifted me to my toes. His fingers dug so hard I could hardly breathe. I grabbed his wrists, tryin to pull myself up to catch a breath.

"This is my place. And I done told you it's mine, even if I have to kill you." His grip tightened.

I felt dizzy. Justice couldn't move. I took in what air I could and whispered, "Calvin, just like Momma, I will always love you. Despite yourself, I will always love you."

My eyes closed as I gasped for one last taste of night air. That's when I heard a grunt and Calvin's grip eased on me. My feet hit the ground and Calvin fell to his knees. An arrow jutted through his chest.

I grabbed him and twisted him to his back. "Calvin. Don't you dare die." Blood seeped like teardrops around the arrow.

Justice crawled to his knees and made his way to me. "Was it you? Did you shoot him?" He pressed his hand into the gash on his side.

Out of the shadows walked Ellie. A bow hung from her fingers. She looked at Calvin as he strained to get a breath.

"I'm carryin your baby." She stared hard into his eyes.

Calvin took in a breath and went to laughin. His body went limp.

I broke into hard sobs, not just for Calvin but for Ellie.

Trigger pulled me loose from Calvin and walked me into the barn. "You alright?" he asked.

"Justice?" I screamed.

"He's fine. Ely has him. He's gonna be fine."

I couldn't find words. What I'd just seen was beyond what I could take in. "How in the name of all that is good did Ellie manage this?"

"I ain't sure, other than we come up here to help if Calvin showed up. I was in the cabin lookin for you. I reckon Ellie come upon the fight. She wasn't about to let you die. She picked up Calvin's bow, aimed, and shot."

Ellie sat on the ground, sobbin and broken. I run to her and wrapped my arms around her. "It's alright, honey. It's alright."

"I couldn't let him kill you. You are like my momma."

Like her momma. I couldn't think of sweeter words.

Calvin was dead. The nightmare was over. Done. I shoulda had some peace, but I didn't. I guessed it would come.

It wasn't long till daybreak come, and along with it was Pastor Jess and the sheriff. Ely took that same shovel he'd used to dig Daddy's and Momma's graves, and went to diggin Calvin's.

There was no words. All I could do was watch from a rock by the springhouse. I took out Momma's notes and read them from beginning to end. The very last one, Momma wrote:

From the book of Genesis, the first chapter, the twenty-seventh verse. The good Lord said this.

So God created man in his own image, in the image of God created he him; male and female created he them.

You ain't children from my loins, but you look just like the good Father. Love one another, forgive the trespasses. Remember, you are all Momma's children. Always Momma's children.

Epilogue

1879—SOURWOOD MOUNTAIN, TENNESSEE

They wasn't a soul any more surprised than me when Pastor Jess come pullin up with an elderly woman. She was dressed in fine clothes, a hat tilted to one side of her head. Her hair was so silver it glistened in the afternoon sun.

I pulled my apron up and wiped my hands. Ely climbed outta the back of the wagon and slid a box to the side for a step. He put out his hand, and between him and the pastor, they managed to ease the old woman from the wagon.

"Pastor Jess." I nodded. "Ely." I leaned and kissed his cheek. "Who you draggin up on the mountain?" I reached to take her hand.

The woman grasped both of her gloved hands around mine. Her voice was weak and she spoke right soft. "Is this her?" she asked.

Ely smiled.

"For a child that wasn't birthed by my daughter, she sure is the spitting image of her."

I shook my head. Had I heard her right? Birthed by her daughter? Was this woman my . . . grandmother?

"This is her, Miss Julietta." Ely pulled me closer. "Worie, this here is Miss Julietta Morgan. This is your momma's momma."

"My grandmother?" I asked.

The woman smiled. "One and the same. It's my pleasure to meet you. I've wondered for years what Louise did with you and your brothers." Tears formed, and she dabbed them with a dainty white handkerchief.

"I don't know what to say."

"There's nothing to say, dear. I just want some time with my granddaughter."

It was awkward and bittersweet as we stood by Momma's grave. Miss Julietta told me about how my grandfather refused to let Momma bring orphans into his home. Stragglers, he called us. And when we walked by the river, she talked about givin Momma the stones from her necklace so she could sell them if she needed anything.

It was hard to take in the things she was sayin, but I could tell she loved Momma, and I could see her sadness in havin to let Momma go.

Me and Justice spent the bigger part of the day with her until Pastor Jess said she needed her rest.

She stepped up to climb into the wagon and took my face in her hands. "You and Justice. My grandchildren." She nodded. "My only grandchildren. Ely tells me you have taken in this passel of little ones."

Ely helped her into the wagon.

"Yes ma'am," I said. "They're all children with no homes. I guess just like me and Justice was. But Momma took us and loved us. I figure it's the best I can do for her memory."

Miss Julietta watched as the youngins played by the barn. "There's nothing sweeter than the laughter of little ones. How many are there?"

"Sixteen right now. But there's always room for more if need be." I looked over them youngins and felt a great pride. Not for what I had done, but for what Momma had taught me. And what the good Lord convinced me of.

"I'll be sending supplies. The pastor will help assure they get here. And I've put money in the bank in Hartsboro in your name. You'll not want. And those children. They'll all be cared for."

Pastor Jess braced me. "Miss Julietta is sending what's needed to build a nice home for you and these children."

"A home?"

"A home." She smiled and pinched my cheek. "If you need anything, anything at all, you send word."

"Yes ma'am."

She puckered her lips and pressed them against mine. "Pastor, I'm ready."

Pastor Jess climbed onto the bench. Miss Julietta waved to Ely and they were on their way.

She did just what she promised. It was only a matter of days until wagonloads of wood, nails, and hired hands showed up. When the building was finished, Justice come carryin a sign that he hung over the door.

All Momma's Children

It couldn't have been more perfect, cause them youngins all called me Momma. And they was all mine. Ever one loved. Ever one taught to read the good book. Ever one happy.

"Ain't this something?" Justice jabbed at me with his fingers.

"It is. Ever youngin has a bed, clothes, and a blanket. It sure is something."

Doanie stood to one side, scoldin T. J. for somethin. It seemed she had moved on despite losing Farrell, and T. J. just didn't remember what had happened. I suppose the good Lord filled that spot in his head. But my heart . . . my heart continued to ache for that little girl. I wasn't sure it would ever heal.

The years passed and youngins come and went. Some the pastor was able to find good homes for, others stayed until they decided to go out on their own.

It took Ellie a while to get over shootin that arrow, but Pastor Jess helped her understand what she did was outta protectin me. He married her and Trigger on the ridge at sunset. It was right pretty—the sun closing its eyes over the mountain sorty closed out the old.

When the baby come, she was a sweetheart. Abeleen took to helpin Ellie mother the youngin, and truth be knowed, I'd never seen Trigger as happy as he was holdin that little pea pod we called Izzy.

I planted proper flowers on Momma's and Daddy's graves . . . even Calvin's. Me and Justice took some time to talk over Calvin's misgivins. I can't say we missed the chaos he caused, but we both loved him. Despite hisself. We made our peace, and I don't recall ever mentionin Calvin no more. They was no need. The flowers on his grave was reminder enough.

I sat on that same rock where I read Momma's notes and looked over what the years had brung. I saw how the good Lord worked in a woman who was selfish and broke.

Me and Justice hit hard places ever now and again. One that was hardest was losing Ely. I felt like they would always be an empty spot for him. Justice moved Miss Bess up the mountain with us, and she was the extra love these youngins needed.

I never married. Never felt the desire. These children was all I needed. And that was alright. I'd long since learned families ain't always shaped the way we think they orta be.

The time come when I was a little slower and my bones ached a little more. The day I set on the porch foldin clothes and saw a beautiful young woman come walkin up to the cabin, I had to squint. Abeleen was helpin me when she stood and threw up her arms. She bolted off the porch, screamin, "Doanie! Doanie! It's Farrell!" The pastor come behind her, lookin like a cat that just ate his mouse.

I couldn't do nothing but bust into tears. I run off the porch, hollerin to the good Lord, "You brought her home. Oh Lord, you brought her home." Then I cried to the pastor, "You found her!"

He seemed right proud of his surprise. He pointed to the sky, givin credit where it was due.

I grabbed that girl and squeezed her till I thought the life would pour outta her. Doanie was beside herself. Right in front of me was a prayer answered. It was like that note Momma wrote:

> *From the book of Luke, the fifteenth chapter and the sixth verse, the good Lord said to me, And when he cometh home, he calleth together his friends and neighbours, saying unto them, Rejoice with me; for I have found my sheep which was lost.*
>
> *Good Father, bring them lost and hungry children home to me.*

And He did.

Author Note

This story has bubbled in my heart for some time, and I simply wasn't able to approach the many facets that it held. That is, until God blessed our entire family with a child we did not expect. She came to my niece and her husband when their only hope of having a child was left in the hands of God. This child changed the face of our family, and she is loved just like we love all the other children.

I also have friends who have adopted children. Some from overseas, others from right in our own backyard, and still others who are fostered until their families heal. The impact these individuals have made on me has been nothing short of amazing. What surprises me about these families is they rarely stop at one child. Their hearts and shoulders are bigger than most can imagine. What a sacrifice they have made to bring wee ones into their homes and love them with all the love they deserve.

Adoption is not for everyone. Neither is fostering. But whether you choose to do those or not, you can be supportive, loving, and faithful in your relationships with these families. Remember, they need your support. Pray for them. Encourage them. Walk by them.

We can all change the lives of another when we take time to love unconditionally. Faithfully. Fully. Just as Christ loves us.

Acknowledgments

My acknowledgments can only begin with praise and gratitude to our Father in heaven. My prayer for years has been, "Lord, will You allow me to be a writer? My work will always be Yours." He has blessed me by answering that prayer. First and foremost, may the glory be all His.

There are many who support me in different ways. My agent for many years and for this novel, Diana Flegal. She was the first to believe in my work. I wish her joy in her retirement. I will miss you. To my current agent, Bob Hostetler, who has been a faithful prayer warrior and friend, standing in the gap long before he became my agent.

To Lonnie Hull DuPont, the editor I have anticipated working with for years. She has encouraged me, led me, and become an Appalachian convert as we worked together. Welcome to the Appalachians via this novel. This has been a dream come true and an answered prayer.

If I could say that God led me into perfect hands, then it is to Rachel McRae's. It's a bit unnerving when an author is introduced into a new publishing house, but to have this sweet thing bounce up to me and tell me who she is, then say, "I speak you as a second language!" . . . well, it is a God-thing. Thank you to Rachel, Lonnie, and Jessica English, and to Revell for bringing me into the fold and making me feel as though I have always been there.

There are never enough thanks for the support of my husband, Tim, and my sons, Chase and Cameron. Also Trevor, Justin, and our sweet Jamie, the best daughter-in-law ever. They are the source of encouragement that keeps me going.

To those special friends who stand behind me, pushing for the next work. Robin Mullins, my good friend and faithful prayer partner, who daily helped me meet my goal by keeping me accountable in word count. Ann Falcinelli and LaTan Murphy—who are we without those who care about us in a sweet and intimate way? Linda Bambino, my day-job boss, who excuses me over and over again to travel and teach at conferences. Thank you so much for allowing me the necessary time to develop my writing career.

And finally, to those readers who have fallen in love with the Appalachian culture. Those who read these works and feel the soft mountain breeze, smell the sweet scent of lavender and honeysuckle, and long to see the hawk soar on the wind. Without your faithfulness, my writing would simply be thoughts in a notebook instead of living words on a page. Thank you with all of my heart for keeping the Appalachian stories alive. My mountain mamaw thanks you.

Cindy K. Sproles is proud of her mountain heritage. Born and raised in the Appalachian Mountains, she has a desire for the "old ways" of the mountain people and life to never be forgotten. Cindy is the cofounder of Christian Devotions Ministries and serves as a project manager for Lighthouse Publishing of the Carolinas (LPC Books). She is the director of the Asheville Christian Writers Conference and executive editor for ChristianDevotions.us and InspireAFire.com, as well as a mentor and editor with Write Right, a private editing service.

Cindy is a storyteller, speaker, and conference teacher. She is also a bestselling and award-winning author. Her first novel, *Mercy's Rain*, was named IndieFab Book of the Year, and *Liar's Winter* was named the Golden Scrolls Book of the Year and was a Carol Award finalist. Her devotions have been published across the eastern seaboard, and she writes monthly eldercare articles for *The Voice* magazine.

A mother of four and nana of two, Cindy lives in the mountains of East Tennessee with her husband.

CINDY K. SPROLES

Speaking and Writing from the Heart

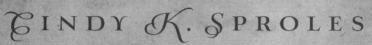

GET TO KNOW CINDY AT

CindySproles.com

- Sign up for her newsletter
- Read her blog
- Learn about upcoming events

f cksproles

🐦 CindyDevoted